2022

PAY OR PLAY

Also by Howard Michael Gould

Charlie Waldo series

LAST LOOKS
BELOW THE LINE

PAY OR PLAY

Howard Michael Gould

SEVERN
HOUSE

First world edition published in Great Britain and the USA in 2021
by Severn House, an imprint of Canongate Books Ltd,
14 High Street, Edinburgh EH1 1TE.

Trade paperback edition first published in Great Britain and the USA in 2022
by Severn House, an imprint of Canongate Books Ltd.

severnhouse.com

British Library Cataloguing-in-Publication Data
A CIP catalogue record for this title is available from the British Library.

ISBN-13: 978-0-7278-5085-0 (cased)
ISBN-13: 978-1-4483-0588-9 (trade paper)
ISBN-13: 978-1-4483-0587-2 (e-book)

All Severn House titles are printed on acid-free paper.

MIX
Paper from
responsible sources
FSC
www.fsc.org   FSC® C013056

Typeset by Palimpsest Book Production Ltd.,
Falkirk, Stirlingshire, Scotland.
Printed and bound in Great Britain by
TJ Books, Padstow, Cornwall.

for Andrew Lazar,
who never gives up

ONE

I t wasn't the sex that set Waldo's woods on fire, it was the afterglow.

Surrounded by forest, nearly all its structures made of wood, his mountain town of Idyllwild had already seen five homes destroyed, the remainder evacuated. Route 243 was closed on both sides, leaving Waldo and all the other residents cut off and fearing the worst. As the record temperatures of summer 2018 scorched California, infernos blossomed up and down the state. Six people were dead in the one up north, the one called the Carr.

Watching clips of his wildfire, the Cranston, from a hundred miles away and the safety of Lorena's house, Waldo knew it would take a miracle to keep the rest of Idyllwild from being consumed. He didn't know whether his own cabin was already lost. He didn't know if his chickens were still alive.

What he did know was this: the conflagration was all his fault.

Not literally, of course. It wasn't like he'd lit the match. And he hadn't set the tinderbox. The planet was rebelling. Climate change had made this fire season hotter and drier. Forest-management practices left more fuel on the ground, too, the unintended repercussion of conscientious wildlife protection. *Those* were the reasons Waldo's mountain was burning.

Those and, according to the news, arson.

But Waldo knew better. Call it karma, call it moral justice – Waldo knew his own wobbling had something to do with it, too.

Four years earlier, Waldo learned in an instant the precariousness of the world, the damage one man could do, the damage *he* could do, when his own zealous police work had led to the death of an innocent man. His life since had been a daily struggle not to do any more.

He had resigned from the force, ghosted his girlfriend Lorena and everyone else he knew, and bought twelve acres in Idyllwild, in the San Jacinto mountains, where he lived for three solitary years in self-sustaining austerity, making a near religion of his commitment to a zero-carbon footprint and to owning no more than One Hundred Things. And that worked for him, at least until Lorena showed up and triggered the chain of events which drew him away from his refuge and back into civilization.

She'd hoped to coax him into joining her expanding PI business, and back into their relationship, too. The latter took; the former, not so much. He did work one case with her, a missing-persons that turned rancid and left Waldo with no taste for more. She eventually stopped trying and seemed to accept the relationship as it was. He'd come down the mountain for a visit about once a month, usually for a few days when Willem – the male model she'd married during Waldo's absence, estranged now but still her housemate – was out of town on a shoot.

It was a delicate equilibrium: less than Lorena wanted, but enough; a constant test of Waldo's punishing minimalism, but within bounds he could handle.

Then Willem, wanting to cash in on the overheated L.A. real estate market, insisted that Lorena agree to sell their jointly owned Koreatown bungalow as a final condition of their divorce. He moved out the day the papers were signed.

The next time Waldo came to visit, the common spaces looked barren, Willem apparently the owner of most of their thousands of Things, including almost all the furniture.

Lorena looked lost in the empty house. That plucked at Waldo in ways he didn't expect, and he ended up staying in town longer than he ever had before, almost two weeks. One night, after love-making fierce and profound even by their standards, Lorena said, 'What if we got a place together?'

In a sense, it was reasonable to muse on.

In another, it was absurd. How could that work? In L.A., just as in Idyllwild, Waldo maintained his exacting rules for living, not allowing himself even an extra toothbrush to leave at her place. Meanwhile, in the face of his asceticism, Lorena clung to her consumerist pleasures all the harder. So, did she mean for him to give up his cabin, and to battle out all their joint decisions, item by item, precept by precept? Or did she mean for him to *keep* his cabin, and cohabit a second home, profligate beyond imagining?

That these questions were even on the table was a sign that

Waldo had gotten too comfortable here. His heart starting to race, he silently recited his catechism, the covenant with the world which he'd devised and repeated aloud regularly for his first few months alone on his mountain until it had become ingrained:

Don't want, don't acquire, don't require.

Don't affect.

Don't hurt.

The answer was not complicated. It was not ambiguous. He needed to hold fast. Every time he hadn't, every time he let his resolve slip, every time he compromised the principles which had redeemed him, something had gone wrong.

And this compromise would be bigger than anything Waldo had ever contemplated, the consequences surely bigger, too. He had to say no. *Of course* he had to say no.

He looked over at Lorena, her eyes closed, her lip curled in a gentle smile, and before he knew it he too was lost in the afterglow. That ruinous afterglow.

And what Waldo said was: 'Maybe.'

By the next afternoon, his mountain was in flames.

Four days later, alone in Lorena's barren kitchen, Waldo scoured the internet for any morsel of new information. Evacuated – what did that actually mean? Had anyone remained to support the firefighters, or was it a ghost town? Not that he knew any of his fellow denizens anyway, even after four years, other than his batty neighbor Hilda Flitt, who kept an eye on his chickens when he was away. And Hilda wasn't answering her phone.

Nor was Lorena, for that matter. He shot her another text and went back to surfing.

Surfing and blaming himself for the fire.

Not that he could talk about his guilt with Lorena. She'd already said something about him 'getting worse' and one time (at a downtown Szechuan restaurant, after he questioned the waiter as to why a restaurant that puts *Environment Friendly!* on the menu still tops the meal with plastic-wrapped fortune cookies), even asked whether he 'ever thought about talking to somebody.' Sure, why wouldn't she want that? It'd be so much easier to have that 'somebody' browbeat Waldo into complaisance than to develop some environmentally responsible habits herself.

Maybe, though, this *was* what 'getting worse' looked like. Holding to rules was one thing, magical thinking another entirely, and after all, it was the guy with the barbecue lighter and the WD-40 who'd set the mountain ablaze, not Waldo.

Still.

It all happened just hours after Waldo's *maybe*, and it was Waldo's town about to be devoured, and Detective III Charlie Waldo had never believed in coincidences.

As the day wore on, the news from Idyllwild began to improve. Firefighters, dropping retardant from the sky, managed to cut the inferno just before it reached the Arts Academy, and suddenly they were using the words 'mostly contained.' Deep into the night, Hilda Flitt still wasn't answering her phone. But the authorities had reopened 243, so Waldo could go back in the morning to see for himself whether his home was safe, whether he even had any Things left, save the ones on his back.

Waldo waited up for Lorena like he always did. He sprawled on her bed with his Kindle, chipping away at Richard White's massive history of the late nineteenth-century United States, specifically a grim chapter about how American 'progress' killed off the bison and pushed the Native Americans to the reservations. Even though Waldo enjoyed the book greatly – it filled multiple lacunae in his knowledge and was peculiarly relevant to the U.S. in 2018 – tonight he struggled not to put it down.

What he itched to do instead was stream another episode of his new addiction, the sinfully titillating *Judge Ida Mudge*, which Lorena had told him about just this week and which instantly wormed its way into Waldo's limbic system like none of his favorite junk television shows ever had, not even prime *MTV Cribs*. But he'd already watched two, using up the daily hour he allowed himself.

Waldo pushed to the end of the chapter and checked Lorena's bedside clock. It was past midnight, later than he ever stayed up in his woods. Was his junk TV 'day' defined by his sleep schedule, or by the clock? That is, could he allow himself to watch 'tomorrow's' *Judge Ida*s now? If he was going to spend much of the next day traveling, he might not have time to watch anyway – so why not allow himself a smidgen of ethical squinching and stream an episode? Or two.

The sound of Lorena's key in the door saved him from the lapse.

He went out to meet her in the living room. 'Sorry I didn't answer your texts,' she said. 'I got caught up with something.' Her vagueness didn't throw Waldo like it would have during the jealous years. She added, 'I don't want to talk about it.'

He shrugged, *You don't have to.*

Apparently she did, though. 'Something with an op. I had to take over a tail.'

'Fat Dave?' Lorena had three part-time operatives, two LAPD washouts and a wannabe. She swore they carried their weight but he found that hard to believe. Fat Dave Greenberg, whose rep as a world-class douchebag radiated far beyond Foothill Division, was the worst of them, as far as Waldo was concerned.

She repeated, 'I don't want to talk about it,' and Waldo repeated his *you don't have to* shrug, but again she did. 'Reddix,' she said. Lucian Reddix was a young African American, the only one Waldo didn't know from the force and the one for whom Lorena had the softest spot. 'He was on a marital tail, followed the subject into a bar. Caught her with her boyfriend, was starting to shoot them on his phone . . . but the bartender came over and he asked for a beer.'

'So?'

'So they carded him. He's not twenty-one until November.' And this was her *star*. 'It turned into a thing. Kid was sure he was made. Don't say it.'

Waldo didn't have to; he'd said plenty in the past. These jokers were one more reason not to enmesh himself in Lorena's business.

'Anyway,' she said, 'I went over and picked it up for him.'

'Get what you need?'

'And then some. Too cheap for a motel, these two. Got it on right in his car. Anyway, I wasn't checking my texts – sorry. Listen,' she said, changing the subject, 'I could use a favor.'

He tensed; something in her voice told him it had to do with work. 'Yeah?'

'I've got a meeting with a prospective in a couple days. It'd help to have you there.' It was the first time in half a year she'd tried to coax him onto a case. 'I'm pretty sure you'd like this one.'

He'd heard that before.

Waldo said, '243's open.'

'Oh. Fire's out?'

'Contained enough, I guess. I've got to get up there.'

She drew a breath at the rejection. It had cost her something to ask again.

'How?' she said. 'Not on your bike . . .?' Since Waldo basically restricted himself to transportation that was either public or self-propelled, each trip from L.A. to Idyllwild meant a bus and then a tortuous, torturous bicycle climb. She said, 'I could drive you.'

And then, she was no doubt thinking, she could drive him back down, once he was assured that his property was all right. Back to L.A. and her prospective client meeting. Back to L.A. and looking for a place for them to share.

He couldn't do it. Besides, he had long ago decided that he'd grant himself a waiver to ride in a private automobile only with someone who'd already have been making the drive without him; clearly that didn't apply here. He said, 'I'll be fine.'

'With the smoke and everything? That's *so* not healthy.'

She was probably right, but he tipped a shoulder anyway, a second rejection.

'Waldo . . .'

'I'll be careful.' Waldo knew he should hit her with a third, to rip off the Band-Aid quickly and tell her straight out that he wasn't going to move in with her.

But she stopped him cold with the lopsided quarter-grin that grabbed him every time. 'Last night in town is usually pretty good,' she said, and headed to the bedroom, grazing the back of his neck with her fingertips as she passed.

He heard her start the shower. He knew he wouldn't be able to tell her tonight. Not even if that meant the winds would pick up, the fire would jump the retardant line, and his woods would be imperiled all over again.

Maybe this time it *would* be the sex that burned it all down.

TWO

I t was ninety-five on the desert floor when Waldo started up from Banning under a yellow sky. Over the year he'd gotten steadily better at the climb, handling longer intervals between rests, but Lorena was right: he had no business biking the twenty-four miles up 243 under these conditions. Even his sunglasses (a Thing he'd added when his discovery of an eco-friendly shampoo-body wash combo allowed him to renounce his bar of soap) didn't protect his eyes from the gritty ash. After only a few miles it scratched at his throat and his breath came harder, too. He scolded himself for his stubbornness, dismounted and folded the Brompton and hitched a ride, something he'd resorted to only once before.

A white Lexus SUV stopped for him – a hybrid, at least, better than the fuel truck that rescued him the other time. A trio of floppy-eared hounds barked at Waldo from the rear. The driver, a thirtyish woman with a bleached undercut and granny glasses, lamented the animals lost in the flames. Waldo assumed woodland creatures knew how to flee to safety, but she had to be right, some unlucky ones must have perished. Waldo tried to tell himself he hadn't killed them.

She let him off near the top of the mountain. Waldo rode to his property. The odor of smoke and burning pine hung heavy, but otherwise everything appeared disconcertingly normal. By the time he turned off the pavement and onto his private, curving dirt road, it was clear the fire hadn't reached his neck of the woods. Still, he sighed deep relief when his eight-by-sixteen-foot home came into view, unharmed.

The chickens were fine; in fact, they had a full feeder and water bottle. Hilda must have come back and checked on them already. Or else she never left. Either way, it was a sign that she was fine, too.

Ash covered the cabin. Waldo went inside. Fortunately he had shut and latched the windows against animal visitors before leaving for L.A., so the smell didn't permeate the way it might have. He'd still need to give everything a good cleaning, but before that he wanted to go out and scope the damage.

From the center of town, the only abnormal trace he could see was a smear of cotton-candy pink on one of the highest overlooking ridges, residue of the retardant. After watching firefighting videos online, Waldo had researched the colored liquid the planes were dropping and learned that the EPA had labelled the substance 'practically non-toxic.' Wheeling now through the main streets, he considered the cycle of fires, human expansion, rising temperatures, bigger fires, and scientific advances to keep them under control, enabling, in turn, still more expansion. Most would call that progress. He wondered what the bison would call it.

Waldo took 243 to the far end of town. The fire had come up this way, from the Hemet side. He'd only been over here once before, when he was first looking for land to buy. A mile or two past the town center he was brought up short by large swaths of pink which carpeted the road, the foliage, street signs, even parked cars. Just beyond the pink, black: husks of trees, charred and denuded. The town had been saved, but by little more than inches.

Tamping down the nagging sense of his own culpability, Waldo tried to wrap his mind around the notion that a human being had done this, had set out deliberately to ravage all the life that he could, human, plant and animal.

Waldo had read all he could find about the fire. You'd think, from the coverage, that the act of arson was but a minor sidelight, the rage behind it not even a footnote. Was that, he wondered, because nobody had a chance to interview the accused yet, or was it that living in a *time* of rage had left us inured? Rage over everything that was changing, rage over everything that never changed, rage over what the government was doing, rage over what it wasn't, protests and counter-protests, hate and counter-hate, and an American president who actually seemed to glory in it. Throw in the dolorous catalog of crushing new epidemics – mass shootings, homelessness, opioids, suicides – and even a part-time hermit could see that the nation was collapsing under a collective mental health crisis.

Of course someone tried to burn everything down, and of course nobody cared why. In the shit show that was 2018, the Cranston Fire barely registered as a metaphor.

*   *   *

Waldo scrambled an egg and steamed vegetables from his garden. Dinner time was television time, and now, happily, that meant *Judge Ida Mudge* time. It also meant that Waldo needed to subscribe to DigiTV, the streaming service for which he'd never seen the need until he got hooked on *Judge Ida* at Lorena's. The $7.99 a month didn't violate any of his rules per se, but that didn't mean it was entirely without environmental cost. Waldo lived cheaply off of investment income and made a practice of sending his monthly excess to a rotating list of nonprofits, like the National Resources Defense Council and The Story of Stuff Project. This new expense would leave that much less left to donate. Waldo rationalized it by offsetting it against last year's work on the Alastair Pinch case, for which Pinch's network donated $16,000 to the Sierra Club – enough to cover Waldo's *Judge Ida* habit for almost 167 years.

Waldo sat down in front of his MacBook and cued up the first episode he hadn't watched yet. He loved the modest way each started, the courtroom spectators polite and respectful, with a voice-over announcer setting up the case. For the first half-minute, it looked deceptively similar to all those other legal reality shows, none of which had ever gotten purchase on Waldo's imagination.

Today's plaintiff, a pasty-faced, mop-haired emo type, slumped to his podium. *'Trent Reinhardt is suing his ex-fiancée for return of a diamond engagement ring. He also wants damages to replace an electric guitar, which he claims the defendant destroyed.'*

That defendant was a gum-chewing blonde, overweight, as were so many of the litigants in Judge Ida's courtroom, especially the women. This one wore an unapologetically unflattering tank top and shorts and sported a line of nose rings that had to be problematic during allergy season. Like her ex, she looked to be in her early twenties. *'Sandy Phillips is countersuing for sixteen hundred dollars in back rent.'*

Waldo felt a frisson as the announcer went into his customary bellow – *'Now y'all rise . . . 'cause Judge Ida Mudge is IN . . . DA . . . HOUUUUUUUUUUUUUUSE!'* – letting everyone know they weren't in *The People's Court* anymore. Electronic blues funk kicked in, the crowd leaped from the benches, and Judge Ida bopped in from the wings and up to her bench.

She was an African American who looked to be in her late

fifties. Her hair was straightened and tousled atop her head, high-lighting, invariably, a pair of magnificent earrings – today, golden hoops. She always wore a bold collar necklace, too; today's was electric green. Waldo assumed she'd had some prior career as a real-life judge, but he'd never wanted to research it. It was enough to know her this way, in the element of her full flower, presiding over a well curated parade of tawdry cases, mostly relating to family law: paternity suits, restraining order violations, small sums contested with incommensurate bitterness. That area had been far removed from Waldo's own experience with the legal system, but it was perfect for television, as family law, when you got down to it, was almost always about sex.

'Bailiff Man, everybody sworn in?' she said to her sidekick.

'Hell, yeah.' He was a tall man with a hard look: complicated braids, tattoos visible even on his deep ebony face, muscles popping out of his muscles. He always wore a tight black T-shirt; his multiracial three-man support crew wore white and looked like they worked out at the same gym. (Those guys weren't visible yet, but Waldo knew they'd materialize when the time was right.)

Judge Ida's first words were to the emo kid: 'So y'all were engaged?'

'Yes, Judge Ida.'

'How long?'

'Three years.'

Judge Ida drew back like that was the stupidest thing she ever heard. She held the pose until the spectators' laughter subsided. *'Three years?'* They laughed again. 'What kinda *bullshit* is *that?'* The audience started whooping.

The salty language was the show's initial boundary breaker. The other streaming services had been pushing the same envelope in other genres, with profanity-laden talk shows and even audience sitcoms, but cussing in a TV courtroom was something new. Waldo chuckled aloud and took another bite of his eggs.

When the hoots died down, the defendant, Sandy, tried to ride the wave. 'That's what *I* kept saying.'

But the judge wasn't having it. 'Am I talking to you? And spit out that gum.'

The girl sneered. She looked a little glazed; Waldo guessed she was on something. Regardless, Judge Ida had no patience for attitude. This was about to get good, you could feel it.

She said to the boy, 'She wanted to get married?'

'Yeah. That's why I proposed.'

'*Proposed?* Son, a young lady does not want to be proposed to, and then . . . *nothin'*. Young lady says "yes," she wanna be sayin' "*I do.*" Remember that next time: shit or get off the pot. Feel me?'

The audience whooped again.

'Now tell me 'bout this ring.'

'It was a family heirloom. It belonged to my mother, and my grandmother.'

The girl turned to him and said, 'You never told me it was your grand—'

Judge Ida banged her gavel, miked to be extra loud. It always quieted the room and always made Waldo jump.

'Bup bup bup,' said Judge Ida. 'You don't talk to *him* when you're in *my* courtroom.' She pointed two fingers at her own eyes. 'Nose and toes face *me*.'

'He told me it was his mother's. He never said his grandmother's.'

'Bullshit!' hollered the boy. 'I told you—'

'Nose and toes!' snapped Ida. 'Nose and toes! Which'a them words you too stupid to understand?' The audience ate it up.

The boy said, 'Sorry, Your Honor.'

'Did you owe her money?'

'No.'

'So that ring wasn't to cover a debt or nothin'.'

'No, Your Honor.'

'Was it a Christmas present?'

'No.'

'Birthday present?'

'No.'

'Valentine's Day? President's Day? 4th of July?' The way she said it – *Ju*-ly – drew another titter.

The boy smiled. 'Just an engagement ring.'

'Who ended the engagement?'

'She did, Your Honor.'

'That correct?' she asked the girl.

'Uh-huh.'

'Don't uh-huh me.'

'Yes, Your Honor.' More attitude.

'So you gonna break up with this boy, then you gonna keep his family ring?'

'It was a gift.'

'Engagement ring ain't no *gift*. In the eyes of the law, an engage-ment ring is a *contract*. And law aside, somebody who'd keep a family heirloom like that is what my mama would call no-'count. You know what that means?'

'Not really, Your Honor.'

'Means *trash*.' The audience chortled. 'You wanna be no-'count trash?'

'No, Your Honor.'

'You got that ring with you today?'

'No.'

Judge Ida froze, but slowly raised an eyebrow. Waldo loved when she did that. 'Where. Is. It?'

'I don't know.'

The boy exploded: *'You're a lying slut!'*

The girl spun and lunged at him, fists flying overhand. She was no fighter, but somehow one shot landed cleanly on his nose and drew blood. The boy turned away and tried to cover up while she kept flailing. The spectators leapt to their feet, the ones in back standing on their benches for a better look. In sudden unison, they all started chanting, *'Judge! – Ida! – Judge! – Ida!'* Waldo wondered how they were able to launch that so neatly every time. Bailiff Man rushed in and wrapped his arms around the girl from behind, lifting her clean off the ground and placing her back behind her podium. Judge Ida just sat back and shook her head slowly, like there was nothing she could do with this tomfoolery but hover above it and wait it out.

When the courtroom settled, the boy was snuffling. Judge Ida said, 'What you cryin' 'bout?'

'I still want to get married.'

Judge Ida looked at him in disbelief. *'To the "lyin' slut"?'* The audience laughed.

'I still love her, Judge.' The audience *ooh*'d.

Judge Ida turned to the girl. 'You wanna marry him?'

'Fuck, no.'

'She don't wanna marry you, son.' The boy, holding back tears, nodded resignation. 'But I gotta tell ya,' Judge Ida continued, 'from here, that don't look like much of a loss.' The audience guffawed and jeered. The girl turned crimson.

They turned to the matter of the guitar, which the boy said he found 'busted up' one day when he came home from work. The judge asked for details about the instrument and what it cost, and the boy provided the original receipt and photos of the damage. The girl claimed that the guitar had been vandalized by her step-brother, whose name was Kyle Fenner.

Judge Ida turned to Bailiff Man. 'We got Kyle Fenner?'

'Shit, yeah,' said Bailiff Man.

'Get that boy's ass in here.'

This Kyle Fenner sauntered in, a skinny punk with a turquoise Mohawk. The audience greeted him with lusty boos, having already made up their minds about him.

The jilted boy charged right at him. They tumbled to the floor and commenced thrashing one another. The production captured it artfully with a turning overhead camera. The spectators chanted Judge Ida's name again. It took Bailiff Man's whole squad to pry the two apart and then hold them back. Waldo noticed that the crew tended to be aggressive about breaking up fights between young men, but let young women go on longer. That was fine with Waldo, because the scratchy, hair-pully girl fights were generally more entertaining. Waldo didn't particularly like it about himself that he felt that way, but he did.

The skinny punk said, 'He's a pussy, Your Honor!'

'Whoa!' said Judge Ida. Waldo could feel the big moment coming.

'And he can't play guitar for shit!'

The boy tried to go at him again, but two of the bodybuilders restrained him.

Judge Ida said, 'Settle yourself down, boy!' It was definitely coming.

The punk said, 'And he fights like a bitch!'

And here it was: Judge Ida slammed down her gavel three times, torqued her body, tilted her head, and let loose the command everyone was waiting for: '*Sit the fuck down, and shut the fuck up!*'

The audience went wild. It was a high point of every show, Judge Ida knowing just the right moment to drop her catchphrase, an instant television legend like *The tribe has spoken*, or *Is that your final answer?* or even Walter Cronkite's *And that's the way it is.*

It took a while to restore order. The Mohawk kid said, 'He's just jealous, Your Honor.'

'Of what?' said the judge, at which point the punk pulled his stepsister, twice his weight, into his arms and planted a deep kiss on her. The audience howled in astonishment, though they must have seen it coming; Waldo certainly had. Judge Ida, giving up on the whole motley mélange, flipped her gavel over her shoulder. The sort-of-siblings were all over each other now, practically grinding on the evidence table. The tattered boyfriend watched them, his sobbing unchecked, Bailiff Man's powerful hand on his shoulder in simultaneous sympathy and restraint.

Waldo's taste in reality generally ran to brainless, shameless celebrations of wealth or gluttony, not this kind of grotesque emotional pornography. Jerry Springer's smarmy irony never did it for him, nor did Maury Povich, Springer Lite.

But somehow *Judge Ida Mudge* planted deep hooks. And Waldo wasn't the only addict: the show had set the internet ablaze and lifted DigiTV into the conversation with Netflix and Amazon and Hulu. Some of it was the swirling in of an actual story, a legal case demanding a winner and a loser. Some of it was the jaunty juxtaposition of the staid faux-courtroom with this bloodthirsty Colosseum mob howling for blood. More than anything it was the outrageous star herself, a little Judge Judy, a little Wanda Sykes and a whole lot of magisterial badassery like nobody had ever seen. She and her producers had found the miracle elixir and with it, no doubt, a fountain of gold.

If you squinted, Waldo thought, you could almost see the end of civilization. But he couldn't stop watching.

As Judge Ida banged her gavel to break up the make-out session, Waldo thought he heard a car outside. He hit the space bar to pause the video and went to his doorway.

Sure enough, a Cadillac Escalade was barreling up his dirt road. Waldo recognized it. His heart sank.

Two men got out, men he knew better than he'd like to. The smaller of them said, 'Miss me, Waldo?'

In the months that followed Waldo's initial return to civilization, he and this man, a Latino trafficker who went by Don Q, had amassed a raveled series of debts in both directions which ranged from cold-blooded murder to influencing private-school admissions. Don Q's helpmate, an Inuit boxer named Nini, didn't talk, but had made an impression nonetheless by beating Waldo senseless on more than one occasion.

Waldo hadn't seen or heard from them since the ugliness on the case he'd worked with Lorena a year before. He said, 'Less than you'd think.'

Don Q cackled. 'You should see the look on your face. Like you think I'm 'bout to ask you for a favor or shit.' He tipped his chin at Waldo's cabin. 'See your castle's all good. I half expected to find a pile a' ashes. True some muthafucker lit this all up?'

'What they say.'

'Whole world losin' its damn mind. Trump, right?' The first time Don Q and Nini came up the mountain to introduce themselves, they dropped what was left of a fellow dealer in front of Waldo's cabin. Waldo didn't recall that having much to do with the Republicans.

They approached the door. 'Gonna invite us in?' said Don Q.

Waldo held his spot in the threshold, nonchalantly blocking them. Better to keep the conversation outside. The two had developed enough of a détente that Waldo didn't think Don Q would make an issue of it.

It was a misjudgment. Nini threw an elbow to Waldo's throat too fast to see coming. Q sauntered into the cabin. Waldo followed, sucking for air. Nini took Waldo's place in the doorway.

'Don't fuck with me, Waldo.'

'OK,' Waldo managed to croak, 'What *is* the favor?'

'I told you, man: no favor. I'm here as a payin' customer, lookin' to procure your services. As a straight up private investigator.'

'I'm not in that line of business.'

'Shit, Waldo, you were the *last* time. When *you* called *me* for a favor.'

'That was an experiment. I decided it wasn't my cup of tea.'

Even if Waldo had any interest in it, Don Q was the last man he'd want to take on as a client. Lorena had made that mistake once, and it was all Waldo could do to keep her from getting killed, by the dealer himself.

Don Q noticed Waldo's open computer and frowned at the frozen image. 'Fuck you watchin', Waldo? *Judge Ida Mudge*? Man, that shit'll rot your head right off your shoulders. You got time on your hands, read a muthafuckin' book.'

Waldo, embarrassed, said, 'I read plenty of books.'

'Yeah? 'S the last novel you finished?'

'I read non-fiction. History, biographies . . .'

'You need to get into fiction, Waldo. Improves your vocabulary. Builds empathy.' He nodded toward the MacBook. 'Can't get brain stimulation of that nature watchin' trailer trash takin' their earrings off.'

'Send me a reading list. But I can't help you.'

'Damn, Waldo. After the shit I done on *your* behalf? Least you can do is a little fact-findin' in return.' He had a point. As did Nini's elbow.

'Sure sounds like a favor.'

'Ain't, if I'm payin'. What you get, like five hundred a day?'

'Two thousand.' Don Q's jaw dropped. Waldo said, 'That's what I get. And *if* I take the case, I'd want it to be a donation to the World Wildlife Fund.' He was still thinking about the animals lost in the fire.

Don Q said, 'Muthafucker, I ain't in this to help you game the IRS.'

'That's not why—'

'You get cash, like all my other vendors.'

'Fine,' said Waldo. 'But know I'll be making the donation myself. I don't do this for profit.'

'Sherman Oaks, two days ago, boys in blue pulled a John Doe out a fountain.'

'What do you mean, a fountain?'

'Kind you throw pennies with your kid, she be wishin' on some overpriced shit she plays with twice.'

'Like at a mini-mall?'

'It's Sherman Oaks, Waldo, not the fuckin' Piazza Navona. *Yeah*, a mini-mall.' Don Q had a way of making him feel under-educated. 'How'd he die, who was involved – I wanna know all the shit the police know. And all the shit they *don't* know.'

'Why?'

'Waldo: do *I* ask *you* why a muthafucker can make two G a day wanna live in the forest like some kinda badger?'

'If you did, I'd tell you.'

'But I *don't* – 'cause that's *your* business. Understand what I'm sayin'?'

'How do you know it's a John Doe?'

'*Pay fuckin' attention*: I ain't askin' you to investigate *me*.'

Most likely Q had killed the guy in the fountain, and now he wanted to use Waldo to help him get away with it. Waldo said, 'Pass.'

The dealer walked right up to Waldo, forehead to chin, and looked up at him. 'This is important shit to me, Waldo. It got me seriously agitated. 'Case you forgotten, I already dropped two bodies in matters related to you.' Don Q pulled an old-school flip phone from a pocket and held it in front of Waldo's face. 'This for you and me to contact each other, nobody else. I got my own burner just for this, too. Number's already programmed into yours.'

'I can't – take – '

'Don't tell me you still doin' that Hundred Things shit.'

Waldo eked out a nod. His throat still throbbed.

Don Q looked around. 'No problem.' He shut and unplugged Waldo's MacBook. 'I'll take this. You get me some answers, we can trade back, keep everything nice and level for you.' He started out, then turned, holding up the computer. 'I'm doin' you a favor, too. *Judge Ida Mudge*. Man, you disappoint me.'

Out the open door Waldo saw them climb back into the Escalade and drive away, kicking more dirt and ash into the air.

He'd spent an entire year grappling with Lorena to keep himself out of the private eye business, and here he was back in it anyway, and on a case that was bound to be morally indefensible.

Plus now he'd need to install DigiTV on his iPhone.

THREE

F our years prior, Waldo, then the LAPD's brightest star, discovered a tragic mistake of his own making, the wrongful arrest and conviction of a teenager named Lydell Lipps for a multiple homicide in a 7-Eleven. While Waldo fought prosecutors and his own department to secure his release, Lipps, who'd already done fourteen years, was stabbed to death in the yard at Pelican Bay. Waldo went public, quit the LAPD and blasted it loud and long, destroying every department friendship he had before withdrawing to his Idyllwild hermitage. He'd been drawn into two cases since, and both times had managed to outshine and embarrass the department. If anything, he had to be even less popular than when he left.

So asking the police for their take on the body in the fountain, the natural place to start, wasn't an option. Riding the Greyhound out of Banning, Waldo thought about alternatives. He might be able to get some help from an old ME buddy, Freddie Dellamora, who'd slipped him a coroner's report on the Pinch case the year before. Of course, this was a John Doe, not the wife of a famous actor; there was a good chance they hadn't even done the autopsy yet. Going over to the coroner's would eat up much of the remaining daylight, time better spent finding the fountain and doing a neighborhood. Waldo decided to phone, instead, on Freddie's old cell, see whether it was still good and whether he'd take the call.

Freddie let it ring for a good while, probably trying to decide. He answered with, 'Haven't seen *this* number in a while.'

Waldo said, 'You know anything about a John Doe in a fountain, Sherman Oaks?' and immediately regretted the abruptness. Close as they used to be, and long as it had been since they'd spoken, Waldo owed Freddie at least a little small talk. But Waldo still hadn't found his way back to social interaction, especially with people from his old life. Lorena was the exception, and even that had taken some time.

There was a pause on Freddie's end. He was probably miffed. 'No,' he finally said.

Self-conscious now, Waldo didn't want to ask Freddie straight out to check. But shifting to personal chitchat would be transparently manipulative. Stuck between the two, Waldo was frozen into his own silence.

Waldo heard a click and Freddie was gone. Did he hang up on him? Waldo checked his phone: it looked like Freddie just put him on hold. Waldo looked out the window of his bus, watching cars pass it by, one solo driver after another kicking out carbon, unabashed, learning from the fires not a goddamn thing.

After a few minutes Freddie came back on the line. 'Yeah, we got him. No rush on the autopsy.'

'Shot?'

'*Shot?* No. Drowned, is the guess.'

'Drowned, in a mini-mall fountain.'

'John Doe, sure. We get one every couple years. Urban outdoorsman, fishing for coins in the middle of the night, maybe a sponge bath? Slips, bangs his head, too loaded to save himself.'

Why would Don Q care about that?

Waldo was also surprised by the commonness. 'Every couple years?' he said. 'I never caught one.'

'Too small for a rock star like you. Why you interested, anyway?'

'No reason.' He realized how abrupt that sounded, too.

After a few seconds, Freddie said, 'That it?'

This time Waldo figured out to say, 'How you been?'

'Eh,' Freddie sighed. 'I fucked up.'

'With Barb?' Freddie's wife had left him.

'Yeah.'

Waldo wondered if he should suggest a beer while he's in town. Somehow he couldn't quite get himself there. Instead, he said, 'Do me a favor and let me know if you hear anything.'

Freddie, sounding confused, said, 'Yeah, sure,' and hung up. Waldo hoped Freddie knew he meant about the John Doe.

Waldo had decided that he'd manage Don Q later, that if he learned anything that might help cover up a crime, he just wouldn't share it. The new news, that this was some drug- or alcohol-related homeless death, took a little wind out of all that, but made the whole thing more curious.

Waldo located the fountain through a three-day-old article on
the Sherman Oaks Patch, which had the address but no information about cause of death. He took a second bus into the Valley
and from there biked to the mini-mall. It felt strange to be back
in town so quickly without Lorena knowing he was there. That
was something else he'd need to figure out.

The fountain sat between a Pinkberry and a poorly named
Mandarin restaurant, The Bamboo Wok on Inn, with a few outdoor
tables. Water trickled down from a bowl at chest level into a round
lower tier about five feet in diameter, with Spanish tile ringing the
sides. A small bouquet of daisies sat soaking in the upper bowl,
an informal memorial, left either by someone who knew who the
dead man was or someone with a heart big enough to mourn a
stranger.

Waldo spotted a stray wooden chopstick on the ground. It
reminded him of another thing about that so-called green restaurant
he'd taken Lorena to: they issued disposable chopsticks, as if they
had no idea that single-use chopsticks were deforesting east Asia
at a rate of twenty-five million trees a year. Well, no single use
for this one, at least. Waldo picked it up and measured the depth
of the fountain. If the man indeed drowned, as Freddie's colleagues
surmised, he'd managed it in two inches of water.

Waldo entered the Pinkberry. A pair of young women behind
the counter eyed him warily. He was used to that in L.A.: people
either recognized him from the news or they didn't, and in turn
treated him either as a celebrity or a derelict. He didn't introduce
himself, but politely asked if they knew anything about the man
who'd been found in the fountain.

'Was he a friend of yours?' asked one.

Waldo shook his head. 'Just curious.'

They said they heard he was discovered early in the morning,
long before any of the stores were open, there being no coffee
shop in the mini-mall. People had been talking about it, but nobody
knew the man's name or anything. Neither of them had been
questioned by a policeman, even though they'd both been on the
first shift every day since.

Rather than go store to store and collect more of the same
nothing, Waldo decided to work a different part of the neighborhood. He biked over to Fulton and the nearest entrance to the

walking trail that ran alongside the Los Angeles River, roughly parallel to Ventura Boulevard in this section of the San Fernando Valley.

Whatever it had been in eras past, now the 'river' was basically a giant open storm drain running from Calabasas to Long Beach. Every few years it would engorge under heavy rains and wash roiling waters to the Pacific. Invariably the local news would cut into programming to show some knucklehead who tried to swim it, only to learn there was no way to stop the ride or to get out; often as not the guy's fifteen minutes of fame would be the last fifteen he knew.

On sweltering summer days like this, though, you could theoretically climb down and walk the concrete for miles without getting your shoes damp. *The mighty L.A. River,* Waldo thought, looking down at a lonely McDonald's cup in a tiny, murky puddle. *Roll on, roll on.*

The city had been 'revitalizing' the river since before Waldo had fled to Idyllwild. What he found on his return was a beautified homeless encampment, that problem having metastasized during his years away. The walking trails were peppered with cheap tents and shopping carts warehousing vagrants' belongings, with thicker clusters under the overpasses. Other citizens generally stayed clear, except for those walking dogs big enough to feel safe.

In the middle of the trail a shirtless man bowed as in prayer, his knees tucked up under him and his elbows and forehead on the asphalt. His back was burned red to the point of blistering but he stayed in the sun, not ten feet from the shade of the underpass, writhing, silent and clawing at his scalp.

More promising was a pale-skinned man in a soiled yellow T-shirt, sitting atop a pile of belongings under an oak. His thinning but unruly hair and graying stubble made him look older than he probably was. He was cutting his toenails with a large pair of paper scissors.

'Hey,' said Waldo.

'Hey,' said the man.

'Hot,' said Waldo.

'Nineties again. Least we're not on fire.'

'Yeah,' said Waldo. 'Listen, you know anything about a guy they found in a fountain, couple blocks up?'

'The Professor?'

'You knew him?'

'Yeah.' It was almost too easy.

'Know what happened to him?'

The guy considered Waldo for a moment before answering. 'So there's this fight? Guy goes, "We have to tell them. *They have to know.*" But he didn't want to.'

'Know what?' said Waldo.

'That it's not true. That they're making the whole thing up. To keep the kids in line. And he says, "You can't tell them. They think you're Santa Claus."'

'Wait, what? They think the—?'

'Because he's *playing* Santa, see? In the movies.'

Waldo squinted. 'The Professor was an actor . . .?'

The man shook his head violently. 'The guy playing Santa in the movies! And he wants them to tell kids that Santa isn't real. And then this other guy, this homeless-looking guy, picture the Professor – he goes, "You can't say that to kids. They're counting on you."'

'The Professor is saying this . . .?'

'No! I'm just saying it *could* be.' He'd left Waldo in the dust. 'It's a movie,' the man explained. 'A pitch. I'm a screenwriter. You think it starts strong enough?'

'Actually, I'm trying to find out about—'

The writer wasn't interested. 'It's like a buddy movie, between the guy who *plays* Santa Claus in the movies, and this *homeless* guy, who turns out to be the *real* Santa. Write what you know, right?'

'You mean you're the real Santa?'

The guy looked at him. 'You're fucking with me.'

Waldo said, 'I don't mean to. It sounds like a cool movie.'

The man brightened. 'Right? Four quadrant.'

Waldo didn't know what that meant, either, but it didn't sound useful. 'Listen, do you happen to know what the Professor's real name was—?'

'*Leave him alone!!*' Waldo turned and saw a white woman coming at him on a bicycle, with a shopping cart braced to it like a sidecar, and brandishing some kind of stick. '*Leave him alone!!*'

Waldo had to jump out of the way to keep from being clobbered.

The woman stopped the bike-sidecar combo with her feet and painstakingly turned it back in Waldo's direction. Her clothes were filthy. She walked the bike toward him. Now he could make out that what she was waving around was half a rake.

Waldo got the screenwriter to vouch that Waldo wasn't doing anything to hurt him, and the woman started to calm. The two didn't seem to know each other. Waldo suggested he try out his Santas pitch on her. The screenwriter eagerly launched into it again, letting Waldo back away and continue down the trail.

'It starts in Wisconsin . . .' said the man, then called after Waldo, 'I should've told you that part!' Waldo didn't turn around.

Twenty or thirty yards along, another woman's voice startled him. 'Yo!' she said, and scrambled out from under a blue tarp. She was African American, with wide eyes and hair teased up from her head, a shock of white just off center. Waldo stepped back, ready to be accosted again. But she spoke calmly: 'I heard you asking about the Professor. You his son? Told me he had a son lives in Atlanta or someplace.'

'You knew him?'

'You his son?' she repeated.

'No. Where'd you know him from?'

'Panera. Bunch of us meet up around five thirty most days. You can join us if you want.'

He said, 'Thanks. The Professor – did you know his name?'

'Nah.'

'Why'd they call him that?'

'Probably 'cause he knew stuff. Like, he'd be all in his head most of the time. He was pretty messed up. Then all of a sudden he'd start in on somethin', you couldn't *believe* how much he knew. Like he read every book in the library. Or maybe he was makin' it all up, I don't know. Whatever, he could talk real good.'

'Have you heard anything about what happened? With the fountain?'

'Just that he was dead when they found him. For all I know, cops killed him, too.'

'The cops? What do you mean, "too"?'

'They killed Israel.'

'Who's Israel?'

'Israel, pretty sure it's Cisneros? He was another guy out here.

Cops hasslin' him for nothin' – I was there, over by Woodman. All he did was ask some lady for money. Ended up takin' his tent.'

'Who did, the cops?'

'Then I heard he got shot, like, three nights ago, up on Magnolia by the laundromat.'

'I heard the Professor wasn't shot.'

'Maybe so. But I heard Israel was definitely shot.'

It felt off, but shooting sounded more like Don Q's game than drowning a homeless man in a fountain, so maybe it was something. 'And you're sure it was the cops?'

'I assume so, the way I saw 'em get into it with him.'

'But could be someone else who shot him?'

'Could be dogs go oink, pigs go woof.'

Could be also that what Freddie's colleague told him was wrong, that this Professor was shot, too. There weren't a lot of fuck-ups working at the coroner's, but with the indifference the cops were showing the dead vagrant by the Pinkberry, it wasn't hard to imagine an ME also giving him the back of his hand.

Waldo said, 'You know any more about the Professor's son . . .?' She shook her head. 'Anything else at all? Was there a shelter the Professor went to . . .?'

'I told him about the one I stay at sometimes on Lankershim, but they wouldn't let him, 'cause of his dog.'

'He had a dog?'

'He found a empty house. He showed it to me once. He didn't hardly tell nobody, though. I'm only telling you 'cause it don't matter no more.'

'You know where it is?'

'One of them streets off Moorpark.'

'What color was it, you remember? Did it have a fence, unusual trees . . .?'

'Yeah, there was a fence. A white fence. And the garage was green, and there's like a second little house in back, same color green. I didn't stay there too long. It got weird, bein' alone with him, know what I'm sayin'?' Waldo tried to look like he knew what she meant. 'He didn't try nothin', just, you know, Professor went off the chain sometime, screamin' stuff I don't understand.' Suddenly she gave Waldo a suspicious look. 'Why you wanna know?'

'A friend asked me to find out about him.'

Somehow that was enough. 'Well, you find out what became'a that pooch of his, I'd like to hear somethin' 'bout it. Ain't easy out here for a dog, you lose your person.' She turned and headed back for her tarp.

Waldo said, 'Thank you,' to her back.

Waldo could probably get away with telling Don Q only that the corpse in the fountain was that of a drowned homeless man nicknamed 'the Professor.' He'd try to tease a little more out of Don Q in return, though, out of his own growing curiosity. He decided to wait for the next day to make the call, so as not to seem like he'd rushed the job.

Out of the same curiosity, he tried Freddie's cell. This time Freddie didn't take the call. Waldo left a voicemail: 'Hey, me again. I got another one, with a name – "Israel Cisneros." Sounds like this one *was* shot. Anything else you can tell me, I'd appreciate it.' He was about to press *end call* when he thought to add, 'Sucks about Barb,' then, feeling extra awkward, hung up as quickly as he could.

The sun was setting. He hadn't let Lorena know that he was back in town. It wouldn't go over well that after a year of resisting her entreaties, he'd taken a case, let alone for a trafficker, let alone the trafficker who had once looked to kill Lorena and driven her into hiding.

To procrastinate, Waldo started googling. It was becoming an automatic response to all sorts of negative stimuli, hunting reasons to get more upset about things which already agitated him. *Getting worse.*

It wasn't hard to find a cascade of sad facts. There were now over fifty thousand homeless in L.A. County, more than the populations of Palm Springs or Biloxi, Mississippi. Their deaths had gone up seventy-six percent over the last five years. Homeless persons were fully one percent of city's population, and sixteen percent of its homicide victims.

When he couldn't stand to learn any more, Waldo phoned Lorena. He told her the whole story, including the Don Q of it, and braced for her reaction.

She said, 'Whose license are you doing that under?'

'What do you mean?'

'You're not licensed to do PI work on your own. So are you taking this job under mine?'

Waldo chuckled. 'I guess I have to be.'

'Gee. Then you're going to have to do something for me,' she said, with a suggestive lilt.

'What do you have in mind?'

'Mm, it's pretty good. Should I tell you now, or wait until you get here?'

'Tell me now. Give me something to think about on the ride.'

'OK.' She held for a beat, then said, 'You can do that meeting with my prospective.' She made it sound so salacious that it took Waldo a second to catch up.

'Wait—'

'That's the fee,' she said, pleased with herself, 'for working under my license.'

He groaned.

'Come on, Waldo. It's a celeb. Showing your face'll make a difference. Besides, it's somebody you'll want to meet.'

Not likely. In fact, Lorena often teased him for being the least star-struck person in L.A. 'You're kidding, right? Who do you think *I'd* want to meet?'

'Judge Ida Mudge.'

FOUR

They'd gotten into the habit of cooking together almost every night, Lorena gently mocking his severe food regimen, especially his rule about never using ingredients that had been packaged. The activity was simple, pleasurable, one of the first things about their reunion that felt easy. Tonight, though, the domesticity of chopping onions and zucchini side by side felt oppressive.

They hadn't returned to the question of cohabitation since Lorena first raised it. She was either waiting for his answer or considering it a fait accompli. It felt like the latter, and Waldo resented it. He resented too the way she'd set him up, turning him on to *Judge Ida Mudge* the week before, fully intending for him to get hooked. For that matter, he also resented that he was prepping vegetables right now instead of watching the episode which DigiTV teased at the end of the last one, about a pair of married-then-divorced cousins, suing each other over their common grandmother's diamond brooch.

Lorena said, 'So I found an apartment downtown. A rental.' Before Waldo could speak, she said, 'For myself. You haven't said you wanted to live together – no news is news. Besides, one big change at a time is enough.' She read his confusion and clarified: 'We are kind of working together.'

That made it sound more official than he thought it to be.

'Baby steps,' she said. 'I'm trying not to jam you, Waldo.'

He did feel jammed, though. He was equally uneasy about living and working together; the rope she was giving him now on the one was snaking around his wrists on the other.

Over dinner, Lorena brought up the subject of how to handle the financial aspect, which she'd clearly given a lot of thought. On the Rose case, which they worked jointly, they'd simply split the fee. Now they had two pieces of business, one completely his and one that was still indeterminate. 'What if we go "eat what you kill"? We'll split the Judge Ida fee if you stay on it—'

'I didn't say I'd—'

'I know, I know. But we'll split the daily for tomorrow. And whatever days you actually work. You know, if you do. My ops come out of my end. And on your scumbag case, you can keep whatever he's paying you. I wouldn't touch his money anyway.'

'Anything I make is still going to non-profits.'

'Your choice.' She took another bite of the stir-fry. 'Oh, one more thing,' she said. 'Can I put your name on the door?' Lorena was still doing business as *Very Private Eyes*, which Waldo believed locked her into exactly the kind of marital gigs she was constantly trying to transcend. 'It would really help.' She'd always hoped a partnership with Waldo would make them the go-to agency for L.A. celebrity work.

Waldo changed the subject, asked her to tell him more about Judge Ida. Lorena was surprised that he hadn't already boned up on his own.

Waldo said, 'I didn't want to . . . *demystify* her.'

Lorena laughed and told him everything she knew.

Ida Mudge grew up in Baltimore, to which she returned after law school, eventually becoming a family court judge. She came to the attention of a talent scout working for the makers of a mildly successful legal reality show, *Judge Joseph*, who were looking to launch a spinoff. They brought her to L.A. for an audition session, where she went big, and then financed a pilot episode, where she went bigger, including her first blurted, *Sit the fuck down and shut the fuck up!* That gave the producers the idea to sell the show to the fledgling DigiTV, where Judge Ida's expletives would not only go unbleeped but could even be promoted as a point of distinction. The show was an instant sensation, the kind of megahit you could build a network around.

But then Judge Ida developed a legal problem of her own, involving, to Waldo's surprise, Bailiff Man. Lorena explained that Immanuel ('Man') Nickerson appeared only on the first season, which Waldo was still in the middle of watching. Nickerson, a former Grape Street Watts Crip, had done stretches in Corcoran, for credit card fraud and other bad habits, and San Quentin, for aggravated assault, before deciding to go straight and seek out a legitimate career, something stable and reliable. Naturally, he chose acting.

His good looks and authentic hard edge landed him a couple of tiny roles in urban crime dramas, and then an audition for the new *Judge Ida Mudge* show, whose producer envisioned a combination sidekick-bodyguard, Ed McMahon crossed with Mike Tyson. Thus Man Nickerson became Bailiff Man and, in turn, a celebrity in his own right. It was reported that Judge Ida was so appreciative of his contribution to the show's chemistry that she arranged for him to receive five percent of her salary as his pay.

Unbeknownst to their legion of new fans and most of their co-workers, that wasn't the only chemistry in play; all through that heady first season, Judge Ida and Bailiff Man were also carrying on a torrid affair. Apparently it ended poorly, and when the show was renewed, Bailiff Man's contract was not. Now Immanuel Nickerson, twenty years his ex-boss's junior, was suing for sexual harassment, claiming that Judge Ida initiated the relationship and that he understood his sexual performance to be a condition of keeping his job. Nickerson, spicing his allegations with the requisite tawdry claims (the judge, he attested, had a bent for presiding au naturel beneath her robe), was seeking five million dollars in damages, on the grounds that he wouldn't be able to find comparable work in 'his area of special skill.' The suit was filed by powerhouse attorney Fontella Davis, mouthpiece to the stars and Waldo's personal antagonist since they'd worked together, nominally, on the Alastair Pinch case.

Perhaps the most intriguing aspect of all was the fact that Davis and Judge Ida had a personal connection: forty years earlier they'd entered college together as freshmen at Mathewson, a small, prestigious liberal arts school in the upper Hudson Valley. The shared history was not, apparently, enough to make Davis a *Judge Ida Mudge* fan. In fact, at the initial announcement of the Nickerson case, she made news on top of news by remarking that the show 'makes Black people look like clowns.'

Waldo hadn't considered that critique until hearing Lorena repeat it now. To the extent he'd thought about *Judge Ida Mudge*'s racial message at all, his impression was that the show's litigants were a conscientious ethnic mix, as if trying to demonstrate that America, at least when it came to moral squalor, was truly a land of equality. Which, of course, meant that Fontella's rough shot was directed at Judge Ida personally, and raised a flood of questions about their history.

Lorena told him too about the recent press conference, a Fontella classic. There she unveiled four more male claimants, going back to Judge Ida's days in private practice, during which she'd allegedly pressured paralegals for sex, as well as a junior associate and even a client who couldn't pay.

A politically heterogenous army of commentators began calling on DigiTV to cancel *Judge Ida Mudge* . . . but that hadn't happened. As an intrepid reporter from *Variety* discovered, the streaming service was still clinging tightly to the show, as it had since before the lawsuits, when Judge Ida's agent had asked them to let her buy her way out of her modest contract so that she could increase her earnings mightily. According to the article, a first-run syndicator had quietly offered Judge Ida a five-year contract for two hundred sixty million dollars.

That potential annual salary, fifty-two million, would have been eye-catching on its own, but *Variety*'s breakdown of the practical implications amplified the buzz. Given the show's production schedule – five episodes, a week's worth, shot back-to-back each Tuesday – it meant that Judge Ida Mudge, who only two years ago was being paid $77,390 a year by the City of Baltimore, could start making a cool million dollars a day.

Lorena pulled her Mercedes into the driveway of Judge Ida's house in Malibu, off Kanan Dume. Waldo said, 'Seriously, the guy gave you no preview at all?'

'This is the third time you're asking.'

'Oppo on the new plaintiffs,' Waldo speculated, also for the third time.

This time Lorena came back at him. 'Cleaner than covering up a murder for a drug dealer.'

A high-pated white man in his forties with rimless glasses was waiting in the doorway. The expensive suit at ten in the morning in Malibu gave him away as an agent. 'Lorena,' he said, 'good to meet you in person. Rick Rothbell.' Turning to Waldo, he repeated, 'Rick Rothbell. Big fan. Privilege to be working with you.' He shook hands firmly with each of them. 'Come, let me introduce you to Judge Ida.'

The house had a New England vibe, with wide plank floors, oil paintings and lots of gingham, nothing like the *Judge Ida Mudge* show at all. Judge Ida herself – Waldo couldn't think of her without the honorific – rose to greet them. She wore a white poplin shirt and khakis, sneakers covered in rhinestones the only glimmer of her television flash. But with her effortless dazzle, she didn't need more. Or maybe Waldo was just buzzing off meeting his obsession in the flesh.

She gave him a hard once-over, making him atypically self-conscious about his unmanaged mountain look. His hair and beard were as long as he'd ever let them grow, and he was wearing literally half the clothes he owned.

'Nice place,' said Lorena.

Judge Ida broke off from her appraisal of Waldo. 'I rent it, for when I'm in town.'

'You mostly live back east?'

'Half and half, when we're in production.' This confused Waldo; the *Judge Ida* episodes were peppered with outdoor shots of an inner city and harbor which Waldo recognized as Baltimore, so he assumed the show was produced there.

Waldo and Lorena sat on a sofa, Judge Ida and Rothbell in club chairs. The agent recapped the harassment case, including the recent batch of additional allegations. Except for Immanuel Nickerson, he said, with whom she'd had a consensual relationship as unmarried adults, the judge never engaged in any kind of sexual relations with any of the plaintiffs; these were false accusations by opportunists who saw a defendant with deep pockets and were trying to position themselves for a payoff to make the nuisance go away. Though three of the four had gone to law school, only two had passed the bar and only one was still practicing, with, as Rothbell described it, a third-rate firm.

They wanted Lorena and Waldo to do deep-dive background checks on the new plaintiffs, to put them under a microscope and find anything, related or otherwise, that might embarrass or discredit them and force them to withdraw from the suit.

It was precisely the dirt-digging Waldo predicted. He glanced at Lorena. She didn't look back. Instead, she said to Judge Ida, 'Did you know these men? Do you remember them?'

Rothbell spoke for her: 'She recalls them, but only vaguely.'

That set the pattern for the rest of the meeting. Judge Ida, so voluble on her bench, was virtually mute. But as Lorena asked questions for their side and Rothbell did the answering for the other, Waldo watched the shimmer behind the judge's eyes. Even silent, she dominated the room. And mostly she focused on Waldo, fairly silent himself.

'Fontella Davis smells money,' said Rothbell at one point.

'Speaking of money,' said Lorena, 'is it true what was in the trades? The syndication offer – two hundred sixty million?' It was ballsy to ask flat out. Waldo knew she was measuring them for the fee.

'Absolutely true. Two sixty, pay or play,' said the agent.

'Which means . . .?'

'Once the deal's signed, the money's guaranteed, whether they end up making the shows or not.'

'Wow.'

'Unfortunately, it's irrelevant. DigiTV isn't going to let Judge Ida out of her deal. Especially now, with the streams they're pulling since this bullshit started. The judge is getting dragged through the mud, and DigiTV's getting fat on it.' Rothbell was poormouthing, his own eye on the fee, too.

But that wasn't what Waldo was interested in. 'What exactly are we getting into,' he asked Judge Ida, 'between you and Fontella Davis? I'm sure it wasn't coincidental that Nickerson hired someone you knew.'

Judge Ida puffed air through her nose. If her silence spoke volumes, her snort spoke libraries. She waved off the question – or was it Fontella? – with the back of her hand.

Lorena said, 'I assume you'll be willing to talk to us about the other complainants? Exactly how you knew them, and the like?'

Rothbell again jumped in. 'The judge knew each of them only in passing; that's all that's relevant for your purposes. We'll give you their names, plus dates of professional overlap, and you can do your background checks without disturbing her. I'll also handle the interface with Judge Ida's attorney.'

Waldo wondered why the judge bothered coming to the meeting at all. This last stonewall looked particularly suspicious. He'd bail on the whole thing right now, if it were up to him.

But it wasn't. 'Understood,' said Lorena. 'Should we talk about a retainer?'

'Let's,' said Rothbell.

She had charged their last clients, the Roses, three thousand per day, but came to believe she should have asked more. Now Waldo could see visions of Judge Ida's syndication offer setting off the terpsichore in Lorena's head. How could it not? It was why plaintiffs were coming out of the woodwork.

Lorena pushed it: 'Our fee for the complete, dedicated resources of our firm – that is, Waldo, myself, and our three operatives full-time, is seventy-five hundred a day, plus expenses. We'd like a ten-day retainer – any unused portion, of course, to be refunded.' Seventy-five thousand up front, just to start. Talk about ballsy. Especially given that Waldo hadn't agreed to work the case beyond this meeting.

Judge Ida narrowed her eyes at Lorena, then glanced at her agent, stood – without a word, of course – and walked out of the room.

Lorena turned to Rothbell, trying to look like she wasn't panicking, like she hadn't just overplayed her hand and lost the biggest opportunity of her career. 'We could do a smaller daily fee for less manpower,' she said, casually as she could. 'But with the full team you'd get faster results, and I actually believe it would be more economical.'

Rothbell said, 'I'll share that with Judge Ida. I'll get back to you.' He rose. Waldo did, too.

Lorena was the last to stand, knowing that it equaled surrender. She said, 'Is there maybe a business manager I should talk to?'

Rothbell said, 'No,' and walked them to the door.

Lorena said, 'Look, if you guys would rather do this on a weekly, we could work out a rate—'

They heard footsteps and turned. Judge Ida was walking toward them down a long hallway, carrying banded stacks of American currency. She said, 'I'll want a receipt.'

As she tried to hand the unwieldy piles to Lorena, one packet of fifties – it looked like a hundred of them – dropped to the floor. Rothbell said, 'Maybe we can find something for you to carry that in,' and they all went into the kitchen.

Judge Ida found a plastic shopping bag from Gelson's market. Waldo said, 'If you have, I'd prefer paper.'

Rothbell drew up a receipt and had Lorena sign it. He handed

Waldo a manila folder with a page of information on each of the plaintiffs. Then everyone said their goodbyes and Waldo and Lorena got into her Mercedes.

As Lorena backed out of the driveway, Waldo started thumbing through the file. 'So?' he said. 'Where do you want to start?'

'Shit, Waldo, I've got seventy-five grand in a fucking Gelson's bag. We start at Wells Fargo.'

FIVE

The nearest Wells branch was at the Malibu Country Mart, where they didn't know Lorena and surely had never seen a mountain man walk in with $75,000 cash in a grocery bag. The branch manager came over for a chat, ostensibly to make certain they were being well taken care of. Waldo knew they'd be sharing the serial numbers with the IRS, who'd be passing them on to the FBI. He and Lorena were taking a leap of faith that Judge Ida Mudge wasn't using them to launder money for counterfeiters or terrorists.

Lorena wanted to celebrate over lunch. They picked a burger joint in Pacific Palisades which had a lot of words in the window like *local* and *organic* and *grass-fed*, though Waldo did wonder where exactly in the Palisades they were keeping the cows. Lorena took out her phone and in about a minute and a half managed to secure a meeting room for that afternoon, invite the ops and confirm that they'd all be there.

'This is exactly what I needed to get my back away from the wall,' she said between sloppy bites of her Breakfast Burger, topped with a fried egg and bacon. (Again: where were the pigs?) 'It's been so tight – I'll have a good couple months, but then one bad one and I'm screwed. Two bad months, I'm practically back to zero. Now I can start looking like a real agency.' Waldo pushed the beets to the side of his ponzu salad. 'Looks are everything,' she said. 'Especially in L.A. But it takes capital, which I've never had. Finally, I can get past this phone-number-and-website shit.'

'What do you mean – an office?'

Mouth full, Lorena flashed her eyes and grinned.

The thought of the emissions, not to mention the scores of Things needed to appoint it, set off alarm bells. Fortunately Judge Ida had given them plenty to do; there'd be no time to run around town interviewing realtors and checking out potential locations. And if a case this size went well, it might itself be proof that they could succeed without one. That alone was reason for Waldo to stay involved.

Lorena slathered a fry in ketchup. 'We have some time before the meeting. Can I show you the space I've been looking at?'

A short man in an orange windbreaker waited for them in front of a glorified pizza joint on Melrose, near Paramount. 'That's the realtor,' Lorena said as they got out of the car. 'He told me this used to be Desi Arnaz's private office, for when he'd sneak away from Lucy for a hookup. Some history, huh?'

Waldo had rarely seen her so bubbly. Even in four-inch stilettos, she bounded up the two flights. The realtor unlocked the door and left them alone. There was a reception area and a pair of offices plus a little room that could be used for a kitchenette. The corner one faced the studio. 'Classic, right? We should find out what detective movies they shot over there, maybe get a big poster.' *We.* 'And we could put a partners desk right here. I think we could squeeze four small desks in the other one – fit everybody, with a little room to grow.'

'What's the size?'

'Fourteen hundred square feet.' Seventy thousand pounds of CO_2 a year. 'We can fix it up, give it some style. That guy Tejano I used to work for? It was a dump like this, and he kept it that way. Like it's in the PI manual, your firm has to look like a shithole. But we could knock through that wall, put a big window between the staff room and the break room, make it feel more open. Get rid of the paneling, do the walls all white, get white desks, white lamps . . . then paint the doors bright colors. What do you think? It's everything I wanted,' she said, rendering an answer from Waldo unnecessary. 'And once we have the space?' More *we.* 'We should put a little money into marketing. You can target really efficiently online, but I was thinking maybe we could do, like, an announcement brochure, and spring for a direct mail campaign to criminal lawyers. There are three thousand in this town – that's a lot of business sitting out there.'

Three thousand brochures! Six thousand Things, counting the envelopes. He said, 'You know, over a quarter of the solid waste in municipal landfills is discarded paper.'

Lorena's face fell. 'OK, fine, we'll stick to online. But, Waldo, being environmentally responsible can't mean we just give up. Believe me, the agency that eats our lunch is not going to be worrying about municipal landfills.' *Our* lunch. 'A business needs what a business needs,' she said, and went to take another look at the break room.

Waldo, aching for a break of his own, walked out and down to the street and kept walking.

A business needs what a business needs. Like how BP *needed* to drill exploratory wells below thousands of feet of water, then thousands of feet deeper into the earth, and how they *needed* to plug a gas leak quickly, so they *needed* to use sea water instead of the proper drilling fluid, and *needed* to skip the cement testing because it was just too damn expensive. They *needed*, and Halliburton *needed*, and Transocean *needed*, and that's how a wellhead blew out on the *Deepwater Horizon* – eleven workers killed, five million barrels of oil pumped straight into the Gulf, marine life massacred in record numbers, plus deformities, mutations, oh, and a third of the children living within ten miles of the coastline bleeding from their ears and noses or menstruating early. But hey: a business needs what a business needs.

Waldo stopped walking. *Easy*, he told himself. *Easy*. This wasn't five million barrels of oil in the Gulf, it was one tiny office on Melrose. Proportion. Lorena hadn't even rented it yet. There was time for discussion.

Deepwater Horizon, for God's sake. Eight years ago. Why even go there?

Getting worse.

He took a few deep breaths and started back.

For forty-five dollars, Lorena booked one hour in a LiquidSpace conference room in a new office building on Hollywood Boulevard near the Chinese Theater. Waldo had managed to avoid her ops for the whole year, but that was about to end.

They took the elevator up. In front of the suite stood a young Black man – *very* young; he looked about sixteen. 'Mr Waldo, sir, it's an honor. I'm Lucian Reddix, but everybody calls me Reddix. Like "Waldo."'

'Did you go in?' said Lorena.

'Yes, but they told me we have our own entrance – right there.'

Lorena headed for the door he pointed to. 'The company's called Alercon. They say they do "online barter"; I'm not sure what that is. They didn't really want to go into it, so I waited out here. But I can go back later. There's one girl I think might talk to me.'

'It's just a meeting space, Reddix. We don't need to investigate them.'

'Right.' He turned back to Waldo. 'You're my idol, Mr Waldo. I'm applying to LAPD as soon as I turn twenty-one.'

Waldo looked to Lorena for help. She was smirking as she opened the door. The kid followed her in.

Waldo recognized a figure slumping down the hall: Dumpster Williams. When he and Waldo were both at North Hollywood Division, Williams, who embraced his alcoholism more than battled it, picked up his nickname after being found behind one. Lorena claimed he was sober now and going by Willie.

'Hiya, Waldo,' said Dumpster, extending his hand. It was a warmer reception than Waldo usually got from old co-workers, but then Williams – dismissed after drunk-crashing his vehicle into, ironically, a second dumpster – was gone before the turbulent end of Waldo's own career. The men took each other in. Waldo was hirsute and unkempt these days; Dumpster had just gotten old. Even his handshake dripped with defeat. 'Good there's a place for castoffs like us, huh.'

Whatever sympathy Waldo was starting to feel evaporated. The department's most celebrated detective, he had resigned from the LAPD as a statement of principle; Dumpster Williams was bumped off the job for being a boozer and a fuck-up. Waldo just said, 'Come on,' and headed into the conference room.

It was equipped with an oval table and six chairs and a raft of audio-visual equipment they wouldn't need. Lorena took one head, Waldo the other. Lorena texted and the men sat in awkward silence while they waited for the third operative.

Dave Greenberg walked in ten minutes late, puffing, toting a 20-oz. bottle of Dr Pepper and an open pack of Red Vines. Without apology he squeezed himself into a chair, folded a candy stick into thirds and stuffed it in his mouth. Waldo hadn't crossed paths much with Greenberg, but his reputation for unpleasantness reverberated far beyond Foothill Division. According to Lorena, Fat Dave's wife surprised him with divorce papers the day after his retirement became official, spiteful timing which left him financially vulnerable in a way he hadn't anticipated. Without the typical network of ex-cop friends to help him find a second career, he swallowed his pride and took a twenty-hour-a-week guarantee working for a woman half his age, and did his best to keep his resentment to himself.

'Charlie Waldo,' he said, through a mouth full of half-chewed Red Vine.

'Dave.'

'Thanks for dressing up for us.' Fat Dave himself had on a threadbare brown suit overdue for the cleaner.

Lorena explained the case. At Waldo's insistence she forwent photocopying Rothbell's pages for the men and instead used her phone to text them photos. She assigned each of the ops one of the new plaintiffs and said that she and Waldo would handle the fourth plus Man Nickerson. Reddix took page after page of notes as she spoke, Dumpster occasional ones; Fat Dave didn't uncap a pen. Two of the plaintiffs lived in other parts of the country, so the task was to do as much as possible electronically and by phone. Lorena said they should start with the database sites and then concentrate on legal records, both criminal and civil, especially looking for histories of filing lawsuits. Then they should go deeper. 'If they ever changed jobs, why?' (Waldo noted Dumpster shifting in his seat.) 'Credit reports, bankruptcies. See who'll talk to you on the phone. Anybody: former wives, former girlfriends, former boyfriends, former pets. Did they use drugs? Did they drink?' (Dumpster shifted again.) 'Did they owe money, gamble, screw around? Use the people search sites. Work their social media hard.'

'Um . . .?' said young Reddix, raising a hand.

'Yes?'

'Clarification on the pet thing?'

'Joke.'

'Thank you.'

Lorena avoided Waldo's eye. But she told the kid she'd double up with him on his plaintiff to start. Then she said that they were going to be moving into actual offices on Melrose very soon, and still avoided Waldo's eye.

* * *

Out on Hollywood Boulevard, she said, '*Waldo-Nascimento*, or *Nascimento-Waldo*? Your name *should* be first, but it kind of sounds more powerful second. What do you think?'

Waldo said, 'How did this office become a done deal?'

'I closed on it while we were waiting for Greenberg. By text. Why – you have a problem?'

'I guess not; it's your office.'

'Well, I think of it as *our* office. But if you don't want any part of it, then yes, I guess it is my office.'

'*Why do you need it?!*'

Startled at the outburst, she stopped walking and spun on him. 'I told you why I need it!'

'That office is going to pump seventy thousand pounds of carbon dioxide into the atmosphere every year!'

'Whether I use it or someone else does!'

Passers-by craned to watch them argue, street entertainment alongside the Darth Vader and Marilyn Monroe and Deadpool posing in front of the Chinese for photos and tips.

'That's the self-justification that's choking the planet.'

'Please . . .!'

'If you didn't use it, and the next person didn't, and the next, they wouldn't build the *next* office that nobody needs!'

'I need it! To build this into the agency I want, I need it!'

It was an echo of the old, fractious days, when the points of contention were usually other women, other men.

'You can be different,' Waldo said. 'You can be better.'

'I'm an East L.A. girl trying to play with the big boys. It's hard enough without being "different." Jesus, why can't you just be supportive?'

'Trying to play with the big boys. With Fat Dave Greenberg and Dumpster Williams and a nine-year-old.'

She didn't have a comeback, which he could tell made her angrier.

Deadpool walked up to Lorena and put a comforting arm around her shoulders, clowning for a gaggle of laughing tourists to take pictures with their phones. 'Fuck off,' she said, and elbowed him in the solar plexus. 'You, too,' she said to the tourists, and they did.

She and Waldo started walking again, leaving Deadpool on all fours on the pavement and Marilyn Monroe tending to him. Waldo said, 'This case is a turd. The client won't even help us. She probably *did* harass those guys, and Fontella Davis probably has a dozen more on the way.'

'Good!' said Lorena. 'More work for us!' Waldo recoiled. 'It's the job, Waldo. You don't get the luxury of waiting for cases that make you feel good. No private eye does.'

'*I* do! It's the only reason I was in this at all.'

'It's the case I've got. I'm sorry I don't have a roster full of high-minded innocents like Don Q!'

'I only *know* Don Q in the first place *because you were working with him!*'

Lorena didn't have an answer for that, either.

This Judge Ida job drove straight to the misgivings he had about PI work when Lorena originally brought it to him the year before. He said, 'I don't want to be a partner. And I definitely don't want to be responsible for the Three Stooges up there. I never even said I'd work *this* case, past the meeting.'

They turned up Las Palmas, where they'd parked. After a bit, Lorena said, 'Look, you can't ask me to give up Judge Ida, and I can't ask you to work it. How about, you let me keep *saying* you're my partner. You come back in when I wrap it up, come with me to deliver what we find, but other than that, you don't have to do anything. I'll give you twenty percent. That's fifteen grand right off the top you can give the Green Earth Society or whoever.'

Waldo grunted agreement.

So he was free of this one. He'd been planning on meeting up with Don Q that night, to put that one to bed, too, but now spending the evening apart from Lorena felt like a bad idea. He'd set something up with Q for the next morning instead, and then head back to his woods.

He knew he'd wounded her, punctured the dream she'd been trying to realize for a year. He said, 'How about we go back to Hollywood & Highland, find an ice cream?' She stopped walking, stunned. Without waiting for her *yes*, he turned and headed back toward the boulevard. She clacked after him on her heels.

'That ice cream gets here in containers,' she said, catching up. 'So do the cones. And I *know* you won't eat it out of a cup. You're doing this for me – really?'

'Don't get crazy. I said we'll find *an* ice cream. And I'll watch you eat it.'

She hip-checked him into a mailbox.

They were going to be OK.

SIX

The guys in the gourmet taco truck in Grand Park held up impressively under Waldo's interrogation about the provenance of their ingredients: even the tortillas were handmade at a bakery right downtown. His conscience clear, Waldo bought three – fish, eggplant and sweet potato – and, to avoid a paper plate, talked them into letting him leave the tacos on the counter while he ate them one by one. They weren't keen on lending him a cloth towel to wipe his hands, but Waldo, intent on not burning through a fistful of paper napkins, offered them an extra two bucks, and one of the guys tossed him a semi-clean rag.

Meals would be simpler once he got back to his cabin. He'd miss Lorena, though. Last night's sex, always their foundation, had a desperate undertone that unnerved him to recall.

He found an empty bench and put his backpack full of traveling Things beside him to save the seat for Don Q. Waldo asked if they could meet downtown, convenient to the bus station, and was gobsmacked when the dealer picked this spot right in the locus of downtown courthouses. Waldo wasn't happy about it, either: there'd be all sorts of law-enforcement types walking through the park in the early afternoon, any one of whom might recognize them both. But Waldo had learned not to argue with Q about the small things. He just wanted this last weirdness off his plate and to get his computer back.

Don Q approached and Waldo cleared his bag off the bench. The dealer laid a copy of the *L.A. Times* on the seat between them.

Waldo said, 'Where's your gorilla?'

'Nini?' said Don Q. 'Gettin' hisself some osso bucco. I can't believe the shit they sell on food trucks now.' Waldo looked over: the Inuit stood at the end of a long line for the one called *Veals on Wheels*. Don Q sniffed in Waldo's direction. 'You been eatin' Mexicano?'

Waldo nodded, then said, 'Thanks for meeting me downtown. Made things easier for me.'

'Man, two G a day, ain't doin' *shit* to be easier for *you*. This worked for *me*. Just so happened, I got things to do 'round here anyway.' There was a bullet-headed man looking their way from across the park. Waldo didn't know the guy, but his suit yawped FBI. 'Wanted to catch my dude Mel, too, and L.A. Phil, but my timin' was off.' Yes, definitely watching them. Waldo nodded acknowledgement. The fed cold-stared back.

'Look,' Waldo said, 'I don't want to know about your friends. Especially their names.'

'Fuck you talkin' bout?'

'Your dude Mel. Phil whoever.'

'*L.A.* Phil. *Philharmonic.* Gustavo Dudamel's the muthafuckin' *conductor.* But it ain't symphony season, what I'm tryin' to *tell* you.' Don Q shook his head. 'You know, Waldo, you wouldn't be such a philistine, you wasn't turnin' your brain to cream'a wheat on fuckin' *Judge Ida Mudge.*' Don Q looked away again. 'Six G in an envelope. MacBook's in there, too. You tell me what you know, then I'm gonna walk away. You gonna carry the paper just like that, don't remove the items 'til you're on your bus and halfway back to Podunk.'

The computer was a Thing and the newspaper was a Thing and the envelope with the money was a Thing, although he didn't intend to accept the cash, and if he left the cash in the envelope, then it was only two Things, but he also had to give Don Q back the burner flip phone, which the dealer would probably tell him to toss, but since Waldo obviously wasn't going to dump all that lead and copper into a trash can to be hauled to a landfill, that meant he had to hang onto it until he found a trustworthy e-waste collection site, which would throw off his day, and still leave him with a Hundred and First Thing – in fact, a Hundred and Second until he recycled the newspaper.

'Fuck your mind at, Waldo? You gonna tell me what you got, or what?'

'Guy died in the fountain. No autopsy yet, but the cops' first take is, he drowned. Reports online say no visible signs of trauma. That must be what the police saw.'

'And who was he?'

'John Doe, like you said. Homeless. Regular around the neighborhood.' Waldo touched the edge of the newspaper and slid it half a centimeter in Don Q's direction. 'Your money's no good. Consider it one more of our mutual favors. All I need is my computer back—'

Don Q slammed a hand down on the paper. '*First of all,*' he said, 'I didn't ask for no muthafuckin' *favor*, I *hired* you. Second, six thousand for *that*? Shit you read *online*? *Where at*, the muthafuckin' *Patch*? And *I* told *you* John Doe, you got the *temerity* to come and sell that shit back to *me*? For *six G*?'

'Not selling. I told you I didn't want your—'

'You didn't find out a damn thing about him? Seriously?'

'There was another homeless guy, killed just a couple days before—'

'You sayin' the fountain man was killed? What was it, killed or drowned?'

If Waldo wanted to suss out Don Q's involvement without abetting it, he had to walk carefully here. 'I don't know, could be both.'

'Cops think they related, these two deaths?'

'I'm not saying that.'

'Then fuck this other homeless muthafucker got to do with *my* homeless muthafucker? I think you know somethin' you ain't sharin', Waldo. I told you this shit got me agitated. You best gimme *somethin'*.' His eyes bore into Waldo's, fierce and unmoored.

Waldo said, 'He had a dog.'

'A dog. Fuck! I want the man's *name*. I want *everything*. Know what? I want his *dog's* name. And I ain't payin' you *shit* for the three days of my time you've already wasted.' He stood, taking the newspaper – and Waldo's computer – with him. 'Do not mistake what you and me got goin' for some kinda bromance, Waldo. This is transactional. You don't bring me what I contracted for, you and me gonna have the same problem I have with *any* muthafucker try and stiff me. And as you may recall, ain't my modus operandi to call customer service and ask for no supervisor.'

He turned and looked toward the food trucks. 'Shit,' he said, 'Nini's still waitin'.' He turned back to Waldo. 'Hey, them tacos any good?'

Waldo left a voicemail for Freddie Dellamora and texted Lorena to let her know he wasn't going back to Idyllwild after all. She texted back that she was with Reddix and that she'd see Waldo tonight at home.

He swung over to Grand Central Market and picked up groceries for a couple days' worth of dinners, then biked the five miles back to Lorena's. He brought inside two UPS packages which sat in front of her door – more Things for her new apartment, no doubt.

There weren't a lot of good moves. He tried Freddie again but didn't leave a second message. He remembered that one homeless woman's offer to join the dinnertime meet at Panera, where he might find some transient who could tell him more about the Professor, but it was getting late to make it to the Valley in time. He'd do that the next evening.

Lorena's empty house silently chided him: she was out working a case for which Waldo was getting paid but not helping. With no idea when she'd be home, he didn't want to start cooking, so he truly had nothing to do. The whole thing made him feel dissolute. Actually, it made him want to watch a couple *Judge Ida Mudge*s. But then, what didn't?

Waldo peeled a cucumber to tide him over to dinner, then connected to DigiTV on Lorena's big screen, the first of her ex's possessions she'd replaced. Today Judge Ida had a paternity suit on the docket, complete with blood test results. When the defendant-father kept trying to talk over her, she followed up her *Sit the fuck down* with a threat to order a second blood test, 'the hard way.' Waldo laughed out loud. What a contrast to her silent glower when they'd met in person.

His second allotted episode was one of the best/worst yet, centered on two little people with two big dogs, getting sued by a truculent plumber, a potty-mouthed woman with full body tattoos, who'd gotten bitten while fixing the little people's toilet. The German shepherds were in the courtroom as evidence and took the entire three-man white-shirted posse to control, leaving Bailiff Man alone to try to stop the little people from knocking down the unladylike lady plumber and then, once they had, from jumping up and down on her. Bailiff Man, laughing like everyone else in the courtroom, wasn't doing much of a job of it.

Lorena got home soon after the episode ended. She was giddy when she saw the packages. 'Yes! My Keurig!' The bigger one held a K-Cup Pod Coffee Maker. 'I swear, the worst thing about the divorce was that the prick took his grinder with him.'

'So how does this work?'

'Brews one cup at a time. You just pop in a pod, and you have your coffee in less than a minute.'

'So no grinder.'

'This is *so* much easier. Way faster, less to clean . . .' She sliced open the second carton: dozens and dozens of single-use pods. He'd read about these. Enough were sold each year to circle the globe ten times.

'You can't be serious.'

'What, because you use them once? Waldo – I've been going to coffee shops. You got a cup, you got a lid, you got a stirrer. This has to be better, right? Aren't they recyclable?'

'Some of them.' He took out a pod and inspected it. 'Number seven. Not these, it doesn't look like. A grinder's better, anyway.'

'So? You can have a grinder at your cabin.'

'I don't have a grinder. I don't have *any* coffee maker. I didn't have the space, plus it was a Thing.'

'Fine: your house, your choice. My house, my choice.'

His first thought was that this was a setup, an extreme prop purchased deliberately to make that point. Still, the point was valid. And with so many of Willem's Things to replace, Lorena would be making terrible choices constantly and each would drive him up the wall. They'd be having the same conversation over and over, and over and over she'd be maddeningly right.

The only way he'd have any legitimate say would be if he were splitting the rent with her.

Was that such an outrageous idea? He still didn't want to live in L.A. full time, but if he were merely taking a share of the place she'd already rented, he wouldn't be adding emissions. It would be similar to the dispensation he gave himself to ride in her car if she was driving to the same place anyway. True, whatever he put toward rent couldn't be donated, but there was a chance that the good he'd do by influencing Lorena's decisions would be as valuable as what that cash would accomplish through a non-profit.

Meanwhile, semi-living together would be a tonic for their again-teetering relationship, offsetting the way he hurt her when he backed out of the partnership. In fact, the release of the pressure of working together actually made this thinkable.

The move felt reasonable, proportional. Well-adjusted. The opposite of getting worse.

'What if,' he began, and laid it out for her. With a smile she couldn't suppress, she challenged him on all the concessions he was making, and he made the case for it being no concession at all.

'By the way,' he said, grinning now, too, 'where exactly do we live?'

Before she could tell him, her phone rang. She checked it and registered surprise. 'Hello?' She listened a while. 'You're sure. Because he'd probably rather—' Cut off, she frowned at Waldo while she listened some more. 'OK,' she said finally. 'He'll be there. Thank you, Your Honor.' She hung up.

'Your Honor?'

'Judge Ida. She wants to meet with you tomorrow. Alone.'

SEVEN

*J*udge Ida Mudge was produced on a small independent lot off Santa Monica that had been around since Laurel & Hardy. The guard at the gate directed Waldo to Stage 4, outside of which a young man waited for him. He introduced himself as DeRaymond, Judge Ida's assistant.

Waldo locked his bike to a rack. The spot closest to the stage door had a sign on the wall that said *Reserved for Judge Ida Mudge – Don't Even F*cking Think About It*. Sitting under it was a couple hundred thousand dollars' worth of Maybach, the subbrand of Mercedes for the driver who can't afford to be seen in an S-Class.

DeRaymond said they were about to shoot their last episode of the day and that Waldo could 'watch from the booth.' He checked to see that the red light of the soundstage door was off and led Waldo inside and through a maze of wooden flats. Occasional glimpses through breaks between them revealed slices of *Judge Ida*'s familiar courtroom. Waldo felt a shiver of excitement despite himself.

DeRaymond brought him to a control room and directed him to a sofa in the back. Four producers or directors or technicians, seated at a console before a wall of monitors, paid him no attention. Eight different camera angles covered the set.

The audience was told to rise; Judge Ida entered and took the bench. Waldo quickly found himself tuning out the technical banter of the quartet in front of him, the better to follow the action on the screens.

The case featured a mismatched trio of separate plaintiffs. Two women were burly and tough, one white, with a severe buzz cut and a braided ponytail down the back, and one Black, with a long red wig which Waldo knew wouldn't survive the episode. The third woman was a fragile platinum blonde from Ukraine. After Judge Ida entered but before the questioning began, some sort of stage manager in a headset ran out and told all the plaintiffs to take off their jewelry and step out of their high heels. Waldo had never considered that bit of melee prep, hidden as it was from the audience at home.

What the plaintiffs had in common, it developed, was that each believed herself engaged to the defendant, a gawky software designer with bug eyes and a nose which looked borrowed from a larger man's face. After months of striking out on Tinder and eHarmony, the ugly computer geek started taking desperate stabs at niche sites to which he didn't naturally accord, like Gluten Free Singles and Farmer Wants a Wife. Judge Ida tapped the defendant's lonely quest for every bit of merriment she could, having particular fun feigning confusion over how J*date*, a Jewish dating app, differed from J*Pay*, the commercial service for communicating with convicts. The geek, it was revealed, had opened accounts on both, the latter after making a pair of romantic connections via Meet-an-Inmate.com, each of which eventually led to a proposal of marriage, conditional on the woman's early release. ('Why *both* of them?' demanded Judge Ida, to which the geek answered, 'You can't blame me, Your Honor. Parole boards are fickle.')

The story grew still more complicated when the geek attained sudden riches by creating an app called Pee-ple Pleasers, a crowd-sourced rating guide to public restrooms. Now he could afford a proper mail-order bride; enter the Ukrainian blonde, who appeared today with a junior college professor to interpret.

The episode took turns both predictable – a three-way brawl among the jealous women, with the little Slav getting the worst of it – and unpredictable – the defendant saying that after all this, he'd like to marry the woman holding her red wig in her hands, right here and now, if the judge would be willing to perform the ceremony. Which, of course, she was. The director, sitting in front of Waldo, somehow barked into existence a bouquet, liturgical lighting and 'Here Comes the Bride' in an R-rated hip-hop rendition.

What luck, thought Waldo, to have gotten to witness this one live.

Judge Ida's office, in a bungalow next to the soundstage, had a cheap and temporary feel dissonant with the show's success. Judge Ida sat behind a desk with a chipping wood veneer. There was nothing personal on the walls.

She said to Waldo, 'You see *USA Today*? They got a poll asking people to name a justice on the Supreme Court. I came in third, behind Judge Judy and Ruth Bader Ginsburg.' She cackled. 'What's that tell you?'

'Women are coming up?' said Waldo.

She cackled again. 'Sit down, sit down.' She called to her assistant: 'DeRaymond! You offer Waldo some water?'

DeRaymond scurried in and got a bottle of water from a mini-fridge in the corner, which he brought over to Waldo. 'Sorry about that.'

'I'd take some tap water in a glass, please, if you have one.'

The assistant looked to the judge, who nodded approval, and DeRaymond trotted back out. Judge Ida shook her head and grinned at Waldo. 'Yeah, I heard all about that shit you do. That Hundred Things – that real?' He nodded. 'Man of principle. Why I believe I can trust you. Why I wanted to see you alone.' Waldo clocked the implicit knock on Lorena.

DeRaymond returned quickly with the glass. He said, 'Rick is here, and Lenny's on his way.' Judge Ida screwed up her face. 'My bad. I double-scheduled.'

'Don't say "my bad" when you mess up. Say, "I'm sorry."'

'I'm sorry.'

'OK. Send them in.'

When Judge Ida was sure DeRaymond was out of hearing range, she said, 'I got a soft spot for a kid comes out of the background he did. Boy fucks up twice a day. Used to be three times, so he's on his way.' Waldo was charmed.

The agent Rick Rothbell entered, hesitating when he saw Waldo, whom he obviously wasn't expecting. Judge Ida said, 'Waldo's here to talk to me about the case. I'm fine with him sittin' in for this meetin'.'

A white fortyish dynamo bounded in with a laptop. He carried himself like a weekend athlete and had hair going silver at the edges. Judge Ida said, 'Lenny West, Charlie Waldo. Lenny's my showrunner.'

Lenny was one of those people struck dumb upon seeing Waldo. 'Oh,' he managed.

'Pretend he ain't here.' Waldo pulled a chair into a corner, to help him with that.

The other three took places around a coffee table, the judge in a chair and the other two sharing the sofa. Opening his laptop, West said to Rothbell, 'Judge Ida and I want to start moving on the spinoff. We looked at all the auditions, then we brought in two candidates for each role and did a mix-and-match. This is the combo we like.' He tapped some buttons and a picture of three judges in robes came up under the title, *Judge Ida Mudge Presents: JustUs 4 Da People.* All of them looked to be in their late twenties: a dark-skinned Black man with a shaved head and diamonds in both ears, a woman of indeterminate race with green dreadlocks, and a white hipster with a twirled mustachio and six-inch chin hairs waxed to a point.

Rothbell said, 'They're so young. These are actual judges?'

Lenny West shook his head. 'But they all had at least a year of law school. We want to take it to DigiTV and push for it now. Go go go.'

Rothbell said, 'I don't know. I don't think we should get in any deeper with DigiTV while the syndication offer is still on the table.' That the million-a-day bonanza remained in play was news to Waldo. 'I'd rather sit on the spinoff and fold it into the syndication deal. If we do that, we can cut out Kovel.' Waldo knew he was talking about Judge Joseph Kovel, the aging jurist from the Bronx with the majestic beard and commanding baritone, from whose show *Judge Ida Mudge* was itself spun off.

West looked to Judge Ida, clearly holding back until he saw how his boss would feel about the defenestration of her former mentor. 'Judge?'

'You know what,' said Judge Ida, 'at this point, *I'm* carryin' *his* ass. People are tired of that Old Testament shit. Man's makin' as much on my show as I am, and you *know* we're gonna have to give him a taste of the syndication money on the way out. I do a spinoff, I ain't givin' that man diddly-squat.'

Now that he knew how the wind blew, West didn't hold back. 'You're right. Fuck Kovel, *and* his plantation mentality. We don't need another old white man show, we need *this*.' He pointed to *JustUs 4 Da People* and its would-be cast of jurists. 'With diversity directors, producers, camera people, the whole crew. A show that looks like America, top to bottom.' Rothbell nodded affirmation.

After that, the meeting wound down quickly. Rothbell and West punctuated their own goodbye with a thumb clasp, chest hug and finger lock.

Judge Ida closed the door again and said to Waldo, 'See how it is? Me against the world.'

'Really? They seem totally in your corner. Down to the handshake.'

She smiled. 'Yeah, they think I like all that smoke they blow up my ass. Important thing? Lenny knows *he* looks good when he makes *me* look good, and Rothbell's the man gonna get me paid. But you, Charlie Waldo – *ha!* You don't give a shit. I got nothin' you want.' She was telling him again that she trusted him. Her charisma enthralled him; her approval gave him a tingle. He'd never experienced anything like it.

He said, 'I wouldn't mind a little something about the plaintiffs.'

'Got nothin' for you; ain't no there there. No, I need your assistance on a whole different matter.'

She took a white envelope from a desk drawer and passed it to him. It was addressed by hand to her, care of the studio, and had an Ocean Park postmark. 'PERSONAL AND CONFIDENTIAL' was handwritten in block letters at the bottom. It had been sliced open cleanly. Inside was a single folded piece of paper. In the center of the page, in Times New Roman, it read simply:

I know.

Waldo looked to the judge for an explanation. She said, 'People hear about a million a day, *somebody's* going to show up, try and jack you. I got no idea what this fool thinks he has.'

'Then he can't jack you. Assuming it's a he.'

'That's why I didn't do anything about it. Then a week later – yesterday – this.' She gave him a second envelope from her desk.

Waldo tried to handle it by the edges. It was similarly addressed, though this one had a Westwood postmark. It too contained a folded sheet, but also a yellowed clipping from the front page of a college newspaper called *The Mathewson Monitor*, dated March 23, 1979.

Waldo read the headline story, about the death of a student

named Anthony Branch, found in a ravine in the woods on college-owned property, beside a drop of almost twenty feet. The death was believed to be related to hazing at a fraternity called Chi Gamma Pi.

'What did you have to do with this?'

'Nothin'.'

'Did you know him?'

'Weren't a whole lot of Black students at Mathewson College in 1979.'

The accompanying page said, in the same style as the first:

Start liquidating assets.

'Tell me about Anthony Branch.'

'Terrible. Terrible. These idiot frat boys, they took these pledges, got 'em drunk, blindfolded 'em, tied their hands, left 'em out in the woods. That was their initiation – the "pledge hike," they called it. Did it every spring. They were supposed to find each other and find their way back. Apparently Anthony wandered off in some crazy direction and ended up fallin' off a cliff or somethin'.' She told Waldo that it was ultimately deemed an accident and that the fraternity was shuttered but with no further consequence to the other students.

'My boyfriend at the time,' she said, 'it wrecked him. He was an upperclassman in the woods. Senior. He only went along to make sure none of the other guys did anything too stupid. He never drank, himself. Not one beer, ever. At least while I knew him.'

'What's his name?'

'Morris Thurmond.' She looked out the window, snagged on a memory.

'Are you still in touch with him?'

'Not for thirty years. He's a minister, up in Oakland. Big community leader. I happened to meet one of his congregants a couple years ago; sounds like he's really made a difference up there. They love him. I'm not surprised. Back then, though, with Anthony – Morris wasn't the same after. He thought he should've stopped 'em from doing that pledge hike at all. Couldn't forgive himself.'

Waldo gave her a moment of quiet before saying, 'Anything else you remember?'

'"Lacerated aorta." I'd never heard that term before. Burned in my mind. Gave me nightmares. And I remember there were three other pledge captains with Morris, the ones who ran it – Matt Fishbein, Carter Gass, and a guy named Hoyt. I don't recall if that was his first name or last.'

'Were you a senior, too?'

'Sophomore.'

'Why would anybody think you had something to do with it?'

'No idea.'

'How about Fontella Davis? Did she know Anthony?'

'She knew him. But I'm sure she don't know anythin' I don't.'

'Who else has seen these?'

'DeRaymond's only seen the sealed envelopes. He doesn't open 'em when they say "Personal and Confidential."'

Waldo took another look at the newspaper article. 'If you really didn't have anything to do with this, let it go. If there's nothing to say except that you happened to go to a college where another student died, they can't hurt you.'

Judge Ida shook her head. 'Oh yeah, they can. I'm tryin' to close a two hundred sixty million dollar deal. You put a scandal, even a bullshit one, on top of Fontella's bullshit? That money's goin' bye-bye.'

'Then be proactive. Take this to the authorities.'

'Come on, you *know* some cop's gonna tip off TMZ. No, I want you to handle this. Look into Anthony's death. Find out if somethin' happened out there, somethin' bad nobody heard about. And I need you to figure out what it is somebody thinks they know.'

'And if it turns out it *was* a crime?'

'*Then* we bring in the law, and a publicist, and we get ahead of the story. That's the only way to make this thing go away: solve it, and make me look like the hero.' She reached into her desk and pulled out a sheet with the show's letterhead. 'Start by goin' up to see Morris. I'm gonna write you a note.' While he began to consider the environmental consequences of a trip to Oakland, Judge Ida wrote on a piece of letterhead from the show:

Morris – For old times' sake, please help this man any
way you can. Ida.

She drew a heart over the *i* in *times'*. 'He used to tease me some-times for doin' that. This way he'll know it's really from me.' She handed Waldo the sheet.

Not taking it, he said, 'Can't you call him instead?'

'You got a problem with this?'

'Hundred Things.' Waldo had determined during the Pinch case that temporarily held evidence would not count, whereas Judge Ida's note – not evidence but a tool to make his work easier – did.

'Damn,' said Judge Ida, 'you are hard core.' She looked him up and down. 'How bad you need that belt? I'll hold it for you till you get back.' When he hesitated, she snapped, 'Come on: *off.*' He unbuckled and surrendered his belt to the judge.

He said, 'You'll need to call Lorena and talk business.'

'Nuh-uh. I'll give you another five grand a day, personally, on top of what all I'm payin' her on the other thing. But you keep everythin' about this a stone secret. Even from that girl.'

EIGHT

S ucker.

Would he have said yes if he weren't starstruck? Not likely. And he didn't just take the case, he tacitly agreed to lie to Lorena, without even an objection. All he'd been putting into making things work with her, all the effort and compromise – sold out, just like that.

Sucker. Spineless fanboy.

Then there was the travel. The trip to Oakland might only be the beginning. In the years since he took control of his carbon footprint, Waldo had never left Southern California. The people worth talking to had to be scattered about the country. Fontella Davis lived right in L.A., of course, but just the thought of her made Waldo's fillings hurt.

About three blocks from Lorena's house, Waldo's phone buzzed. He pulled onto the sidewalk and checked it. 'Freddie,' he said.

'Cisneros.'

'Yeah?'

'This guy wasn't shot, either. Where you getting this shit?'

'How'd he get killed, then?'

'Hyperthermia. Heat stroke.'

'And what about the John Doe?'

'Nothing yet.'

Heat stroke. The cops didn't kill Cisneros and neither did Don Q. In all likelihood his death had nothing to do with the Professor; that was just some free association by a woman who lived next to the river.

So it was back to a random transient too hammered to keep himself from drowning.

Why the hell was Don Q worked up over *this*?

'OK, Waldo,' Freddie said and hung up. Waldo realized he'd blown another opportunity to be even passably sociable.

The cops had taken away Cisneros's tent, and then he'd died of exposure. It started Waldo googling again. With temperatures on the rise, record numbers of homeless people across the country were perishing from heat stroke and heat exhaustion. About two percent of the people on the streets of L.A. died every year. Their life expectancy was about fifty years of age – *fifty!* For women, less than that.

Meanwhile L.A. had voted hundreds of millions of dollars for homeless relief but couldn't agree whose backyards they could spend it in. In Sherman Oaks, where both those men died, an informational meeting about a proposed shelter turned into a near riot. Sherman Oaks, which in the last election voted seventy-five percent Democrat.

Waldo put away his phone, hitched up his pants – he wanted that belt back – and biked the rest of the way to Lorena's. Another package from Amazon waited in front of her door. The Keurig coffee maker would still be inside, he was sure, sitting in its box.

Waldo let himself in. He was surprised to see Lorena standing in her living room, sweaty in her exercise wear. The look always worked for him; more often than not, she didn't end up showering alone. He was sure that was the main reason she didn't do it at the gym.

'You must've walked right past this.' He put the package on the coffee table.

'How'd it go with Judge Ida?'

'She didn't give me anything we didn't already have.'

'Why'd she want to see you alone?'

'Just wanted to shoot the shit about Lydell Lipps, Alastair Pinch.' He walked over to her with a smile. 'She's a starfucker, like everyone else in Hollywood.' She laughed. He kissed her, hooking a thumb under each strap of her tank top and sliding them over her shoulders.

Nothing could render the world uncomplicated like Lorena Nascimento. No rules, no Things, no Google, just her mouth, her nakedness, her softness, her strength. If he'd only let it, life could be simple as this, and all the time. Stop fighting it, start now, just let go . . .

Lorena broke away from him and said, 'Wait – first let me see what I got.' She threw him a teasing smile as she re-strapped herself and went for her package. 'Yes!' she said, dislodging a box from the packing carton, cardboard to hold more cardboard.

'Handcuffs,' she said, and, with a twinkle, 'Don't get any ideas, they're for the office.'

Waldo took the box from her: a ten-pack of Safariland Disposable Double Cuffs. '*Plastic?*'

'Come on – they're smaller, and ten for the price of one. And how often are we going to use them?'

'Exactly. So get yourself one good metal pair.'

'I've got three ops.'

'You're giving them cuffs? I wouldn't trust them with forks.'

'Hey, you didn't want to team up – this isn't your call.'

'But—'

'No "but." The apartment, yeah, but not the business.'

It was the opposite of the move she put on him with the coffee maker. She was trying to jam him into working with her, too.

Nothing could loosen his grip on his values like Lorena Nascimento, either. Seconds ago he was ready to let it all slide for her, like he did when he stayed here night after night after night until his town almost went up in smoke. How much more warning did he need?

'OK, then,' he said, digging in, trying to re-anchor himself. 'No single-use coffee maker. For our apartment.'

Lorena sputtered, but said, 'Fine.'

'And we can get rid of some of this other stuff, right?' he said, crossing into the kitchen.

'What's left? Willem took everything.'

Waldo opened one of the picked-over drawers. 'Two spatulas?'

'You can't flip a pancake with the little one, and you can't use the big one in the single-egg frying pan.'

'You don't need a separate single-egg frying pan. And I can't remember the last time I saw you make a pancake.'

'You're not here every morning, are you.'

'So, what, you make pancakes when you're alone? That's one frying pan and one spatula you can get rid of. For starters.' He started looking through the cabinets for more.

'Can't I grandfather the stuff I have? Who's it going to help if I throw my spatula in the garbage?'

'You don't throw it in the garbage! You take it to Goodwill, and somebody gets a spatula *there*, instead of buying a new one!'

'It's one little spatula!'

'Do you know one-twentieth of the *petroleum* consumption in the world goes toward manufacturing plastic? And the neurotoxins! Ninety-five percent of the adults in America have BPA – bisphenol A – in their urine. Think about that.'

'OK, Waldo. There's two ways we can play this. Either you can keep talking about neurotoxins in our urine until I throw up . . .'

'Or?'

'*Or*, we could take a shower.' She went into the bedroom, leaving the door open behind her.

Listen to himself. Bisphenol A. This was definitely what *getting worse* sounded like. Credit Lorena for staying steady this time and not rising to his bait, for de-escalating with the shower move.

Besides, she wasn't the one twisting him in knots, it was Judge Ida. Well, Lorena, too, but it was everything that the judge laid on him that put him over the top tonight: the travel she expected, the secrecy she demanded. Plus his pants kept sliding down and annoying the crap out of him, and that was her, too.

He heard the shower start and started to unbutton his shirt. But before he gave in to that distraction, which he knew would stretch deep into the night, he needed to call Judge Ida, back out of this blackmail business, and set a meeting to trade her note to Rev. Morris Thurmond for his belt. Not only the note, he reminded himself, but also the newspaper clipping, which he now felt a little guilty for having taken.

He went to his backpack and carefully removed it. It gave the case a tangibility; holding it in his hands, with its age and brittleness, it was almost like he was bypassing Judge Ida and making direct contact with the young man who died.

That young man, in his high school cap and gown, smiled from a boxed obituary Waldo hadn't studied in the judge's office. It began on that front page and continued at length on its back. Waldo took his time and read the whole thing.

Anthony Branch had been a protean superstar: a two-sport athlete, a Big Brother volunteer first in his native Brooklyn and then again at Mathewson, a graduate of prestigious Stuyvesant High School, to which he traveled every day by bus and subway. He was the first in his family to go to college.

And someone seemed to think somebody killed him . . . though you'd never know it from the *Mathewson Monitor*.

Was it properly investigated at the time? Or underattended, because he was Black, or because he didn't come from money?

An old feeling was coming back, that achy tooth former Detective III Charlie Waldo knew he wouldn't be able to stop teasing with his tongue.

It had been some time.

And not that he needed the rationalization, but there was this too: what was Judge Ida Mudge, after all, but a million-dollar-a-day damsel in distress?

Waldo heard the water turn off. Lost in himself, he'd left Lorena hanging.

A minute later, she emerged, a towel around her torso, her long, black hair hanging wet. She rested a hand on a cocked hip, and gave him a look that said, *Seriously?*

Waldo said, 'There was more to it with Judge Ida.'

Lorena said, 'No shit.'

NINE

Waldo wheeled through Sherman Oaks, taking the grid streets between Ventura and the 101 one by one, south to north, over one and then back the other way, hunting for a green garage and a white fence. He wanted to find out enough about the Professor to satisfy Don Q before going to Oakland.

Lorena, meanwhile, was trying to locate Rev. Morris Thurmond and also Anthony Branch's parents. If the latter were still alive and in Brooklyn, Waldo would have to consider flying. Carbon dioxide, carbon monoxide, hydrocarbons, black carbon, sulfur oxides, nitrogen oxides, lead. How could he do it? Then again, when he'd set the rule for himself to use only transportation which was public or self-propelled, he'd never specifically excluded planes; Lorena claimed it wasn't fair to the client – or, by extension, to the business – suddenly to add that now.

On Mary Ellen Avenue, closer to the freeway than to Moorpark, Waldo found what had to be the Professor's squat house: two stories, white vinyl picket fence and a green garage in more need of a paint job than anything else on the well-tended street. The lawn was synthetic, a positive California trend in response to perpetual drought and the resulting increases in water pricing.

Waldo propped his bike against a wall next to the front door and took a closer look. The house itself needed paint too but otherwise wasn't in obvious disrepair. He walked the driveway around to the back. There were no signs of either person nor dog living there. He tried the rear entrance: locked.

The small property contained, in addition to the main structure, a jacuzzi, a raised firepit and a small guesthouse. There Waldo spotted the only sign of notable damage: a small broken window just above the doorknob. This one turned in his hand. Waldo leaned in and took a peek. The air was close with a corporeal reek, but it was empty, no furniture or random belongings.

Waldo heard voices, pedestrians on the street side of the house.

He closed the door, waited for the people to pass, then got on his bike and rode to Panera.

There Waldo ordered a soup and salad and, learning that they baked their bread on premises, bought two extra bagels to bring back to Lorena's. The evening rush hadn't started and there were plenty of empty tables to choose from. His phone buzzed with a text: Lorena, telling him that she'd learned Anthony Branch's father had died and that his mother had moved to Tempe, Arizona.

A man walked in, unkempt hair and beard much like Waldo's but wearing a hospital gown and what looked like the bottoms from a hockey uniform. The man scanned the room, picked three adjacent, unoccupied two-seat tables and pushed them together. Then he stepped back a few feet, studied the tables, and edged one about a millimeter forward. Then he studied again and re-adjusted back. He moved to another vantage point and repeated the process.

The wide-eyed woman from the wash, the one who'd invited him, appeared at Waldo's elbow. 'Hey, you came. What's your name? I'm Mikaela.'

'Waldo.'

'Come sit with us, Waldo.'

'Thank you.' He followed her to the grouping of tables, which the OCD man was worrying again.

'Waldo,' she said, 'this is Tooch. Leave it be, Tooch. It's perfect.'

'Y'think?'

'Yeah.'

'Y'think?'

'Yeah.'

'Y'think?'

'I'm gonna get some food. Talk to Waldo, Tooch.'

Tooch moved to another spot to study the tables again.

Waldo said, 'It's perfect.'

'Y'think?'

'OK if I sit down?' Tooch nodded absently, so Waldo did.

A light-haired, nervous-looking man in a sweatshirt with *DIVA* spelled out in spangles came over and sat opposite Waldo, setting a coffee and a sweet roll on the table. He looked to be in his twenties. 'Hi. I'm Danny.'

'Waldo.'

'Hey, Tooch,' said Danny.

Tooch studied the tables some more and said, 'Y'think?' Danny looked at Waldo and smiled.

Waldo said, 'You come here a lot?'

'I guess.'

'Did you know the Professor?'

'Yeah,' said Danny. 'That was really sad. You know him?'

'Friend of mine did,' said Waldo. 'He a good guy?'

'Um . . . *interesting* guy. Very knowledgeable. On a wide array of subjects.'

'Did you know his name?'

'No,' said Danny. 'Everybody just said "Professor." He might have been a real one. He was smart like that.'

Tooch looked at Waldo and pointed to himself and nodded.

'What? You know his name?'

Tooch nodded and said, 'Dough.'

'Hmm?'

'Dough.' Waldo fished in his jeans pocket for his money. He took a five-dollar bill and slid it toward Tooch. Tooch looked at it, then at Waldo. 'Dough.' Waldo slid him another five. 'Dough . . .' This time Waldo put down a ten. Without giving him the name, Tooch scooped up Waldo's twenty dollars and headed for the counter. Danny shot Waldo a sympathetic *what can you do?* look.

Waldo watched Tooch leave the dining room, passing the screenwriter he'd met down by the L.A. River. He was carrying a tray with a bowl of soup and a hunk of bread. 'Hey,' said the screenwriter, seeing Waldo and Danny.

Danny said to him, 'We were talking about the Professor.'

The screenwriter sat down and said to Waldo, 'Do you know about the girl? The daughter?'

Waldo said, 'I heard he had a son.'

'She's only seven. She's had to grow up without him.'

'Where?'

'San Diego. The parents split up when she was a baby. He *wanted* to be a good dad, you know? But he just never had the time with her. So now he's got her with him for a week—'

'What do you mean, "now"?'

'On location, in Wisconsin, and he has them put a pool table in his trailer, and a PlayStation with *Grand Theft Auto* and *Manhunt*, and she's bored out of her mind.'

Waldo said, 'Is this your movie?'

'And just when they're about to stop shooting for the holidays, he gets a call from his ex-wife, and she says, "You better have her back in San Diego by Christmas Eve." Maybe she'll get all his custody taken away if he doesn't. Not sure. I'm still working on that part.'

Mikaela came back to the table with her dinner. 'Russell,' she said, 'Waldo wants to know about the Professor. You can tell him your movie later.' Sitting, she said to Waldo, 'It's real good, though. I'll go see it.'

Russell the screenwriter said, 'Thank you,' grinning deep gratification.

Referring to Waldo, Mikaela said, 'The Professor was a friend of his friend.'

Russell said to Waldo, 'Total antihero. Always running afoul of the authorities. They took his shopping cart one time.'

Waldo said, '*Who* took it?'

'The cops. They said he stole it. They do that – they arrest you, and don't give your stuff back.'

Waldo said to Mikaela, 'Is that what happened with Cisneros, with his tent?'

'Hundred percent. Professor said his meds were in there, and his clothes, and some papers. He was suin' the city.'

'The Professor was suing the city? There was an actual lawsuit going?'

'Uh-huh. For seven million dollars. LaLa was helping him.'

'Who's LaLa?'

Russell said, 'L.A. Legal Aid. You know Tim Allen?'

'Tim Allen, the actor? What does he have to do with . . .?'

'He would be awesome stunt casting.'

Waldo, testing for confirmation, said, 'The Professor had a lawsuit going against the city. For real.' Given how wrong Mikaela had gotten the Cisneros death, Waldo doubted this.

'Uh-huh,' said both Mikaela and Russell, Mikaela adding, 'That's what he said.' Waldo looked to Danny, too, but he was staring at the ceiling and not saying anything.

Waldo asked Russell, 'Do you know the Professor's name?'

Someone tapped Waldo on the shoulder. 'Dough.' Waldo turned around and saw Tooch, who in his other hand held a tray of pastries.

Waldo said, 'I already gave you twenty.'

Tooch hiked a shoulder and put the pastries on the table between Russell and Danny. Apparently he'd used Waldo's donation to buy desserts for the gang.

Waldo felt eyes on him from across the dining room, and looked back. Time and context threw him off, so it took a second for the beefy, pock-faced man to register as Pete Conady, even though for years he'd been Waldo's closest friend on the job.

Waldo and Conady had met and bonded at the police academy. It probably shouldn't have surprised Waldo, but it did, that Conady took Waldo's post-Lydell Lipps meltdown as a personal betrayal. Their falling out was ugly and the one Waldo most regretted. At one point on the Pinch case, Conady had even arrested Waldo for a murder he surely knew Waldo didn't commit. Now his ex-pal was frowning at him across Panera, where he sat over a sandwich and chips.

'Lena,' said Mikaela, 'you know Waldo?' pulling him back to the conversation at the table.

'No. Pleasure to meet you, Waldo,' said Lena, holding out her hand to shake, the first of the group to do that. Waldo realized this was the woman on the sidecar bike who'd come at him with a rake. Either she was on something then that she wasn't now, or she was on something now that she wasn't then.

Mikaela said to Lena, 'Waldo's asking about the Professor.'

Lena said, 'That poor man. Anybody seen Sancho?'

Mikaela shook her head.

Waldo said, 'Who's Sancho?'

'His dog,' said Lena. That would be something, at least, for Don Q.

'What kind is it?'

'Dough,' said Tooch again.

Mikaela said, 'Tooch, leave the man alone.'

Waldo said to Lena, 'Any chance you knew the Professor's name?' Lena shook her head.

'*D-O*,' said Tooch. '*Do*. That's his name, fucker, son of a fucker, cockmothershitfucker. How many times I have to—? Dorian. Short for Dorian. *Fuck.*' He reached for a coffee cake and studied it from all angles before taking a bite, docile again.

Waldo opened Google on his phone, typed in *professor dorian* and went to *images.* He slid the phone in front of Mikaela and Lena, who leaned over and studied it while Waldo slowly scrolled down the dozens of thumbnail photos.

Mikaela pointed to one. 'That's him, right?'

Lena said, 'He was younger then, but definitely.'

A few more clicks and Waldo had his man: Dorian Strook, onetime Professor in the Department of Hispanic Studies at University of California Riverside, a lesser jewel in the UC system, fifty miles east of Los Angeles. That would be enough to hold off Don Q and free Waldo to start work on Judge Ida's blackmail.

He wanted to help the group out, beyond the pastry tray. After the money he gave Touch, he had two twenties and three ones remaining in his pocket. He carried a credit card; how much cash (which he counted as one Thing, regardless of the amount) would he need on top of that, with travel looming, and how ought he divide up the rest among them?

While he pondered, he heard, 'Waldo,' and realized Pete Conady was standing over him, brow still furrowed. 'You doing OK?'

'Yeah, Pete. I'm fine.'

Conady glanced over at Danny, who was sitting quietly with the back of his *DIVA* sweatshirt pulled over his head and past his chin, covering his face.

The others all stared at Conady, the interloper. 'OK,' said Conady, shifting his weight. 'Good.' He held out his hand to Waldo, who started to shake it until he realized that his friend was slipping him something.

Conady took a couple steps backward, then hustled out of the restaurant.

Waldo looked down: two twenties, a ten and Conady's business card. Waldo would get change at the register and pass around the fifty; the business card he'd have to leave on the table, lest he add a Thing.

It wasn't until later, after Waldo left Panera, that it occurred to him he should have asked Pete how *he* was doing.

TEN

Whil Lorena put away the last of the dishes, Waldo tried Don Q again. He wasn't answering and the burner wasn't equipped for voicemail.

Lorena had accessed the archives of the upstate New York newspapers. The *Albany Times-Union* had the most thorough reporting on Anthony Branch's death, including quotes from both detectives assigned to the case. Neither was still alive.

There were two people Waldo wanted to talk to in person, and fortunately they lived in western states: Anthony Branch's mother outside Phoenix, and Judge Ida's ex in Oakland. Both were close enough to L.A., in fact, to weigh the various methods of getting there. The first website he found claimed that rail, mile per mile, trimmed the damage of plane travel by ninety percent, largely because airliners kicked their CO_2 directly into the upper atmosphere, where it did double the harm of an equal amount emitted on the ground. Another site had it at only fifty percent better, factoring in the fleeting impact on climate of planes' vapor trails and tropospheric ozone emissions. Still another emphasized a fundamental counterpoint that Waldo hadn't considered: that the environmental injury per passenger was highly dependent on the occupancy rate of the vehicle; that is, fully booked trains or even buses were far better, but on average sold only around forty percent of their seats, which actually made them *worse* than planes.

Waldo allowed the EPA to have the last word (despite the perversion of that organization's mission under the present administration): for travel over seven hundred miles, rail and air travel had comparable impact, but for shorter trips, buses were better than either, especially if they were full. L.A. to Phoenix was 373 miles, so he'd take the bus. Phoenix to Oakland was 743 miles, so he'd fly.

Lorena said, 'Where are you going to stay?' subtly referencing the fuss he'd made, during their case in Orange County the year before, over ostensibly 'green' hotels, each of whose shortcomings seemed to tick him off more than the last. Waldo sighed and went back to his phone to see what he could find in Phoenix. 'You know,' she added, 'if you slept on the bus, you wouldn't even have to worry about that.' He knew she only said it to taunt him, but she also happened to be correct, and a few minutes later Waldo surprised her by announcing that he had a ticket on a Greyhound for that very night, leaving at 11:50.

Then Lorena thought of something else: 'You don't have a driver's license. How are you going to get on a plane?'

It was true, he'd made room in the Hundred Things neither for a license nor an alternative ID. He studied up on this new problem and learned that boarding would indeed be possible for a domestic flight, so long as he arrived extra early to go through a TSA interrogation. All of this underscored how he'd be even more reliant on his iPhone on the road.

He thought of something else. 'Can I leave my gun here?' He didn't always bring it with him to L.A., but this time he had, not knowing what Don Q was getting him into.

Lorena nodded but looked unhappy.

'What?'

'I wasn't serious about the all-nighter. I thought you'd be here until tomorrow, at least. What do you have, an hour until you have to leave?'

'Maybe two.'

'Good.' She slid into his lap.

Reaching for his phone, he said, 'I ought to update my IOS before I go. But I can multitask.'

'Asshole,' she said, unbuttoning his shirt.

Waldo dozed intermittently through the night, getting off the bus to stretch his legs at both desert stops, east of Palm Springs and west of the Arizona border. Still, accustomed to Greyhound trips a third the duration, it left him much stiffer than he expected to be, with a crick in one shoulder and knees unready for biking to the north end of Tempe. He fetched his Brompton from the storage compartment and removed his breakfast, the last Panera bagel and a hunk of Jarlsberg, from his backpack. He munched as he shuffled across the street, taking the first hundred yards on foot in hope of walking himself loose. It was already in the mid-nineties in the Valley of the Sun, at six thirty in the morning.

After about twelve miles on his bike he made his first stop, at a convenience store, to replenish his canteen. (The counter kid accused him of filling it with Mountain Dew from the fountain rather than water; Waldo placated him by purchasing three overripe and overpriced bananas.) Five miles later, nearing the address Lorena gave him, Waldo saw a dilapidated sign that read *Sonora Esta es*. He tried to decode the Spanish, with which he'd always struggled for competence, but then realized it was the remains of a sign for *Sonora Estates*, the development where Anthony Branch's mother supposedly lived. Waldo rode in and had a look around.

It was a trailer park in full death rattle. Some units were defaced by graffiti; others were gone entirely, leaving empty cement pads and utility hookups. There was no visible sign of occupancy. Then Waldo heard the unlikely screech and laughter of a toddler, and followed the sound.

Between two trailers, an old Latino man in a straw campesino sat on a mesh folding chair beside a small inflatable pool. A little girl in a diaper splashed about. 'Can I help you?' the man said.

'What happened to this place?'

'They sold it,' said the man. 'Condominiums. *Luxury* condominiums. Want to buy one?' He laughed.

'So everyone just left?'

'They took the money.'

'From the owners?'

'State. Eighteen hundred if you got out by first of the year. But how far is that going to get you?'

'How long will they let you stay?'

The man was quiet for a moment, then said again, 'Can I help you with something?'

'You know Hortense Branch?'

'She's still here.'

'Know where her trailer is?' The man gave Waldo directions to a spot on the other side of the park.

It wasn't hard to find, alone in a stretch of deserted pads, looking vestigial and vulnerable. Waldo leaned his bike against the trailer and knocked on her screen door. 'Mrs Branch?'

Hortense Branch opened her interior door but kept the screen one closed. She was in her seventies, at least, with tightly cropped white hair. She wore a print housedress and peered down at Waldo through thick metal-rimmed glasses.

'Mrs Branch?'

'Who are you?'

'My name's Waldo. May I talk to you?'

'You can say your piece from out there. I'm keepin' this door locked.'

'That's OK.' A gentle breeze from inside cooled his face.

'You look shady. You need a haircut. And a bath.'

Waldo smiled. 'No argument there. But I'm not shady, I promise.'

'You ain't allowed to push me out for another two weeks.'

'I'm not here to push you out. I'd like to talk to you about your son, Anthony.'

She straightened. '*Anthony?* Why?'

'I'm interested in how he died.'

'You law? Don't look like law.'

'I used to be. Los Angeles Police Department. Now I'm a private investigator. I was hired by a friend of your son's.'

'What friend?'

'One of his fraternity brothers.' The lie wouldn't hurt and might help. 'He's always had some questions about what happened that night.'

Mrs Branch tilted her head. 'Why now?'

'I honestly couldn't tell you. This is just when he hired me.'

'Hmmph.'

'I'm starting from scratch, and it's a lot of years. Could you tell me a little about Anthony? What he was like?'

'He was a prince. I was blessed. A prince. Never got in trouble. Got himself into that Stuyvesant school in Manhattan. His father and I didn't know nothin' about schools like that until Anthony went and did it. Loved all the sports.'

'Did he have brothers and sisters?'

'We had an older girl died when she was four.'

'I'm sorry. How?'

'Pneumonia, right after Anthony was born. So he was our only one, most all his life.'

'You were living in Brooklyn when he went off to college?'

'We were.'

'And did you talk to him much while he was there?'

'No, not much. Long distance was expensive. But Anthony wrote us a letter every single week. And I used to bake him shortbread he liked, first Sunday every month, sent it in the mail.' She recalled something and her expression darkened. 'Last one came back, they wrote on it, "Undeliverable." That's all they thought to do. Can you believe that?' She looked at Waldo like she was blaming him. 'None of y'all came around askin' back when it was new.'

'The police didn't do their job?'

'Didn't talk to *us*, tell you that. My husband, Anthony Senior, he believed they was coverin' up somethin'. Somethin' some rich white boy did. Like it was enough they even let Anthony *into* a college like that, and nobody owed him to live through it.'

'Why did your husband think that?'

She wasn't saying.

Waldo looked at the empty space behind him, abandoned by a neighbor. 'You didn't want to take the money from the state, huh? Can't blame you. Better to hold onto the air conditioning long as you can, right?'

'I got asthma, too.'

'You spoken to legal aid?'

'What's that?'

'Lawyers for people who don't have money. Some of them do eviction rights work. You have a phone?'

'They had a pay phone outside the office, but somebody busted it up. Probably the landlord, tryin' to hurry us on out.'

'I'll try to call for you. No promises, but if somebody comes around from *legal aid*, you talk to them, OK?'

She didn't say anything.

'So why'd your husband think they weren't telling the truth about Anthony?'

'They told us it was alcohol-related. Anthony didn't drink.' Judge Ida had said the same of Morris.

'Did your husband talk about his suspicions to anybody?'

'Anybody who'd listen. 'Course, that was mostly people in the neighborhood. He tried to get the upstate police on the phone, but they didn't want to hear it. Ate him up. Died himself not two years later.' She tipped her chin at Waldo. 'Thirty-five years, nobody gave a damn. What's the point now, comin' 'round? You can't bring either of 'em back.'

This felt different from the other two cases Waldo had worked since he came down the mountain. On both of those the victims were secondary, almost afterthoughts. This moment, though, felt more like the old job. He said, 'Maybe it's time somebody speaks for Anthony.'

The old woman said, 'What was your name again?'

'Waldo.'

'Waldo, you think the person hired you wanted you speakin' for Anthony? *Now?*' Hortense Branch shook her head. 'Nah. Somebody askin' you to mess with this after thirty-five years, somebody up to somethin'.'

She closed the door.

ELEVEN

At Sky Harbor, Waldo found the ticketing counter for a newish discount airline which offered one direct flight a day to Oakland International at less than half the price of the majors, for anyone willing to live without leg room or overhead bins. More passengers crammed into less space meant fewer tons of CO_2 per passenger-mile, so for Waldo, it sounded like a win-win.

The carrier's economy meant only one ticketing desk, with a dozen and a half travelers already in line. While he waited, Waldo researched on his phone and found a legal services agency which included among its specialties both housing and seniors. A woman with a voice like a teenager took all the information he could provide about Hortense Branch and her situation. When Waldo said someone would have to go out to her trailer park, though, the woman hesitated and said they'd try but couldn't make any promises. He hung up feeling like he hadn't done enough, but knew Hortense Branch wasn't a project he could assume. His job was to understand what happened to her son.

Waldo pocketed the phone and took stock. He'd never worked anything so cold: thirty-five years in the past, understood at the time to be an accident. On top of that, it would be impossible to access police or medical examiner files without the publicity Judge Ida was desperate to avoid.

Still, unique as it was, the case would be framed by the usual trinity: means, motive, and opportunity.

Means – if this indeed *was* a crime, and if Judge Ida's recollection of the basic facts was correct – would be the clearest: either a push off a cliff or a fatal blow followed by a push to disguise it.

Motive might be the most fertile territory for investigation, all these years later: who might have had reason to kill a gifted honor student?

But the most curious question at this point pertained to opportunity: what would give a blackmailer reason to believe that Judge

Ida had somehow been waiting for Anthony Branch's fraternity hazing out in the woods, or had collaborated with someone who was?

The agent said, 'Next,' and Waldo realized it was his turn. He asked for a ticket to Oakland. When she insisted on his ID, Waldo explained that he was allowed to have TSA interrogate him instead, search his bags, and fill out a form. The agent said, 'Why would you want that?' Waldo explained his minimalism and the One Hundred Things, and, at her further confusion, the environmental value.

'What,' she said, 'are you one of those "global warming" people?'

'Have you seen what's happening in California? The town I live in—'

'That's because your state takes all its water and diverts it into the ocean to make the tree-huggers happy. And now it's backfiring on you.'

'What? Where did you hear *that*?'

'Watch the news. Learn something.' She pushed his credit card across the desk, a rejection. Waldo asked if there was a supervisor he could speak to. The ticket agent gave him a slack-jawed, baleful look, then headed behind a door, turning the line behind Waldo restive.

A supervisor emerged. Conveniently, she had heard of Waldo, and looked up a photograph of him on her own phone to compare and confirm. She told the agent to print Waldo a boarding pass before quickly disappearing again.

'No,' said Waldo to the agent. 'Please don't.' She gave him the slack-jawed look again. 'Could you please email it to my phone instead?'

The agent sounded disgust with her glottis, but tapped her keyboard. Waldo's phone buzzed in his pocket with an incoming email.

Waldo decided to go through security before calling Don Q. While he waited, he tried to open the boarding pass on his phone. But as soon as he hit the *Mail* app, the device went black, reducing itself to a stubborn hunk of unresponsive plastic. Waldo pressed the *on* button, waited for it to fire up, tapped in his security code, went right to *Mail* . . . and the phone shut down again. He did this a few more times while absently shuffling along with the line.

Before he knew it, he was in front of a TSA agent. 'Boarding pass?'

'It's on my phone . . . but I'm having a problem with it.'

'ID?'

'Sorry, I don't have that, either.'

The TSA agent groaned and called for *his* supervisor.

As it turned out, this supervisor, a cheery middle-aged woman, was 'a big recycling person myself' and even admiring of Waldo's explanation for not carrying ID. She confirmed that he'd just need to answer some questions, and asked for his boarding pass. He told her about his phone malfunction, and she said that wouldn't be a problem, either: all Waldo had to do was go back to the ticketing desk, and ask the agent there to give him a printed one.

The need to wait on the ticketing line, again, and the TSA line, again, almost made Waldo miss the flight entirely. In the stress, he decided not to count his phone a Thing so long as it was dead. Even before takeoff, though, he castigated himself for the rationalization: not only a Hundred First Thing, but a Hundred First *plastic* Thing. At that point, though, penned into a window seat, there wasn't anything for him to do about it. He tucked the boarding pass in the pouch in front of him and tried to pretend it wasn't 'his' until they landed and he could recycle it. He shifted in his seat, wretched and guilt-racked, all the way to Oakland.

At that airport, Waldo found the rental car area, chose the least busy desk (Hertz, it turned out), and cajoled directions to Berkeley, which he committed to memory. If he had to go much longer without a phone, he'd need to shed a couple of Things and replace them with a pad and pen.

Night had fallen. Fortunately, he had a reservation waiting at a remarkable boutique hotel called The Bancroft, environmentally friendly down to recycled carpet tile and towels manufactured at a wind-powered plant. Waldo found his way, checked in and fell into the kind of slumber he could only enjoy on organic and fair-trade cotton sheets.

In the morning he awoke thinking of Don Q, whom, in the stress of travel, he'd forgotten to try again. Waldo called now but got only a pair of ticks at the other end, like Q answered and hung up right away. The man was making this too hard.

Meanwhile, the Rev. Morris Thurmond's information was all locked away on the dead phone. Fortunately Waldo remembered the name of his parish, and a lobby clerk was able to draw a route on a map, which Waldo, of course, declined to take with him.

Before leaving L.A., Waldo had studied up on the minister. After college, Thurmond went to Costa Rica with the Peace Corps. He followed that with a Divinity degree at Yale, then a return to his hometown of Oakland, where he co-founded Wellspring AME Church, at which he now held the title of Senior Pastor. There he'd launched programs touching almost every aspect of urban life, from early childhood centers to career training for the formerly incarcerated to hot meal delivery for seniors. He'd been married once, briefly, without children; the wife had died in a traffic accident. In a profile, the *San Francisco Chronicle* referred to him as one of the most respected men in the Bay area.

Wellspring AME sat on a commercial street in West Oakland, its portal and bell tower more grand, its grounds better tended than anything else in the neighborhood. Waldo followed the sounds of children playing to a broad garden behind the church. He found a couple dozen kids of widely varying ages, most but not all African American, with maybe a third as many adults supervising. A poster read *Happy Birthday!!*

Morris Thurmond sat at a metal picnic table, watching the party and smiling. Waldo dismounted his bike and walked it over to him. 'Whose birthday?'

'Almost all of them. We do this once a month, for kids living in any of the shelters. Doesn't cost us much, just the cake. We ask adults in the church to donate a small gift in their own birthday month – a ball, a doll. Every child goes home with a little something.' Speaking took effort. He looked too old to have been a schoolmate of Judge Ida's or Fontella's; with his snow-white hair and weary eyes, Waldo would have taken him for seventy.

'My name's Waldo.'

The minister nodded. 'I followed the Lydell Lipps business pretty closely. And those things you were involved with last year. It's not often you see a policeman of any color stand up like that for a young Black man. Consider me an admirer.'

The truth was, Waldo always felt in his heart that he'd have made the same mistake – believing Lydell's own brother when he gave false information and testimony about Lydell's part in a quadruple murder – and, later, fought just as hard to correct it whether the suspect was Black, white, brown or hot pink. And even during his days of rage, he thought the LAPD's and DA's resistance to reopening the case had more to do with rigidness and defensiveness than to racism; after all, the Black brass in the department had been just as intransigent as the white. The media extrapolated a racial narrative anyhow, and Pete Conady and the rest of Waldo's friends would never forgive him for the stain.

This from Rev. Morris Thurmond was the flip side of that public take – not absolution, but an unexpected blessing with a moral authority that made Waldo's throat catch. He said, 'Thank you. That means a lot.'

Then Waldo took Judge Ida's note from his shirt pocket and passed it to the minister, who unfolded and read it. 'You know who it's from?'

'Oh, yeah, I know who it's from.' Rev. Thurmond smiled, brushed by private memories.

'I'd like to talk about what happened to Anthony Branch.'

The minister looked at Waldo and blinked. Then he turned back to the children and watched them for a while. 'I could stand some lemonade, couldn't you?' He pushed himself up off the bench. A young woman, probably not twenty, suddenly materialized with a walking stick. 'Thank you, Brandi,' he said.

With the cane, Rev. Thurmond moved pretty well. The other two walked alongside him, Brandi at the ready if he faltered, Waldo wheeling his bike, about half a block, to a low-slung apartment building. 'Mr Waldo . . . will walk me up,' the Reverend wheezed, the words morphing into a brief coughing fit. Brandi gave Waldo a warning look.

Waldo folded his Brompton and the men went up two flights to Rev. Thurmond's apartment. It was neat and clean but spartan, just a living room and half-kitchen, with doors to what appeared to be a bathroom and a single bedroom. Nothing like the multiple homes where his million-dollar-a-day ex resided.

Without excusing himself, the minister went into the bedroom. Waldo could hear him taking hits from some kind of inhaler. When he returned he seemed a little jittery, but still weak and tired. He poured two glasses of lemonade and brought them to the table which divided the half-kitchen from the rest of the room. 'Ida bringing up Anthony after all these years – why do you think that is?'

'Maybe all these changes in her life? She's making some money now.'

'What I hear.'

Waldo said, 'She's wondering whether there's anything the authorities overlooked. I talked to Anthony's mother, too. Apparently she and his father always suspected there was more to the story. A cover-up, even.' The minister frowned at that. 'If you could just share whatever you remember. I know it's been a long time.'

The minister drew a toilsome breath before beginning. 'I was a senior. Chi Gamma Pi – we had this tradition, these pledge hikes. We thought of it as a bonding activity. I'd been through three of them before – once as a pledge, two more as a pledge captain, one of the fellows in charge.'

'So you were one of the pledge captains Anthony's year?'

'No, it was my senior year. I wasn't so active in the frat anymore. I was starting to get more serious about my studies, and what I was going to do with my life. But I guess I was feeling a little older and a little wiser, and I more or less imposed myself, said I wanted to go along as some sort of guardrail.'

The irony hung.

Waldo said, 'Tell me about Anthony.'

'Oh,' said the minister, brightening, 'he was a natural. The star of his class – athletically, academically, socially, you name it. I *loved* seeing a young Black guy come in that way. So few at the time.'

'At Mathewson?'

'Two thousand students at that school, and there weren't seventy-five of us.'

'Was there racial tension within the frat?'

Rev. Thurmond arched a brow and rolled his eyes with his voice. 'Is that what Ida's got in her head now? That this was some kind of racist killing?' Waldo waited for a real answer. 'The fellows in that fraternity came from all over the country, all different back-grounds. You could tell some didn't feel entirely *comfortable* around Black people. But I've seen racial tension – and this wasn't that.'

'Tell me about that night. How did the pledge hike work?'

'There were acres and acres of woods, I think owned by the college. Part of the fabric of the place. There were landmarks everybody knew – an old treehouse, a brook, a thick wall of vines.

'That night – we always did this with a full moon, first one after the snow melted – we locked all the freshman pledges in the basement of the house and gave them each a six-pack they had to drink. Then we blindfolded them and drove them out to the woods. We split up the pledges – each of us took two or three and placed them at different spots and tied their hands behind them. We told them to count out loud to a thousand, and then they could untie themselves and go looking for each other, and find their way back together. *Together* was the key. Partly for bonding, but also for safety. And yes, I realize how idiotic that sounds now.'

'Was Anthony one of your pledges, to place?'

'No, he was with another one of the guys. There were twelve pledges and five of us – *that* I remember. We had flashlights; the pledges didn't, of course. We found our way back to the cars and went back to the house to wait for them. Then it took longer than usual. Hours and hours, they didn't come back. When the sun started to come up, the five of us went out to look for them. We found the other eleven pretty quickly, all together in a group, trying to find Anthony. We split up into teams. Somebody saw Anthony at the bottom of this gully, near a footbridge, and yelled out. I climbed down, me and one or two other guys . . . and he was dead. He still had his hands tied behind him. His blindfold had slipped off part way – you could see one of his eyes, wide open, looking at us.'

'How big was the drop?'

'Ten, fifteen feet?'

'You think there'd be anything to gain by my going there and taking a look?'

'Nah. It's woods, man. If I remember, they even extended the rail of the footbridge so nobody could fall again, even if someone went out there drunk and blindfolded.' He started tapping his leg, trying to decide whether to share something. Finally: 'Anthony had more than six beers. He had nine.'

'Why?'

'We had one pledge who was a Mormon. Anthony and one of

the other guys split his six pack for him. I didn't hear about it until after. That's what Anthony was like.'

'His mother says he didn't drink.'

The minister smiled. 'Maybe that's what he told his mama. He drank. *I'm* the one who'd given it up by that point. That's the problem with what you're doing, Mr Waldo. People believe what they want to believe, and remember what they want to remember. They're sure they've got a moment captured crystal clear in their mind . . . but memory doesn't work that way. It changes as we change. Makes things fit the world as we come to understand it. So, after thirty-five years?' He worked a deep breath. 'I'm sure that's what happened with Ida: she's probably built up in her head that one of those other guys did something.'

'Why do you say that?'

'Why else would she want to investigate this? After all this time.'

Waldo left him his misunderstanding, and said, 'Tell me about the other pledge captains.'

'Four guys: Carter Gass, Hoyt Lelong, Dave Petters and Matt Fishbein. Anthony was with Carter.' Waldo realized he'd need to talk to each of them, and asked the minister if he had phone numbers or addresses. He answered that Petters had died in a skiing accident some years before and that he'd fallen out of touch with Lelong and Fishbein. He did have contact information for Gass, who lived in the Phoenix area, and offered to call ahead. Waldo, wincing at the environmental insult of the double-back to Arizona, thanked him and asked him not to mention Judge Ida to Gass, or to mention this new investigation to anyone else.

He asked about the other pledges. Rev. Thurmond said, 'I might remember a name or two. If that. I was a senior, you know, and not even a pledge captain. Carter might know more names. But honestly, I don't see how those fellows'll have anything more to offer. Remember, they all started out blindfolded and separated, and Anthony fell before they all found each other.'

'What do you recall about the original investigation?'

'The state police came in, I think. There was never any sign of anything but an accident. Not that we heard about. Anthony wasn't even bleeding when we found him. They said it was all internal injuries, from the fall.'

'And the aftermath?'

'The school forced the fraternity to disband, of course. We worried about some kind of criminal prosecution, but nothing happened. I kind of remember hearing about Anthony's parents suing the school, but I believe there was a settlement before that went anywhere.

'You've got a handful of nothing, Mr Waldo. It's just a story about youthful stupidity and waste.' He had another brief coughing attack, then said, 'Do something for me? Don't tell Ida I'm unwell.'

'What's wrong, if you don't mind my asking?'

'Lungs. Sarcoidosis.'

'I'm sorry.' The minister raised a dismissive hand. 'They say facing the end gives you a clarity. That's the saving grace. You come to know some things everybody else doesn't.'

'Tell me one.'

'Beats hell out of me. Guess I'm not close enough yet.' He smiled in a way that warmed Waldo's soul.

Waldo said, 'How long have you and Ida been out of touch?'

'Years. Decades. The way it is with an ex, right? Sometimes the silence takes on a momentum of its own.'

'How long were you a couple?'

'Year and a half. Doesn't sound like much now, but you know how intense those things can be when you're young. It ended before I graduated. It was clear we were headed in different directions.'

Waldo smiled. 'That's an understatement.'

The minister got serious, almost stern. 'Make no mistake: I'm proud of that woman. I'm proud of everything she's—' He went into another hacking jag; this time he kept trying to speak through it, which only made it worse. Finally he got the words out: 'Tell *both* those girls . . . to stop . . . busting on one another. Hard enough . . . for any . . . for *any* of us without . . . *that*.'

'You mean Fontella Davis?'

He nodded through the coughs. 'They . . . were best . . . friends.'

'What happened between them?'

The minister held up his hands at one of the mysteries of the universe. 'What . . . ever happens . . . between girlfriends?'

Waldo hated to trouble him further, but with that revelation it suddenly felt important to know: 'Do you ever talk to *her* anymore? Fontella?'

Rev. Thurmond shook his head, then waved Waldo off, signaling that the interview was over. He pushed himself up from the table and tottered toward the bedroom on his cane. He stopped and held Waldo from leaving with a shaky finger. He leaned on the doorjamb and settled his breathing enough to repeat, with every ounce of strength he could muster: '*Tell . . . those girls . . . to stop.*'

TWELVE

Waldo rushed back to Oakland International, stopping only at a used clothing store to replace his belt, now that he'd offloaded Judge Ida's note. He wanted to get to Arizona and Carter Gass before nightfall. Everything was easier for having just made the trip in the other direction: he knew the route to bike, the airline to fly. At the airport he remembered he'd need a series of boarding passes until he could get his phone straightened out, and regretted purchasing the belt. He decided to get down to ninety-nine again by donating his sunglasses to a squinting skycap.

Waldo got on the ticketing line. Moments later he felt a scratch on his neck and a painful yank at his scalp. He turned and found himself eye to eye with a white-faced capuchin monkey. Waldo drew back his head to reclaim his hair, but the capuchin held fast. 'Hey!' said Waldo.

The monkey responded with a barrage of clicks and screeches.

'Laura!' said the woman behind him on line, on whose shoulder the monkey sat. 'Let go!' Laura the monkey released Waldo's hair but gave him three quick, painful pops on the cheekbone before throwing her arms around the woman and burying her face in her neck. The woman offered no apology, just stroked and cooed at her unhappy pet. Waldo gave her the stink eye. The woman, taking umbrage, said, 'I need her for my work.'

Waldo said, 'Why? Are you an organ grinder?'

'Excuse me,' said the woman. 'You can't talk to me like that. That's ableist.'

'I'm sorry,' said Waldo, 'I didn't realize. Is it a service monkey?' he added, in as neutral a tone as he could manage.

'*She*, not *it*, and, *no* – she's an *emotional support* monkey. It's entirely different. And as for my profession, if you must know, I'm a licensed psychotherapist.'

After Waldo bought his ticket and made his way through TSA's interrogation and paperwork, he called Lorena on the burner and asked her to start tracking down the other two pledge captains, Fishbein and Lelong. He kept the conversation short, lest Don Q try him and get a busy signal.

In fact, the dealer did call him only a few minutes later. 'Why ain't I heard from you?'

'I've been trying to get you—'

'Grand Central Market. Six o'clock, by La Tostaderia. You got me some answers, I'll buy you some octopus.'

'Can't. I'm not in L.A.'

'*What?*'

'Look, you're not my only case—'

'Not your only—? Muthafucker, you are on *my dime.*'

'I have everything you wanted. I have the guy's name, his dog's name, it's Sancho—'

'*Not on the phone.* Where you at right now?'

'Oakland, heading to Phoenix.'

'Shit, man, how long all that travelin' gonna take you? I *know* Charlie Waldo ain't getting on no plane, shootin' out vapor trails and fuckin' up the atmosphere.'

Shamed by Don Q on matters environmental, an unforeseen low. Waldo sighed. 'I'm flying.'

'Waldo flyin'. Well, that's some bullshit right there, ain't it. Client gotta be some *mamacita*, got you all sprung. Lorena met her yet?' Waldo didn't take the bait, leaving a hole in the conversation, which Don Q filled with a dirty chuckle. 'Yeah, I *know* she ain't. Well, I don't give a shit *who* the bitch is. What I *do* give a shit, I see you in the next forty-eight. That's *see* you, muthafucker, not *hear* from you. And you're payin' for your own damn octopus.'

The line went dead.

In Phoenix, the thermometer pushed 110. Waldo didn't think Don Q would try him again, so he called Lorena and got her help doping out a train-and-bus route to Ahwatukee, Carter Gass's part of town. The two-mile bike ride at the end left him dehydrated and lamenting his forfeited sunglasses.

Waldo didn't know where Gass's money came from, but judging by his Spanish-style desert mansion, two stories tucked into the foothills plus an extra level of landscaped terrace and pool, there had to be plenty of it. There was no one to be seen on his street, no sound but the desert wind. Waldo rang the bell.

A college-aged kid in cargo shorts and a green and white Mathewson tee opened the door. Waldo said, 'I'm looking for Carter Gass.'

'Yo.'

'I was expecting somebody older.'

'You mean my dad? Trip Gass?'

'Could be.'

'He's Carter Gass the Third. He goes by Trip, like triplets? Three? I'm Carter the Fourth. They can't call me Quad, because that'd sound like I'm, you know, fucked up.'

'I'm probably looking for Trip, then. My name's Waldo. An old fraternity brother of his sent me, from Mathewson. Chi Gamma Pi.'

'Sweet. I'm Chi Gam there, too. Hey, come in out of the heat. My dad should be home any minute.' Waldo left his bike out front, figuring it safe in the deserted, wealthy neighborhood, and followed the kid into an open, multilevel living area. Floor to ceiling windows made for a breathtaking canyon view, especially with the azures and creamsicles of late afternoon, but they wouldn't do much to hold in the air conditioning, which was already working a good four degrees harder than it needed to be. 'Want a water?'

'Thanks.'

Carter IV went behind the bar, got a half-sized bottle from a fridge and tossed it over.

Waldo said, 'Could I have tap instead? In a glass, no ice?'

Carter IV, thinking it was some kind of gag, laughed and flopped onto a sofa.

Though parched, Waldo left the plastic unopened. 'I thought they shut down Chi Gamma Pi a long time ago.'

'Yeah, it's all underground. School won't let us have a house or anything. But usually like six guys rent a place off campus, where we can do parties and meetings and shit. We got a hella sweet crib this year – on the second floor, there's these, like, French doors, and we took a sledgehammer and knocked out the cement on the balcony? The landlord was *pissed*. But it was so worth it: now we, like, open the French doors, and you can start at the other end of the hall and get a running jump? We stack up these mattresses on the ground and make the pledges play kamikaze, with real kamikazes. Like, the drink?'

'I'm familiar.'

'There are these hedges you got to clear, or you're totally shit out of luck, know what I'm saying?' He laughed, picturing it. Waldo smiled and nodded amiably, and returned the fist bump Carter IV offered. 'One guy fucked up his ankle pretty nasty, but still, it's a good time. If you're ever back east, you should come check it out.'

'Maybe I'll do that.'

'Cool. I just got elected president.'

'Something for your resume.'

'Yeah. Not like I need one, to go work for my dad.' They heard a key turn in a lock. 'There he is.' He lowered his voice. 'Hey, don't tell him what all I told you. He'd bag all over me about the shit with the sledgehammer.'

'What does your dad do?' said Waldo.

'Car dealerships. Like ten of them,' said Carter IV as Carter III entered.

Waldo introduced himself. The elder Gass said, 'Morris told me you were coming.' The younger didn't need a prompt to leave the room, but paused to give Waldo another fist bump, underscored by sober eye contact, underscoring that the invitation for an afternoon of kamikaze was heartfelt.

Gass took an elaborate bottle out of the paper bag he was carrying. 'Tequila?'

'No, thanks.'

'You sure? Sweet for the heat.'

Waldo declined but asked again for tap water in a glass, which this time he received.

Gass said, 'The thing you want to talk about – to be honest, I've pretty much pushed that out of my mind for thirty-five years.'

'I understand. But I'd appreciate your trying to pull it back. As much as you can.'

Gass poured himself two fingers, neat. 'I was a pledge captain,' he said, then corrected: '*His* pledge captain. Anthony Branch's. I'm the one who left him out in the woods. Nowhere near the bridge – but I'm the one who left him out there.

'Thing is, I hardly knew the guy. So the whole incident was

terrible and all, but it was never as real for me as it was for Morris, or maybe some of the other freshmen.'

Waldo asked him to walk through the details of the night. Gass's telling echoed Rev. Thurmond's pretty closely, including the certainty that it was a pure accident. He'd been one of the people who climbed down the ravine along with Morris Thurmond, and also recalled that there were no visible wounds. He also shared the minister's sense that there would be no value in making a trip to see the spot where Anthony Branch fell.

Waldo asked if he could tell him the names of the other pledges. Gass recalled only two in full, plus a bunch of nicknames like 'Power Boot' and 'Kotexio,' which he could haltingly match with a first or last name but not both. Waldo asked to borrow a pen and wrote all of these on the back of his last boarding pass, which he'd kept to use for notes.

Gass said he hadn't stayed in touch with his frat brothers after graduation – probably, he said, because it all ended sourly for them, with their chapter getting closed and all. For him, this seemed mostly a story about some bad fortune which spoiled some good times.

He happened to be in touch with Morris because their paths had crossed recently in relation to some fundraising for the school. He didn't have any contact information for Hoyt Lelong or Matt Fishbein, either. 'And of course,' he said, 'there's poor Dave Petters. That guy had no luck at all.'

'Skiing accident?'

'Yeah, that, but he *never* had luck. Got his girlfriend pregnant while we were in school. Had their wedding a week after his graduation.'

'You're not in touch with her, are you? Did she go to Mathewson, too?'

'Ruthanne? I don't know where she is. Yeah, she was the same year as Morris's girlfriend. A year behind me. You know who that is, right? Judge Ida, from TV?'

'How far from that bridge *did* you leave Anthony?' said Waldo, turning the conversation abruptly, hoping to catch Gass off guard.

'*Far,*' said Gass. 'Must have been fifty yards, at least. And Anthony was the furthest one from the road, too, so when they started calling to each other, he should've been walking *away* from that bridge. I went out there several times afterward, to take a look, and I was sure. I was *sure*.'

Gass drifted somewhere and Waldo let him.

'I'll tell you something, though,' he said at last, 'since you're the only one asked me about it, all these years. Every decade that passes? It feels like maybe it was closer.' He chewed on some ice and on whatever that meant, then went to the bar to pour himself another tequila.

Waldo said, 'You ever talk to your son about that night?'

'No,' said Gass.

Waldo said, 'Think maybe you should?'

Waldo glided down the hill to the bus stop and rested in the shade. Now he had three people confirming Anthony Branch's death as an accident. Waldo was racking up emissions chasing what Rev. Thurmond called a handful of nothing. He took out the burner and called Lorena again, to tell her that he was coming home.

She didn't give him the chance. She jumped right into the research she and the ops had been doing on the harassment plaintiffs. They weren't finding much on the new ones, she said, just an extramarital here, a DUI there. Waldo didn't have the patience to actually listen. What did she expect from those clowns of hers? But then Lorena was saying something about a double murder two, in a different tone, and he asked her which one she was talking about. '*Man Nickerson*,' she said, irritated at his inattention. 'That agg assault conviction? The original indictment was voluntary manslaughter.'

'*And* a double murder two?'

'Yeah, his publicist managed to keep that one out of his bios entirely. Beat it on a hung jury. I wonder if Judge Ida even knows about it.' She didn't need to lay out the implication: Bailiff Man was supposedly reformed by the time Judge Ida found him, but now that he was an adversary, was this violent history something to be afraid of?

Waldo said he'd bring it up next time he talked to her. It gave him the chance to change the subject. 'I'm coming home,' he said. 'There's no case.'

'Before Lelong and Fishbein?'

'They're just going to be more of the same.'

'You're quitting halfway through? The whole point was to get celebrity word of mouth. You bail and piss her off, we get celebrity kiss of death.' He heard an unfamiliar noise in the background – was it that coffee maker she was supposed to return? Unsupervised, Lorena could be doing just about anything with their two new shared spaces.

'What about the pledges?' he said. 'There were a dozen of them – you think I owe it to Judge Ida to chase them all over the country, too?'

'Do you have their names?'

'Only a couple. Unless Lelong or Fishbein remember a lot more, we'd probably have to get access to the original state police records . . .'

'. . . Which we can't do.' They agreed not to pursue the pledges for the time being, and leave it to Judge Ida to decide whether to risk publicity by widening the investigation. 'Look,' said Lorena, 'if this is nothing, it's nothing – but you've got to take it at least through all the captains, before the blackmailer hits her for money and she has a decision to make.' He conceded with a sigh. 'I do have some good news,' she said, her voice brightening. 'Reddix found them for you. Fishbein is in Boston, and Lelong is in Tampa.'

Carbon dioxide, carbon monoxide . . . 'Boston and Tampa are good news?'

'*Reddix* is the good news.' She told him they'd already booked Waldo onto an overnight to Boston and gave him the flight information.

The Arizona heat was suddenly more stifling. He'd always made his own plans, always been free to make his own decisions about questions like planes versus trains. It would've been more efficient, he couldn't help thinking, to go to Tampa first and take better advantage of the jet stream. But he knew to keep that to himself.

The woman beside him on the redeye shared her one seat with not only her toddler but a pair of Persian cats – one, presumably, to emotionally support each of the humans. Waldo spent the entire flight with her three charges taking turns leaping onto his lap. He didn't sleep a minute, instead doing arithmetic in his head minute by minute, estimating how much wreckage, at five hundred miles an hour and 0.24 pounds of CO_2 per mile, his cumulative moments of personal weakness were causing.

He took an express bus to the Back Bay, where he still had half an hour to kill before the Apple Store opened. He was desperate for sleep. His stomach growled, too. Finding unpackaged food on the road was problematic, at times nearly impossible, especially at airports. There was a Sweetgreen in the Prudential Center across the street, but that didn't open until after Apple did. And now there was the New England humidity to reckon with: supposedly the city was twenty-five degrees cooler than Phoenix, but he'd trade this soup for the desert frying pan in a heartbeat.

He chained his bike to a tree in front of a line of Massachusetts rental Bluebikes. Sweating and hungry, dog-tired and miserable, he watched Apple employees bustle behind the locked, three-story-tall glass storefront. What if they couldn't fix his phone? What if these bastards didn't even *want* to? What if this glitch in his system update had been planted there deliberately, to lure him into a store and from there into a full upgrade to an iPhone 7 or 8 or 15 or whatever they were pushing this week, e-waste be damned, conflict minerals be damned?

Pedestrians coalesced into a sloppy line while a polo-shirted Apple worker unlocked the door. Just as she opened it, the burner buzzed in Waldo's pocket. He was in no mood to deal with Don Q, that was for damn sure. He knew better than leave Q's call unanswered, though, not when he still wouldn't be back in L.A. for days.

But it was Lorena. 'OK,' she started, 'I need you not to go batshit.'

'What are you talking about?'

'There's a mistake, OK? It's just a mistake. So chill, OK?'

'*What?*'

'Reddix checked it again. We sent you to the wrong Matt Fishbein.'

'What do you mean, the—? Where the hell's the *right* one?'

Lorena said, 'Dallas.'

THIRTEEN

The Earth tipped off its axis; Boylston Street tumbled end over end. Waldo's heart raced and he gasped for air, air he didn't deserve. Maybe he'd just die right here. He steadied himself on a street sign and waited for the spinning to stop. Something like two hundred extra pounds of carbon – all on him, all in one day – even as his mountain kept burning. If he could get online and find distances he could calculate more precisely how much he'd contributed to the horror, but he *couldn't*, of course, because he had *no fucking phone*, except for Don Q's stupid burner flip.

He staggered into the Apple Store. A bright-eyed young woman with a headset welcomed him and asked if he'd scheduled an appointment.

'No!' he said. 'How can I make a . . . when it . . . *look*.' He tried to turn on the device to show her, but got stuck staring at the white Apple logo while the phone booted up.

'We can see what's available later today or tomorrow—'

'*No!*' he blurted. 'I'm traveling! I need a— *I'm traveling!* I can't get on a— They won't let me – the security lines – and it just goes *dead*!'

Gently, she said she'd try to get a Genius or tech to help him as soon as she could, took his name, and told him he could wait on the third floor, where someone would find him.

The spiral staircase dizzied him more. He climbed, one hand over the other clinging to the banister to steady himself, and when he reached the top flopped into a seat at the first hardwood table. A thirtyish couple sat opposite, talking loudly, but Waldo couldn't focus on anything they were saying. All he could think about was the *space*, the capacious, unnecessary gaps between sleek devices – without all that, who'd need three stories, who'd need *two*, you could do the whole store on one and save two-thirds the emissions, but the better the products looked, the more you'd want, the more you'd think you *need*, plus all the other Things that come with it, all the crap on the wall and on the floor below – the cases and adapters, the docks and cables and jacks, the charging pads and selfie sticks, the speakers, the cameras, the gaming controllers, *more* and *more* and *more* – and even if you tried to *avoid* tossing your phone and buying another Thing, they'd detonate this virus by remote, destroy your Thing right from Silicon Valley, *without even touching it* – and *where was his fucking Genius, anyway*?!

'You just got the 3 last year,' the man across from him was saying. He had on a Porsche Turbo baseball cap.

'The 4's going to be thinner,' said his partner, with a purse whose design was the Balenciaga logo repeated fifty times on each side, 'and the display is bigger.'

'What'll you do with the old watch? Put it in a drawer, next to the *old*-old one?' the man said, laughing. *Laughing!*

'Nah, that one'll be ready for the landfill.' She laughed, too.

Waldo erupted: '*What is wrong with you?* Everything electronic – you throw it away, lead leaches into the ground, beryllium, brominated flame retardants—'

'We don't *actually* put it in a landfill,' said Porsche man, ever so virtuous. 'We e-cycle.'

'Which means *what*?' They clearly didn't know. 'Half those e-cycle places – you know how much of that poisonous shit they just dump to China? They've got a town called Guiyu – there's laptops in the streets, cell phones piled higher than your head, they just truck more of them in and throw them on top! Families make it a business, drip hydrochloric on your "e-cycled" watch right on their kitchen table to find the copper, strip the parts for re-sale. They got a river there that's *black*. The dioxin in the air is so thick you can *see* it. Eighty percent of the kids in that town have lead poisoning. Do *you* have kids? How *they* doing?'

The couple stood and scurried down the stairs.

Waldo railed at their backs: '*Buy less. Buy less. Buy less.*'

A giant of a man stepped in front of him, six-eight easy, face like a caveman, latitudinous shoulders straining his corporate polo shirt, fists on his hips. The couple slipped away. Since when did Apple have bouncers? Fuck. Waldo braced for a pounding.

The behemoth looked down at him and said, 'Mr Waldo?'

'Yes?'

'You're having a problem with your phone?'

Waldo took a moment to process. 'Are you my Genius?'

The behemoth smiled and held out his hand. 'Felix.'

Waldo's Genius listened patiently while he spluttered through the problem, then told Waldo that it was a minor bug that affected a small number of devices and that he could quickly set things right by re-updating the operating system.

Waldo sat watching Felix work, humiliation beginning to bubble. Yes, those self-involved cretins needed an education, but his conniption was more than the moment called for.

Way more.

Batshit, Lorena would have called it. *Getting worse.*

Then again, if 'mental health' meant serenity in the face of the casual destruction of the planet, Waldo didn't want any part of it.

Besides, this didn't feel batshit. What it did feel *exactly* like was the frantic despair four years ago when he learned that Lydell Lipps was shivved to death after spending almost half his life in a cage Waldo put him in, out of his own vanity and ambition and carelessness. And true, no one died this time. Not directly, at least. But who knew what Waldo's two hundred pounds of carbon was going to do?

What *did* feel like batshit was the notion that Waldo could hold onto the tenuous peace he'd found while trying to have a 'normal' relationship, let alone a career. Trying to give Lorena what she wanted – *that* was what was driving him to the breaking point. He needed to straighten up, to rededicate himself. Now. Put this nothing of a case to bed for Judge Ida, who – Lorena was right about this, at least – deserved to have Waldo see it through. But after that: total renewal, whatever the cost, before he was lost again.

Felix said to him, voice lowered, 'I kind of agree with you about people upgrading too often. For what it's worth, Apple's been really good about converting its buildings to renewable energy. And the packaging is almost all recycled paper now.'

Felix asked him to test the device. Waldo went online, then checked his email and tried a couple of news apps, playing around until he was confident it wasn't going to turn off by itself again.

Felix, without irony, suggested this kind of thing would be less likely to happen if Waldo kept his operating system current.

Waldo, spent, simply thanked him.

His iPhone failed him no more, but his road problems continued. His crisis at the Apple Store made him forget all about the Sweetgreen and he found himself at Logan, starving, scrounging for a permissible meal and coming up empty. There wasn't much time anyway before his flight to Tampa, which Lorena had rescheduled for him, with Dallas to follow.

Somehow he'd been assigned a window seat, beside a couple in their early twenties trying to calm a screaming baby girl. Waldo watched Boston Harbor recede. He lowered his shade and read to distract himself from his growling stomach. His hands trembled, a residual effect of the incident or maybe simply from hunger. He put down the tray table to brace his Kindle.

Reading tapped the last of his mental energy, but he fought to stay awake, tuned out the baby and pushed himself through a chapter. It was a wild one, too, about the election of 1876, in which the Democrats relied on violence and coercion to suppress Black votes, the Republicans countered with voter fraud, and the country waited to see whether the presidency would be decided by shenanigans in the electoral college, by shenanigans in the House of Representatives, or by Civil War general George McClellan putting the band back together and storming Washington. All that, thought Waldo, without the assistance of cable news.

He closed his eyes and finally surrendered to sleep.

When he stirred, a bottle of water, a cup of ice and a tiny bag of pretzels sat on the tray beside his Kindle.

'We thought you might like something when you woke up,' said the baby's mom, a sweet-faced woman with apple cheeks and pixie haircut.

'Thanks,' said Waldo. 'But I don't – I can't – would you like them?'

'Oh, no, thank you. They're for you.' The baby was fast asleep in her lap.

'Please,' said Waldo. 'Maybe your husband wants them.'

The bearded dad leaned forward and said, 'No, thanks.'

Waldo's stomach sounded a mating call for the pretzels.

'You should eat those,' said the young mom.

Waldo rang for a flight attendant. 'Can I give these back?' he said, when one arrived. 'I don't need them.' The bearded dad helped pass everything to the aisle.

'Oh,' said the flight attendant, dumbfounded, as if no such thing had ever happened in the history of aviation. She took the pretzels, unopened water, the cup and the ice, and threw it all into a big plastic bag with the rest of the garbage.

Waldo found the most eco-friendly hotel in Tampa, conveniently located between the airport and Hoyt Lelong's house, checked in and called Judge Ida. He'd been looking forward to this; he knew her star-glow would pick him up. In fact, just having her private number on his own phone made him feel special.

She told him, 'I got more fan mail today.'

'What'd it say?'

'Dollar sign, numeral "1," word "million." That's it.'

'No instructions?'

'I assume that's next. What *you* got?'

'I've met with Morris Thurmond and Carter Gass.'

'Yeah? How's Morris look?'

Waldo remembered the minister's request to keep his struggles confidential. He said, 'Handsome.'

In a flash, her tone went icy. 'Don't fuck with me, Charlie Waldo. You don't know me well enough to fuck with me. He healthy? I saw a photo of him, looked like he had a canc.'

'We didn't talk about his health.' She'd laid a chill on his own tone, too.

Judge Ida snorted, enouncing without speech that she didn't believe Waldo, that he'd fallen from grace, that he'd been moved onto *that* list.

Discomfited, he started pacing the hotel room. 'He had more details about Anthony Branch's death, but he's sure it was an accident. So is Carter Gass.'

'Then what's this fucker think he's got on me?' He knew she meant the blackmailer, but she said it like she was accusing Waldo of something. 'Someone ought to tell him I don't *have* no million dollars, not unless I get my syndication – and that ain't happenin' if he goes and stirs up some phony-ass scandal. What are you

doin' next?' That sounded like an accusation, too. This was the
Judge Ida who'd gotten Waldo hooked in the first place, the scin-
tillating despot of the TV courtroom. Turned out not to be so
entertaining when you were on the wrong end of it.

'I'm in Tampa, to see Hoyt Lelong.'

'Yeah, "Lelong," that's his name.'

'And Matt Fishbein's in Dallas. I'm flying there tonight. There
was one more you didn't mention: Dave Petters?'

'Dave Petters. He was a pledge captain too?'

'You didn't know him?'

'I knew him,' she snapped again. 'Just didn't remember he was
no pledge captain.'

'He passed away. In a skiing accident. He was married to a
classmate of yours; I think her name was Ruthanne. Does that
ring a bell?'

'Vaguely.'

'Would you like me to track her down? See if her husband ever
talked about this? Told her anything that doesn't match?'

'That the best you got? Some damn *widow*?'

'Hey,' said Waldo, 'this is all your call, how wide you want me
to go. I'm doing the captains; I could start chasing down the
pledges, too. But the wider we get, the more chance this leaks.
Plus we don't know how soon this guy's going to call for the
money.'

'*Plus*? I'll tell you *plus*: *plus*, there ain't shit out there for you
to *find*. You talk to Hoyt Lelong and you talk to Matt Fishbein,
and if they ain't got nothin', then fuck it, I'll take my chances.
Let this sonofabitch do his worst, whoever he is.'

'One more thing,' Waldo said, loath though he was to introduce
another tricky subject. 'Immanuel Nickerson – you're aware of
his full record? The indictments, not just the convictions?'

'Don't go mealy-mouth. Say what you got to say.'

'Nickerson's been charged in the past with three deaths – two
murders and a manslaughter. I just want to make sure you understand that the guy you're beefing with is dangerous.'

'I know all that. Ain't nobody hired you to be my wet-nurse.
Do what I'm payin' you for, Charlie Waldo. Other than that? Stop
wastin' my time.'

*   *   *

He knew Hoyt Lelong was in town, at least; he'd insisted that Lorena figure out that much, after the wrong-city debacle. Lelong's office – he was a hand surgeon – confirmed for her that he was seeing patients that day, and would be again tomorrow.

His house was one of the smaller ones on a bayside street, and the only one with solar panels. A Tesla sat in a driveway lined with bright pink gerberas. Waldo rang the bell. The door opened and a tall man with a deep tan and a full head of white hair looked at him quizzically.

'Hoyt Lelong? My name's Charlie Waldo.'

'Yes, I've seen you on the news. What can I do for you?'

'I'm looking into the death of Anthony Branch.'

'Jeez, Louise. Who asked you to do *that*?'

'A relative.'

'Come on inside.' He checked out Waldo's Brompton. 'Cool bike. You can leave it on the side of the house with mine, if you'd like.'

They went around the corner. Lelong had a Bianchi, a high-end model Waldo knew from the research he did before buying his own. 'Nice.'

Lelong said, 'I ride to work every day.'

'What's the car for?'

'Rainy days, mostly.'

They went into the house, which was devoid of knick-knacks and decorations, almost as spartan as Waldo's own. Lelong led him into an all-white kitchen. 'I was arrested once. Up in D.C. A protest against the Keystone Pipeline.'

Waldo couldn't believe it: the guy was trying to one-up him. 'Yeah? How'd you get there?' No way this surgeon with a Tesla rode the bus all the way to Washington.

'On my bike,' said Lelong, catching Waldo short.

So Waldo blurted, 'I only have One Hundred Things,' and immediately felt like an asshole.

'You win,' said Lelong with a warm smile. He hadn't been competing, only trying to let Waldo know they were kindred spirits, which made Waldo feel like an even bigger asshole. He was frayed, a mess. He needed this long trip to be over.

He said, 'What can you tell me about Anthony Branch?'

'So, what, now someone's questioning whether that was an accident?'

Waldo hiked a shoulder.

Lelong rolled his eyes. 'Figures. Everything's about race now, right?' The remark jarred a bit, dissonant with the solar panels and the rest. It brought home that all the pledge captains were Caucasian (it was a safe assumption that Fishbein would be, too), consonant with Judge Ida's and Rev. Thurmond's comments about how white Mathewson had been in their day.

Waldo asked him to walk through the night and morning of Anthony's death. Lelong's recollections matched his frat brothers' closely but not perfectly; he remembered it being well past daylight when they went out to hunt for the pledges, and he was sure there were at least fifteen of them, not twelve. But on the main item, his take was the same as the others': it was a terrible, freak accident, nothing more.

Like Thurmond and Gass before him, Lelong volunteered how popular Anthony Branch was. Waldo said, 'So there was no one who, I don't know, had it in for Anthony?'

Lelong chuckled. 'You mean, besides that girl on TV?' Waldo cocked his head. 'The one making all that money. Ida Tuttle.' He sneered. '"Judge Ida Mudge." They give her a million dollars a day, that girl.' *Girl*, twice. 'How does *that* happen? *Both* of them.'

Waldo acted like he didn't know who Lelong meant.

'Fontella Davis. Those two Black girls – they could buy and sell all of us.'

Waldo stifled a cringe, so as not to shut Lelong down. He said, 'What was Ida's problem with Anthony Branch?'

'I don't remember exactly how it started. But what I do remember – vividly – was her slapping his face at a party. I mean, that was a *slap*. Open hand, but it sounded like a rifle shot. And then she started screaming at him.'

'About what?'

'He came on to her or something, and she turned him down, and then he started telling people he slept with her, maybe? That's what's in my head, anyway. But she went *ghetto* on him, I remember that. Black girls – you do not want to mess with them.'

It could be that, three and a half decades later, racism or something else was twisting Lelong's memory. But if not – if Judge Ida *had* slapped Anthony Branch in front of people – it was a hell of a detail for her to have left out.

'Any chance,' said Waldo, 'that Ida had anything to do with Anthony Branch's death?'

'No. Come on – out in the woods like that? How could she?' He chuckled again. 'I mean . . . if this was about Anthony getting his nuts cut off, maybe. But that girl didn't kill him.'

FOURTEEN

'Lelong brought up something I hadn't heard before – some trouble between Ida and Anthony Branch.'

At the other end of the line, Rev. Thurmond chortled. 'Yeah, they got off on the wrong foot.'

'What happened, exactly?'

'The way I recollect, at one of the first parties when Anthony was rushing as a freshman, he put a move on Ida, and came on a little strong. Anthony wasn't always what you'd call smooth with the ladies.'

'She was your girlfriend at the time?'

'She was.'

'How did you feel about that?'

'I didn't know Anthony yet, and he didn't know she was going with anyone. Not a problem.'

'Was there a physical altercation?'

Rev. Thurmond scoffed. 'Between Anthony and me?'

'Between Anthony and Ida. Lelong says she slapped him. In front of a roomful of people.'

'Is that right.' Waldo could almost hear the minister grinning through the phone.

'You don't remember that?'

'No, I don't. I was definitely not in that room.'

'But does that sound like something that might have happened? That Ida might have done?'

'You ever see her TV show?' The minister chuckled himself into another coughing fit.

Waldo waited it out. 'Lelong remembers it a little differently.'

'Of course he does. What did I tell you about memories?'

Waldo pushed past that. 'He remembers Anthony going around telling people that he slept with her – *that's* why she slapped him.'

Rev. Thurmond held a silence, then said, 'Was there a question?'

'Does that version sound familiar?'

'I don't recollect anything like that,' said the minister. 'But, again.'

Waldo thanked him for his time and they ended the call.

Waldo flashed on Stevie Rose, the fifteen-year-old fabulist at the center of his last case, and all he'd learned then about the transformations, inconsistencies and impulsiveness of the adolescent brain. Every day, thousands of parents asking, *What were you thinking?* and their teenagers answering, *I don't know.* Young Morris and Ida and Anthony and Carter and Hoyt, they hadn't been much older than Stevie. Put whatever happened, captured at the time by their still-developing hippocampi, then bruised and modulated as it bounced around their respective neocortices and amygdalae for thirty-five years, and what of their conflicting recollections could he trust? Could be Rev. Thurmond was right about this much: *People remember what they want to remember.*

Waldo's phone rang: Lorena. They hadn't spoken since the call in front of the Apple Store. 'I've got an address for Fishbein.' No apology; none when she first told him she'd sent him to the wrong city, and none now. Just a street and apartment number, in a Dallas area called Oak Cliff.

'You sure Reddix has the right Fishbein?'

'I found him myself. I called the Mathewson alumni office.'

'And they just gave out his address?'

'I *got it*, Waldo.'

'And you're sure he'll be in town?'

'Did I tell you I got it?'

Not apologizing was strategy. She was trying to pose it as *his* problem, to get him to roll with things better. Could she have even sent him to the wrong city on purpose? Force Waldo to reckon with unnecessary air miles, so that plastic handcuffs and single-use coffee pods wouldn't seem so outrageous? To train him.

But then Lorena said, 'I'm sorry about Boston. I know that had to mess you up,' leaving him flustered and embarrassed at what he'd been thinking.

He said, 'It wasn't too bad.'

Lorena scoffed. 'Right. Tell me how I can make it up to you. I'll do it.'

'Buy a Prius. Used.'

'Done.'

'Really?'

'No.' He could picture her silently snickering, the way she did when she got him like that, her torso bouncing twice, her eyes jiving, her smile even more askew than usual. He missed her, was the truth of it, and the rest fell away. He even missed L.A., the way he'd grown accustomed to missing his woods.

Lorena said, 'Finish up and get home safe.' It was all he wanted to do. And that threw him, too.

Waldo had gotten away with stowing his bagged bicycle in overhead compartments on his previous flights, but the gate agent in Tampa was a hardass who insisted it didn't fit in the carry-on 'bag sizer' (which Waldo felt was dishonestly undersize, anyway). When the agent took the bike and held out a claim ticket in return, Waldo said, 'Don't even,' and went without.

Miraculously, the bike survived the baggage handlers and luggage carousel without casualty, but that did little to improve Waldo's attitude toward the airline, especially after sharing a cabin for two hours with a comfort mastiff four times the size of his folded Brompton.

He lit out to find Matt Fishbein, who lived in a part of Dallas where the signs for non-chain businesses ran about half English and half Spanish, in a housing development in the architectural style Early Box Store.

Fishbein had a second-floor walk-up with, from the look of it, a balcony view of the community dumpster. Waldo broke down his Brompton and carried it up; leaving it unattended here wouldn't be like Gass's neighborhood, or Lelong's.

It was only four o'clock but Fishbein was home when Waldo rang the bell. 'Yes?'

'Matt Fishbein – the Matt Fishbein who went to Mathewson in the eighties?' Fishbein nodded. 'My name's Charlie Waldo.' That didn't seem to mean anything to him. 'I was hoping I could talk to you about the death of Anthony Branch.'

'Oh,' said Fishbein. 'Come in, come in!' He opened the door. Waldo carried his bike inside. The air felt heavy and smelled like mold and canned soup. Paperbacks overflowed from cinder-block-and-plank bookcases. The wall clock was twenty minutes off and the sofa rested on a brick and a book where one of its legs should have been. 'Anthony Branch,' said Fishbein. 'What a tragedy. And there are still fraternity deaths every single year. "The fruitlessness of experience and the confirmed unteachability of mankind."'

Waldo recognized the quote. 'Churchill.'

Fishbein lit up. 'You've come to the right place. But I've got to go to work. We can talk on the way.'

He sped out the door, Waldo on his heels. It wasn't the time of day most people left for work. Maybe he was a professor, teaching night classes at a community college or something. That would explain the crappy apartment.

Waldo assumed he was following Fishbein to his car, but the man strode right through the parking lot and to the street. It was a wide avenue, with few trees to shield them from the pounding Texas sun. Waldo didn't have a chance to unfold his Brompton, and anyway thought it would be tacky to ride alongside a man who was walking.

'Let's catch it!' Fishbein shouted all of a sudden, and broke into a trot toward a slowing bus. Boarding, he talked Waldo through the purchase of a day pass – which, of course, Waldo insisted Fishbein keep – and found them a pair of seats.

Waldo asked the same set of questions he'd asked the other fraternity brothers, and Fishbein gave the same set of answers – everyone liked Anthony, the fall was bad luck and an accident for sure – but he dismissed the questions more hurriedly than the others, because what Fishbein *really* wanted to talk about, especially with a man who knew his Churchill, was fascism, drawing links and parallels across eras and continents, Trump and the Caesars and the Khmer Rouge and Josip Tito and Trump again. No, he didn't remember Ida Tuttle slapping Anthony. Then it was back to fascism.

A half-dozen stops later Fishbein popped out of his seat and made for the door. Waldo followed him off the bus, probably running out of time with this guy and definitely running out of patience. Fishbein was going on about ethnic cleansing in Bosnia and the Muslim Ban when Waldo cut him off: 'When Anthony Branch fell that night – do you have any idea how far he was from the spot where they left him?'

Fishbein was peeved to be yanked out of his dissertation. 'Well,

I didn't see it myself, but I knew where Carter was *supposed* to leave him. I mean, he could have gotten it wrong—'

'What do you mean, "supposed to leave him." It was planned?'

'We had spots. For each of them. It wasn't random. *Nothing* is random. It's just like when the Russians start looking for the emails the *same day* Trump said—'

'*How do you know it was planned?*'

'Because I planned it. This was meticulously designed: each pledge thirty to fifty yards from the next. Close enough to find, far enough that it wouldn't be easy.'

'And who knew the spots?'

'The pledge captains. I showed them.'

'You, Gass, Lelong, Petters, Thurmond . . .'

'Thurmond wasn't a pledge captain, but yes, correct.'

'And nobody else.'

'No way! They'd need to have the map.'

'There was a map?'

'That's what I'm telling you. A map of where each of the twelve pledges was supposed to be placed. But I can't guarantee you that's where Carter left him.'

'The map – one copy?'

Fishbein shook his head. 'One for each of the pledge captains. And Morris. I gave it to them that afternoon.'

'So why are you sure no one else had it?'

'Everybody knew to keep it a secret. The pledges needed to find their way out by themselves. And who else would they show it to?'

A girlfriend, maybe. Or, a girlfriend could sneak a look without the boyfriend knowing.

Which meant there was a way, or at least a glimmer of a sliver of a notion of a way, that young Ida Tuttle could have known exactly where Anthony Branch would be, alone at night in the woods. With a history of animosity, which she'd concealed from Waldo.

Opportunity and motive?

It was possible – *possible* – that she set Waldo on this investigation to make sure that what happened that night was as buried as it looked, before she decided that she didn't really have to pay a blackmailer.

Or, one of the brothers or one of the pledges killed him.

Or, someone else saw Matt Fishbein's map, and went out there and did it. Anyone else.

Or, more likely, it was the accident everybody said it was.

'OK,' said Fishbein, 'we're here.' They were in front of a McDonald's. 'Did I answer all your questions?' He was still irked.

'This is where you work?'

Fishbein heard the surprise in Waldo's voice and turned defensive. 'I *manage* it.'

'Nothing wrong with that,' said Waldo, quickly, wondering whether the fortunate start Fishbein had, the Mathewson education and whatever else, had turned out to be the difference between managing a McDonald's and pushing tables together at Panera.

Fishbein opened the door, then turned back to Waldo. 'On that other thing?'

'Which other thing?'

'This country. "The confirmed unteachability of mankind." I'm glad we talked.' He disappeared inside.

FIFTEEN

Lorena's fingers twitched in a dream, her nails raking Waldo's stomach and waking him, all of him but his left arm, which remained asleep under the weight of her head. He tried to ease it out.

When he returned the night before, there was so much to talk about, and so much not to talk about. Not talking won. He didn't want to know what Things she had bought for their new apartment or the office. Well, he did want to know, but he didn't want the argument that would come with asking – not when, most of all, he didn't want to talk about what he was doing in the morning.

He was going to see Fontella Davis, his nemesis and Judge Ida's former BFF.

Why? he knew Lorena would ask.

Because, he'd have to say, if he were being honest, *I want to hear from someone who'd love to be able to tell me Judge Ida did it.*

And Lorena would say, *You don't build a business by going out of your way to figure out whether your client killed somebody.* And, of course, she'd be right.

He wondered how he'd avoid the conversation now. Fortunately Lorena, stirred by his shifting, reached for him, and not talking won again.

Their lovemaking put Lorena behind schedule and into a morning bathroom frenzy, scrambling to get to an early breakfast with a divorce lawyer who might throw her some business. As she dashed out the door she thought to ask what he was up to; he said he'd spend the morning making follow-up phone calls to the pledge captains. She said, 'Good luck,' and was gone.

In fact, he'd made all those calls before he left Dallas. Morris Thurmond had sounded stronger, his lungs less troubled, but he didn't remember anything about a map. 'I'm sure I didn't have one. But maybe because I wasn't official. What did Carter and Hoyt say?'

'I haven't called them yet.'

'And Matt? How's he doing? I heard he . . .' The minister didn't know how to finish the sentence. Waldo didn't, either, really.

Gass and Lelong also claimed not to remember a map. Which meant . . . what? That they were lying, or misremembering. Or both, in some combination. Or that Fishbein alone was.

Waldo washed and dressed and headed out to Fontella Davis's office in Century City. He locked Lorena's door behind him, unfolded his Brompton and started down St Andrew's Place.

As he turned onto Maplewood, the door of a parked SUV flew open and knocked him off his bike and sent him tumbling into the street. A minivan bearing down in the other direction swerved and threaded the needle between Waldo and his skittering Brompton.

Waldo pushed himself onto all fours. One rough fist grabbed his collar and another his hair. They tugged Waldo to his feet, threw him face-first into the SUV, then spun him around, bringing him eye to eye with Don Q's man Nini, who drove one of those fists into Waldo's solar plexus. Nini dragged Waldo by the arm to the passenger side, shoved him inside and slammed the door behind him. Waldo barely got his shins out of the way.

He sucked for oxygen while Nini drove north. By the time they crested Laurel Canyon and headed down into the Valley, Waldo, still aching, was breathing normally again.

He wasn't surprised that they ended up at the mini-mall in Sherman Oaks, nor that Don Q was standing in front of the Pinkberry, wearing his usual guayabera and gazing glumly into the fountain of death. Waldo said, 'Be easier to set up a meet with a phone call. On me, especially.'

'Fuck that, Waldo. I ain't slept. Not since you dropped that shit on me.'

'What shit?'

'What shit? "What shit," the man say. *Sancho*, what shit.' The dealer squeezed the bridge of his nose, pained. 'Sancho,' he repeated.

Sancho was the name of the dead homeless man's dog, Waldo barely recalled.

'What else you know? I want *everything*,' the dealer hissed.

Nini, who'd been leaning on the Escalade, giving the two men room, sensed the change in his boss's tone and took a step toward them.

Waldo held up a hand to let Nini know that further pummeling was unnecessary. He told Don Q all he'd learned from the gang at Panera: that the dead man was a transient, that his name was Dorian Strook, and that he'd once been a professor in the Department of Hispanic Studies at UC Riverside, east of L.A.

'I *know* where Riverside is, muthafucker,' said Don Q, and actually moaned. He was taking all of this like a knife in the gut.

'What's the problem? What is this about?'

Don Q turned and studied Waldo through narrow eyes, like he was trying to decide whether or not Waldo was the enemy. 'OK. OK, Waldo. I'll confide.

'The other Sunday, I'm goin' bout my business, takin' Dulci for some pancakes.' Dulci was the dealer's delight of a daughter, who would have just finished the third grade. 'Let the wife sleep in. Dulci do like her Sunday mornin' pancakes. So we're walkin' down the street right there' – he nodded in the direction of the busy boulevard – 'and what do I see? Po-lice, rollin' a dead body right out this fountain.'

'And you knew him?'

'No, I didn't know him, fool! I knew him, what I gotta pay you two G a day to find out who the muthafucker is?' Don Q pointed to a spot on the tiled plaza, just beside the fountain. 'Laid the man out right there,' he said.

'And Dulci had to see it.'

'Yeah, which was fucked up, but that ain't what got to me.' He looked straight at Waldo and said, like he was repeating a bad diagnosis, 'He was wearin' my shirt and my shoes.'

Waldo looked at Q's shirt. 'Like that? Like what you're wearing now?'

'No, man, *my shirt. My vaqueros. Mine.* My actual clothing. That I had just given away.'

'To Goodwill or something?'

The dealer screwed up his face. 'Goodwill? No, man, fuck them people! I got *beef* with muthafuckin' *Goodwill.* National Council of Jewish Women. Those bitches are *righteous.*'

Conversationally, Don Q was always a moving target, but this was different. This was unhinged. 'So, fine,' said Waldo. 'You donate some clothes, homeless guy buys them, gets wasted, bangs his head and drowns. And . . .?'

Disgusted, Don Q said, 'You call yourself a detective. You should be payin' *me*, man. Shit. Department of Hispanic Studies? Dog named Sancho?' Waldo shrugged, flummoxed. 'Where you think that name comes from? *Sancho Panza.*' It meant nothing to Waldo. 'Cervantes.' Waldo didn't know him, either. 'I told you to read fiction, man. *Don Quixote de la Mancha*, by Miguel de Cervantes. Building block a' modern fuckin' literature. All the shit you ain't read? Shit wouldn't exist, wasn't for *this* shit you ain't read. I named my daughter Dulcinea off one'a the characters. And Sancho Panza – dude was the O.G. Don Q's wingman. And now *this* muthafucker, laid out in fronta me – in my vaqueros, my guayabera! You still don't get it?'

Waldo honestly didn't.

'He was my *doppelgänger.*' Don Q looked at Waldo with disappointment again. 'And you probably don't even know what that shit *is*. 'Cause you don't muthafuckin' *read.*'

Back on the same defensive ground, Waldo said, 'I read.'

'In fiction, a doppelgänger is a double. A harbinger of bad shit comin' down. Harbinger, that means like a *omen.* Dostoevsky wrote a whole book. Rossetti – I could show you a painting, freak you the fuck *out.* Shelley, you know who that is?'

'Yeah.'

Don Q saw through it. 'You frontin', Waldo, you don't know no fuckin' Shelley. He was a poet, man, a *poet.* Muthafucker actually *saw* his double – next thing you know? Fell out a boat, drowned in the ocean. Abraham Lincoln, same thing. Queen Elizabeth, too.'

'Queen Elizabeth?' Waldo knew that one was wrong. 'Queen Elizabeth is still alive.'

'Not *that* bitch,' said the dealer. 'The *first* one. One that used to fuck Shakespeare.'

It had been a while since Waldo had to think about Don Q's literary aspirations, which had once been the cause of a lot of trouble. 'Hey,' he said, 'whatever happened to that thing you wrote? What was it called – *Beowulf*?'

'I didn't write fuckin' *Beowulf.* I wrote an epic poem *like Beowulf.*' Don Q sucked his teeth. 'Nobody wanted it. 'Parently, ain't chick-lit or YA, you're fucked.' Waldo was confounded again. 'I'm tryin' to adapt it into a screenplay, which is how I saw it in the first place, but it just ain't comin'.' Q's leg was shaking, a new tic. 'You wouldn't understand what I'm dealin' with, Waldo, 'cause you ain't a inherently creative individual. But writer's block? It's like a permanent case'a tequila dick.'

'Is that what's getting to you?'

Now it was the dealer on the defensive. 'What you mean?'

'This . . . doppelgänger business. I think you're being—'

Don Q silenced him with a glare that brought to mind the corpse he'd once left in front of Waldo's cabin.

Waldo tried again: 'I believe . . . it's just a coincidence, you seeing the guy wearing your clothes.'

'Ain't no coincidence. It's a *omen*. It's a *portent*.' He bit off the words: 'What – fuckin' – happened to him?'

'Maybe he was bathing. Maybe he was looking for coins, and—'

'*No. Sancho.* The dog.'

'I have no idea. Truly.'

Don Q chewed on that. 'You done with that other case?'

'Just about.'

'I ain't payin' you for the days you was runnin' round for nobody else. But I'm gonna start payin' you again now.'

'Listen—'

'You gonna find me that dog.'

'No.'

'Wrong answer, Waldo. My little girl been on me for a dog for her birthday, and you gonna find her Sancho. That be like a good deed, me takin' in a homeless man's dog, improve its standin' in the world. That be some genuine fuckin' *Oliver Twist* shit. Good deed like that, counteract whatever bad I got comin' on account'a this doppelgänger.'

'I am not looking for a dog.'

'You don't take care'a my girl, you won't be able to take care'a *your* girl.' There once was a time Waldo believed Don Q had actually killed Lorena.

'Seriously, this again? If I don't locate a stray dog, you're threatening . . . what?'

'You oughta know by now, Don Q don't threaten.' With that,

the dealer walked away. As Nini opened the car door for him, he added, 'And don't be bringin' me no phony-ass dog, neither. You bring me that bitch, he better answer to "Sancho."'

Nini closed the door, opened the rear hatch, extracted Waldo's Brompton, and chucked it toward the fountain. The Escalade peeled off onto Ventura Boulevard.

Waldo checked to make sure the bike was rideable, then started for Century City and Fontella Davis and *that* world of pointless bullshit.

Which had suddenly become his *good* case.

The midday traffic was light on Sepulveda, no cars in either direction for long stretches. Running alongside the 405, with its gentle curves and two wide lanes in each direction, it was the easiest of the passes through the Santa Monica Mountains, as comfortable as his ride could be, at least in the August broil.

Waldo glided downhill from Mulholland with nothing in front of him. He heard someone coming up behind and pulled to the far side of the slow lane, not that the car would need all that room. Something gave him a funny tingle, though, and he glanced back and saw what looked like a cherry red Range Rover hugging the same line and, of course, gaining fast.

As it was about to pass, Waldo jerked to the right and onto the narrow shoulder. The Range Rover buzzed him, dangerously close – Waldo didn't just feel menaced by its breeze; he could swear the side mirror tickled his hair. Waldo bumped the curb and toppled into the brush.

The Range Rover disappeared around a bend.

Waldo got up and straddled his bike. A couple of passing cars made him flinch but left plenty of room as they passed.

Still shaken, he started pedaling and accelerated on a downhill straightaway.

Then a big red SUV appeared around the curve up ahead. Waldo glanced over his shoulder: nothing behind. He hoped to hell it wasn't the same guy coming back for him.

That wish faded fast. The northbound Range Rover slid into the southbound lanes, barreling unapologetically into what would be oncoming traffic, if there were any. Waldo had nowhere to hide.

He made a choice.

Waldo steered straight toward the SUV and pedaled downhill fast as he could, impelling a game of chicken, folding bike vs. Range Rover.

At the last second Waldo swung the handlebars to the right. The SUV tried to match him but a split second late. Waldo wiped out into a tangle of rocks and weeds, the top of his right arm taking the brunt.

He looked back to see the Range Rover decelerating on the wrong-way shoulder. From around a far curve, eight or ten cars, probably released together at the same stoplight a way back, sped southward, boxing it in.

Waldo jumped onto his Brompton and pedaled back out onto the road, making deliberate swoops across the slow lane and through the passing lane, then back again, forcing the traffic behind him into a jam. Those cars began honking in chorus, soon joined by more caught behind, a sweet serenade of outrage that carried Waldo all the way to the safe harbor of Westwood Village.

SIXTEEN

His shoulder blossomed purple. Waldo found an ice pack in Lorena's freezer, dragged one of the two dining table chairs into the empty living room, and, much out of habit now as compulsion, fired up the next episode of *Judge Ida.*

A couple, immigrants from Moscow without much English, were suing their former tenant, a dominatrix whose 'renovations' required wall and ceiling repairs far in excess of the security deposit. Juicy stuff, but his attention wandered:

Something happened to Anthony Branch that night, Waldo thought, *and someone didn't want him to figure out what.*

And the fact that someone tried to kill him was pretty much the only clue that he had.

Judge Ida was irritated by the Russian husband's halting attempts to explain a contractor's written estimate, which was handwritten and partially in cursive Cyrillic. 'What you write this in, secret code? How am I supposed to understand this diddly-bop?'

Who would want to shut Waldo down? Who even knew he was looking into Anthony Branch's death?

Judge Ida. Lorena. Rev. Thurmond and the pledge captains, scattered around the country.

Which meant the pledges could probably be ruled out. That was a start.

Judge Ida was saying, 'That's way too much for replacement paneling. She owes you a hundred dollars, and that's it.'

'Hundred dollars? But written here—'

'It's not written in English! I know what paneling costs. And you're *lucky* she ruined it. That tired shit was butt-ugly.'

The audience whooped.

Lelong, going on about the 'Black girls.'

Gass, the one who placed Anthony in the woods.

And Fishbein's map – did it ever exist? Or did Fishbein make it up to expand the suspect pool, make it appear possible that anyone at all could have known where to look for Anthony Branch, blindfolded and vulnerable?

The landlord tried to say, again, 'But written here—'

Judge Ida said, 'I – can't – read – that – gobbledygook!' Building . . .

'He is licensed contractor—'

'You're not listening to me.' Building . . .

'To replace, cost us—'

'You – are – not – listening – to me. Now, *sit the fuck down, and shut the fuck up!*' The audience exploded. The poor Russian couple, not understanding *her* diddly-bop, looked lost and frightened.

She was a bully. She needed to dominate. That's what the show was built on: her fascist control of this phony little realm.

She must have been like this all along, even if she knew she had to hold it in – an African American woman, that young, that time, that place.

How powerful was it, deep down, that need to dominate?

Enough to murder?

But if she had killed Anthony, and hired Waldo only to see if she'd been found out, and by whom, why would she try to kill him as soon as he started getting some traction?

Unless that option had been part of her plan from the start.

The Range Rover attack came the day after he learned about the map. How would she know that he had?

Could Rev. Thurmond have told her? Could they be speaking again now? Could they have been in touch all along?

Possible. For sure, Judge Ida was hiding a couple of cards. Maybe half the deck.

Waldo heard Lorena's key in the lock and paused the TV. The episode had already moved on to a second case but Waldo hadn't registered any of it.

Lorena entered with a bag from Pavilions and a small cardboard box, which she handed to him, excited. 'Check this out,' she said. He lifted the top: inside were matte-finished business cards which read *Nascimento-Waldo*, black on pale green, in a muscular typeface. 'I didn't think you'd mind my name being first. It really does sound stronger.'

Waldo frowned and handed her back the box. 'I'm not going to—'

'Carry business cards. *Obviously*. I had them make an electronic version you can send to other people's phones. It's even got a little animation. I'll email it to you. What's with the ice pack?'

Waldo told her about his adventure with the Range Rover and brought her up to speed on the rest. He told her about Fishbein's map and his creeping suspicion that Judge Ida may indeed have had a hand in taking Anthony Branch's life, and perhaps today's attempt on his own.

He watched that sink in, then added, 'I want to talk to Fontella Davis.'

'Why?'

'Because she doesn't like Ida.'

Lorena studied him. 'And the point of that is . . .?'

Waldo shrugged his eyebrows.

Carefully, she said, 'And if you found out that Ida *did* kill somebody thirty-five years ago? What would you do with that information?'

Just as carefully, he said, 'What would you *have* me do with that information?'

Lorena pursed her lips. Her house had never felt so silent. This was bigger than coffee makers or business cards.

She said, 'I would have you . . . not go out of your way . . . to learn that information in the first place. I would have you not talk to Fontella. I would have you simply tell Judge Ida that you couldn't learn anything.'

'Disengage.'

'Yes.'

'Back off. Turn a blind eye.'

'You're in the private investigation business now. The private investigation *business*.'

'Your idea, not mine.'

'You signed on. You accepted this assignment. Working for a client. You don't turn around on your client and nail her for a cold case.'

'Even if the client reopened that case herself? What if she's using us to figure out what evidence is out there, so she can destroy it?'

'Hazard of the trade,' said Lorena.

'Then maybe the trade's not for me. Not that this is the first time I've mentioned it.'

'Fine. But finish the case you committed to.'

Waldo nodded, but said, 'So, you're going to find out if Judge Ida owns a Range Rover, right?'

She stomped into the kitchen and started putting away groceries.

Waldo watched her. He plucked at the paper Pavilions bag.

Knowing what he was thinking – that he'd given her several reusable ones to keep in her car – she said, 'I forgot to bring one of yours into the store. Big deal, Waldo. They're disgusting, anyway, after you use them, like, twice. Even the cashiers are grossed out.'

Waldo looked in the bag and plucked out a disposable pepper grinder. He studied its mechanism: plastic on plastic on plastic. 'You can't get a refillable one?'

'I *have* a refillable one. The pepper comes out too fast.'

'So find a better one.'

'I *tried* to find a better one!' She slammed open a cabinet and rummaged for something in the rear. 'Then I tried to find *another* better one, and *another* better one!' She pulled out a pepper mill, then three more, smacking each on the counter in turn. She glared at Waldo, challenging him to challenge her.

Instead, he smoldered, then walked out of the house.

On foot, he thought, he'd be a marginally harder target. Still, his eyes darted both ways down St Andrews before he even stepped onto the sidewalk. He decided to head up to Melrose, and relative safety among more pedestrians and more cars.

Two cases, both absolute shit, taking turns being worse from one day to the next. Fucking PI work. He'd gotten lucky on Pinch and Rose, both times, in the end, doing more good than harm. But that was pure luck. Sooner or later he was bound to wind up on the wrong side of something, and this Anthony Branch business was feeling like it.

And then there was Lorena. Bit by bit she kept wearing him down until everything went her way: living together, working together, disposable bags, heedless travel, bad news clients. She'd apologize again, sure, but then it would be back to the same old same old, Waldo doing all the compromising.

He walked Melrose all the way to City College, then up Vermont, wishing that he had his bike and his backpack and could just keep going, all the way downtown and straight to Idyllwild. Let Judge Ida and Lorena and everyone else fend for themselves.

But when he got to Santa Monica he turned left without really thinking about it, and the same when he hit Western, and after about an hour and a half he'd stewed himself out and was back on Lorena's block.

Just inside her door he found a bunch of random items in little piles: all the unsatisfactory pepper mills, a partially melted spatula, a wicker tray, a laundry basket with a broken handle, half a dozen green plastic clothes hangers, a Dodgers giveaway beach towel, an ugly stuffed turtle he'd never seen before, a stupid number of sunglasses, two pairs of boots, a denim jacket and what looked like some blouses.

Lorena came out of the kitchen carrying the Keurig, which he was sure she'd been using in his absence, and put it with the rest. 'I'm giving this all away, OK? I'm not going to count my Things or any of that shit. But whatever I buy from now on, I'll trade off: I get a pair of shoes, I give away a pair of shoes.

'Here's the deal, though: even if you don't care about sabotaging our business, if you walk away, you're sabotaging *my* business. And that's not fair.

'That frat kid died thirty-five years ago, Waldo, and if it weren't for me pulling you into this, you'd have never even heard of him. So, please: let it go.'

Boots. Lorena Nascimento was giving away boots.

He'd have to figure out what he was going to tell Judge Ida. But for now, Waldo was in the dog-catching business full-time.

SEVENTEEN

Waldo took a train to the Valley and a bus the rest of the way to Sherman Oaks. It was hot on that side of the hill, Arizona hot, and between that and his adventure on Sepulveda, he decided to stick to public transit as much as he could.

He tried to reconcile himself with the day's abasing work. Don Q was a dangerous man, and if he was out of his tree, somebody could get hurt. Especially in this barbarous heat. Besides, Q was paying top dollar, which, given the temperatures and the fires, Waldo thought about redirecting to the Union of Concerned Scientists.

He went on the San Fernando Valley Animal Services website and clicked on *Finding a Lost Pet*. The Valley had three shelters holding almost a thousand lost cats and dogs among them, a lot more than Waldo would have expected. Buttons on screen let you sort by animal, sex and more. *Dog, male*, and *no preference* for age, size, color or breed brought up photographs of over two hundred dogs, with descriptions, sizes, the names of the shelters housing them and the dates they were received.

Waldo got off the bus, unfolded his Brompton, and headed for Fulton and the same entrance to the L.A. River walking trail. He got lucky: Lena wasn't far from where he'd left her the first time he was down here. Better still, she appeared not to be in whatever chemical condition would have her maiming him with a rake. She sat against a tree, drawing on a large pad. That screenwriter Russell sat cross-legged beside her, barefoot again. Waldo laid down his bike and walked over toward them.

'But wait,' Lena was saying, 'if he's the real Santa, why doesn't he just get the reindeer and the sleigh? Then he could fly the movie Santa home. And his daughter, too – they'd all fit.'

'But it's more interesting if they have to fight their way there however they can. Like *Miracle on 34th Street* meets *Midnight Run*. Two Santas and a little girl in, like, an old crop duster? There's your poster.'

'Yeah, but it has to make sense for the characters. It has to be about what *they* need, not what the *movie* needs.' She looked up. 'Hey, Waldo. Where you been?'

'All over.' He nodded at her pad. 'Can I see?'

'If you want.'

He crossed behind and looked over her shoulder. It was somewhat abstract, but on closer look Waldo thought he could make out a garden, with a child pushing a wagon down a dirt path. Beyond, there was a stream, with a grove of orange trees on the other side. She rubbed her way down the water with two fingers, blending red and blue and green into brown. There were only five colored pastels on the ground beside her, which somehow she'd managed to make look like a full palette.

'Where'd you learn that?'

'Just always did it.' He realized that the bend in her stream echoed the concrete river in front of them. What she'd turned into a garden was the patch of weeds next to the asphalt, and the wagon was her bike and sidecar shopping cart.

Waldo said, 'Hey, my friend who knew the Professor? He'd like to start taking care of Sancho, if I can find him. I thought I'd check out the shelters, but I don't know what he looks like. What breed, even.'

'He was like a husky or something, but could be mixed?'

Waldo took out his phone. 'Check out the animal services website with me? Maybe you'll see him.'

'Sure.' Lena helped him with some specifics, and soon they were able to narrow it down to about seventy dogs, ten to a page. On the fifth page Lena pointed to a gorgeous animal, mostly white, with a slate gray crown angling to a point between his eyes. Lena was certain it was Sancho. The website described him as an Alusky, a Siberian Husky crossed with an Alaskan Malamute, and said he was at the Van Nuys shelter.

Waldo thanked her, and gestured toward her pastel.

'What do you do with a picture like that when you're done?'

'Some I save. Some I give away.'

'You ever sell them?'

'No, but I would.'

It made him glad he hadn't replaced his sunglasses yet.

*   *   *

Fortunately the woman at the desk at the Van Nuys shelter didn't know who he was. The last thing renowned detective Charlie Waldo wanted to do was explain why he was working a missing canine.

Waldo told her that he lost his dog, and pulled up Sancho's picture on their website. She looked up the records, and was able to tell Waldo that he'd been brought in three days ago, that they'd wanded him and hadn't found a microchip. She turned back to Waldo and gave him a once-over. She asked if he had any kind of proof of ownership, like papers or vet bills.

'No,' he said. 'I'm outdoors, pretty much. But I take care of him.'

'There's a seventy-two-hour rule. If you can bring us proof of ownership by five o'clock, we can give him to you. After that, he's up for adoption.'

'So I can come back at five and officially claim him?'

She shook her head. 'There's someone in line ahead of you – the person who brought him in. They get a window from five o'clock until eight, when we close. If they don't, then you can come in when we open in the morning. There are fees, though,' she made sure to tell him. 'For microchipping, and some other things—'

'But you're saying I don't have a shot anyway.'

'You never know. Some people say they'll take an animal if it isn't claimed, but they never come back.'

Waldo asked if he could have a look at his dog, at least, and she brought him back to the cages. Most of the others barked at him, but Sancho didn't, just stared up at Waldo with plaintive, Arctic-blue eyes. Waldo would have been drawn to him right away, without the photo. Dulci would be mad for him, if Waldo could figure out how to get him for her.

Waldo thanked the shelter woman and went back outside. He was looking at a couple of unstructured hours in the worst of the afternoon heat. He'd already gone through most of his canteen. Lena, Russell and the others had to kill time like this every day, at least on the days they didn't have to spend fighting their way through the maze of forms and rules and agencies for modest assistance. And the ones whose executive functions were too compromised for all that bureaucracy – well, endless, parched stretches of this kind of nothing were pretty much all they had.

There was a Ralph's nearby, where at least he could cool off. On a less brutal day, he'd indulge the internal debate about the rightness of going into a public space only for its air conditioning, but this wasn't that day.

He stepped in front of the automatic door and was assaulted by the sweet, chemical smell of the refrigerant. He hadn't been in a chain supermarket in four years. He walked aisle after aisle, marveling at the waste, and sickened by it. Bread in plastic, eggs in Styrofoam, fish in plastic *and* Styrofoam. Even the produce, for God's sake: single serving salads in single use plastic shells, with plastic forks inside.

A manager started following him, and soon told Waldo he'd have to leave the store if he wasn't going to purchase anything. Waldo bought a Honeycrisp apple and a banana and left anyway.

He found shade at a bus shelter and ate both pieces of fruit, thinking about the pet care aisle, with its shelves and shelves of canned food. He hadn't had a pet in these years since he changed his life (unless, of course, you counted his utilitarian chickens), and hadn't had reason to think much about their ecological cost. He did some research now.

What he found dismayed him. For one thing, the EPA had labeled dog feces an environmental hazard on par with pesticides. Even conscientious pet owners, the ones who collected every bit of their dog's waste, were laying claim to one twenty-fifth of the space in America's landfills. And pet *food* was arguably worse: American dogs and cats alone consumed more meat than the humans in all but three foreign nations. Food for American pets generated sixty-four million tons of CO_2 a year – climate impact equivalent to that of thirteen million cars.

The carbon pawprint! Why didn't people talk about this? There were things that could be done: dogs could live perfectly well as vegetarians, or at least eat food made from non-cud-chewing ruminants, and poop could be buried. But nobody was doing those things. It turned out that owning a pet was another one of those selfish, Earth-devastating choices that millions of people who called themselves 'environmentally conscious' made without remorse, like using a trash can instead of composting, or traveling for recreation.

Then again, Sancho was adorable.

By 4:30, Waldo had stationed himself across the street from the shelter. At five on the dot, a fortyish white man and a young girl, about the same age as Don Q's daughter, went inside, holding hands. Thirty-five minutes later they came back out, the man leading Sancho on a leash and the girl petting his back as she skipped along beside him. The dad opened the back of a Toyota RAV, coaxed the good-natured dog inside, and closed the hatch.

Waldo got on his Brompton and tailed the RAV. His heart sank at the thought of separating this giddy little girl from her brand-new pet. At the same time, he knew he'd be doing her and her father a service: better the separation be effected by Waldo than by Don Q himself. Especially Don Q in madman mode.

Waldo tailed them to a one-story home in Valley Village, not far from where he used to live himself. The dad set the girl and dog loose in their front yard, surrounded by a wooden fence. The Alusky gamboled and barked. The girl picked up a stick, yelled, 'Fetch, Oliver!' and threw it, but the dog wasn't interested. Maybe he was waiting for her to call him Sancho.

Waldo approached the house on his Brompton. The dad, wary, maneuvered himself between Waldo and his daughter. 'Can I help you with something?'

Again, Waldo was grateful not to be recognized. He said, 'That's my dog. I lost him a few days ago. His name's Sancho.'

'Yeah? Do you live around here?'

'I'm kind of on the street. I stay sometimes at a house in Studio City, or by the river. My friends – you know, other people who are pretty much living over there? They can tell you I take care of him.'

The dad drew back, his lip twisting, like Waldo was a year-old casserole discovered at the back of his fridge. The disgust cut Waldo to the core – as if he *were* the Professor, as if this man – privileged, safe, blessed with a loving daughter and the lucky accident of mental health – were deeming him unworthy of his own pet. As if he were less than human, as if he'd invited scorn by violating the code, by not keeping himself hidden in plain sight, by having the temerity to remind society that he was alive, that he was here.

'I don't know what you think you're doing,' said the man. 'But leave us alone.'

'That's my dog,' said Waldo. 'Look – I'll give you something beautiful.' He took Lena's pastel from his backpack and unrolled it.

'I don't want that. Look, he belongs to my daughter now. We did things the right way. We could've just kept him when we found him.'

'*That's my dog.* I've fed it. I've loved it. Just because my life hasn't been as fortunate as yours, just because I don't have a nice house, just because I have to sleep where I can and eat what I can—'

'What—?' The man shook his head, bewildered. 'You're that detective. You're famous. And you're – what? – lying, to steal a dog from a little girl?' He called to his daughter. 'Honey, go in the house. I'll bring Oliver inside in a minute.' He turned back to Waldo. 'Don't make me call the police, OK?'

Staggered, ashamed, Waldo mumbled, 'Sorry to bother you,' and pedaled away as fast as he could without thinking about where he was headed. A minute later he realized that he'd gone down a cul-de-sac and would have to redouble his humiliation by passing the house again on his way out.

At the dead end, Waldo stopped and braced himself on his handlebars. Tears filled his eyes and his nose started running and he didn't even know why.

The world tumbled off its axis again, like it did in Boston. He laid down his bike and slumped to the curb, his head between his legs, praying for it to stop.

The word *stress* popped into his mind – a concept he generally didn't think about.

Stress? Over what? Chasing a homeless dog?

God, what would Lorena say to this pathetic show? She'd be back on *talk to somebody*, or worse. Meds, even. A doctor had once wanted to put Waldo on an antidepressant, back during the struggle to get Lydell Lipps's conviction overturned. That guy talked about stress, too. 'Stress,' the doc said, 'is fundamentally about lack of control.'

Well, control – *that* Waldo understood. Control was how he'd rebooted his life: control over what he owned, what he ate, what he used, how he traveled, what he did with his time. And that's what was being stolen from him now, by Don Q, but by Lorena even more. They were both forcing him into detective work – into a *mockery* of detective work. Stealing dogs from children? Covering up old murders? No wonder he was falling apart.

He pulled out the burner and speed-dialed Don Q.

'You got my dog?'

'No,' said Waldo, his voice thick from crying. 'I found out what happened to him, but it's not good. He got hit by a truck on Riverside.'

'What kinda truck?'

'Garbage truck. The recycling one.'

'Shit, man. I already told Dulci she was *gettin'* that dog.'

'Why would you—'

'She's been takin' doggie-care classes. We bought chew toys – one's shaped like a fuckin' sushi, and a ice cream cone for dessert.'

Waldo said, 'Sorry.' Then, 'Are we finished?'

'Yeah, Waldo, we're finished.' Only after they both hung up did Waldo recall that Don Q still had his MacBook.

But this wasn't the time to worry about that. This was the time to go see Fontella Davis.

EIGHTEEN

Her assistant put him on a long hold, but came back on the line and said that Ms Davis would see him at six o'clock. He didn't think it would be so easy. Waldo and Fontella Davis first crossed paths on Pinch, and it was dislike at first sight. She didn't care for Waldo's past, his look, or his way, nor he for her mercenary history, her take-no-prisoners style, or her M.O. of burning adversaries in the media, truth be damned and consequences, too.

He took Laurel over the hill. It was a little out of the way, but he thought it would have the most traffic that time of day and make him the hardest target. Still, he kept looking over his shoulder for a red Range Rover.

He breezed through West Hollywood and Beverly Hills and into the chilly glass canyon of Century Park East. He couldn't find a stand – Century City wasn't built for cyclists – and decided to fold and bag his Brompton and carry it inside. He checked in at security, pushed his way past the end-of-workday crush streaming off the elevators and rode up to Fontella's.

Davis, Madeas, Wolff & Heuton occupied the entire floor. Waldo gave his name to the receptionist and took a seat, alone on the four leather sofas that comprised the waiting area.

A few minutes later, a young lawyer in a white bowtie blouse and skirt suit came around a corner, saying to someone walking behind her, 'Thanks for going over all this again. I know it's repetitive, but it'll really help the case.' When her interlocutor appeared, Waldo rose in recognition of a familiar face. It took a second to realize it wasn't an actual acquaintance, it was someone from TV – specifically Man Nickerson. The sneer he got in return said Bailiff Man knew *him* from TV, too.

Then the lobby was still for ten or fifteen minutes. At half-past six Waldo asked the receptionist if Ms Davis knew he was here. The receptionist assured him that Ms Davis's assistant did.

Ten minutes after that, a young white woman escorted out a

frail Black woman who looked close to seventy, dabbing teary eyes with a lace handkerchief.

At quarter to seven, the same young woman returned and told Waldo that Ms Davis was ready for him.

'Charlie Waldo, making house calls,' said Fontella Davis, as the assistant led Waldo into her corner office. It was the largest he'd ever seen, and he'd been inside a network president's. He could see all the way to Catalina Island. 'Darkening my door.' She began to open a bottle of wine with an electric device.

'Thanks for seeing me.'

'Cabernet? Hundred Acre, 2007.'

'No, thanks. Is this how you end every day?'

'Not with a six-hundred-dollar bottle of wine, I don't. Only when I've got something to celebrate.'

'Big win?'

'A *very* big win. That police shooting in University Park last week? That kid, got shot in the back?' Waldo had read about it; everybody had. It was another one of those stories, fresh in detail yet numbingly familiar: fourteen-year-old honor student walking at night, cops flashing their lights for no good reason, kid running for no good reason, eight shots fired and a dead teenager carrying a loaded hot dog from Five Guys.

Waldo said, 'You got a settlement already?'

Davis scoffed. 'Even *I* can't make the wheels of justice turn *that* fast. But the case is a lock, eight figures. The grandmother spent the week talking to six different lawyers. And I,' said Davis, lifting her amply filled glass in Waldo's direction, 'just signed her.'

That would have been the old lady in the lobby, crying her way to the elevator.

'You're sitting there judging me. But I'm just doing well by doing good. Getting justice *and* getting mine.' She swirled the wine, tilted her head down and her eyes up. 'And I bet you're not judging your client, are you. How she's using *her* law degree. "Judge Ida Mudge." Who, by the way, sounds like she's about to be way richer than me.'

Davis took a first sip, savored it. 'Mudge,' she said, 'you know where that comes from? She had an auntie Tuttle with that married name. Ida gets onto the family court, suddenly it's "Ida Tuttle-hyphen-Mudge," same as her aunt. That girl had as much "Mudge" in her as the President. Had her eye on TV before she hit that bench, is what she had.'

Waldo nodded gently, letting Davis keep the resentment spewing. He'd barely had to tap the earth and he'd hit the gusher he'd been hoping for.

'And the way she talks on TV. Let me tell you something: *my* daddy was a garbage man. *My* mama cleaned rooms at the New York Hilton. I was Bed-Stuy, do or die. You know where Ida Tuttle grew up?'

'Baltimore, right?'

'"Baltimore," yeah. Roland Park. Both her parents? Doctors. The whole thing – Jack and Jill, cotillion. I had to *teach myself* to sound the way *she grew up. She* taught herself to sound like she's Cardi B's homegirl.' She took another sip. 'Million dollars a day. Well, she always did like to have lots of cash in her pocket. I hear she's spending it before she has it, too.'

'How's she doing that?'

'Line of credit. She better be careful, this lawsuit hanging over her.' Davis grinned like a lioness. 'Which is what you're here to talk about, I assume.'

Waldo shook his head.

Davis pushed back into her chair, surprised. 'I was sure you were going to float a settlement offer.'

'White flag on the harassment suit. I'm here for something else.'

Davis chortled. 'Let me guess: You want to team up again. You miss me that much.'

Waldo couldn't help but smile. He said, 'What do you remember about Anthony Branch, and the way he died?'

Caught off guard, Davis's face softened, fell. She looked stricken, in fact.

Then her countenance changed again and she erupted in a guffaw. 'Why . . . in heaven's name . . . is Ida Tuttle sending you to my office asking about Anthony Branch?'

'I'm doing it on my own. The lawsuit got me curious about the two of you, and I went back to your old college newspapers.'

Davis hummed doubt.

Waldo pressed on. 'There were so few Black students at Mathewson, I figured you both had to know him. And—' This time he stopped himself before saying *Judge*. '—Ida said you did. Then I talked to Anthony's mother—'

Davis hummed again.

'—and she says that she and Anthony's father never believed the finding.'

Davis gave him nothing.

'Would it be all right if I asked you some questions?'

Davis's eyebrows told him, *Take your shot.*

'What do you think happened?'

'Accident.'

'Did you know the other guys in his fraternity?'

'Couple.'

'The pledge captains?'

'Couple.' Whatever he pulled out of her would have to come a word at a time.

'Carter Gass?'

'Mm-hmm.'

'What did you think of him back then?'

'Rich.'

'Hoyt Lelong?'

She took a beat before saying, 'White.'

'Why'd you pause there?'

She hummed at him again.

'Morris Thurmond?'

'Hero.'

'Matt Fishbein?'

'Strange.'

'Was he honest?'

She hiked a shoulder.

'Any of them have gripes with Anthony?'

She hiked the same shoulder.

'What about Petters? Dave Petters? The one who died?'

'Sad.'

'What about his wife?' he said, practically an afterthought. 'Ruthanne.'

Somehow that was the name that drew the lawyer out. 'Oh, *her* I know. Or *knew*, really. We're not in touch. She was a sweetheart, that girl.'

'You say you're not in touch – any idea where she is?'

'Last I heard she was in Topanga Canyon or something. She was *from* here. That was my first taste of California.'

'So you were close in college, then.'

'I was in her wedding. Ida, too, as I'm sure you know.'

Waldo didn't know. In fact, Judge Ida had acted like she barely remembered Ruthanne Petters. And hadn't wanted Waldo to go talk to her, either.

He said, 'Do you remember anyone talking about a map of the woods for the pledge hike? Of where they were going to put the freshmen?'

Fontella Davis took her time, gave it some thought, before saying, 'You heard about the map?'

Waldo tried not to look excited. 'I did.'

'From who?' said Davis.

'I'd rather not say.'

'Who all do you think had a copy of that map?'

Somehow this had turned. Waldo said, 'I was asking the questions here.'

'Is that an objection?'

'Kind of, yeah—'

'Overruled. You heard about the trouble between Ida and Anthony, didn't you.'

'It's been mentioned.'

'Who told you about it? Hoyt Lelong? Did you go talk to him?'

'I—'

'Did you talk to Morris? Carter?'

'I've talked to them—'

'Did you go *see* them?'

Attempting to slow this down, Waldo attempted a Fontella Davis shoulder hike.

She snorted and said, 'You think Ida Tuttle killed Anthony.'

'I'm not saying that—'

'You heard Ida *hated* that so-and-so,' said Davis. 'That he went around telling people she had sex with him. And you think she got the map, maybe *from* Morris, and she found Anthony in the woods, blindfolded, hands tied, and led him to that cliff and pushed him over. *Could* that have happened? Yes, it could. Absolutely.'

She was laying out means and motive and opportunity. The

most important thing, though, was to get clear confirmation of the latter. Waldo said, 'So there *was* a map.'

Davis said, 'Beats the devil out of me. I never heard a thing about a map before you walked into my office.' She cocked her head, a challenge; he couldn't tell whether she was feigning ignorance, or feigning feigning.

She had him off balance, though.

She said, 'But what I *am* pretty sure? You didn't find out about Anthony Branch on your own. Ida put you onto this. And now you're wondering why.' She picked up her wine, which she hadn't touched in a few minutes, and swirled it. '*And* you're wondering what that girlfriend of yours got you into.' His surprise must have registered. 'Come on,' she said. 'How *else* would this happen?' She laughed again. 'Mr Clean goes to work for the Queen of Sleaze – how'd you *think* that was going to work out? Ida probably got you twisted up into thinking she was some damsel in distress who needed you to save her. Am I close? I bet you're flying all around the country to talk to those old frat brothers, too – aren't you, bicycle man. Telling yourself you're speaking for the victim. That's all right, Waldo. I run that same okey-doke on myself, when I need it to get by.'

Off balance, indeed. She was spinning him like she'd been spinning juries and the public for decades, with the gift of ensorcellment that bought her that view of Catalina and six-hundred-dollar bottles of wine.

'I'll tell you one more thing,' she said, 'out of respect for our having shared clients in the past. If Ida Tuttle brought you into this, and wanted you to think she killed Anthony? She's got a reason. Which you may never find out until it's too late.'

She sipped a little more of her cabernet, worked it around her mouth before swallowing. 'You're smarter than I expected before I met you, Waldo. I'll grant you that.

'But Ida Tuttle? She's smarter than damn near anybody.'

NINETEEN

He texted Lorena that he was on his way home, but he was in no hurry. He'd agreed not to go see Fontella Davis, and now he'd have to tell her that he had. Besides, he was eager to start tracking down Ruthanne Petters, to find out if she was still in Topanga and whether he could see her the next morning.

He rode to an indie coffee joint he liked out past Paramount, where Shauna, the owner, sold steeply priced but defiantly sustainable coffee. Waldo made it there a half-hour before closing time, ordered and took out his phone.

Ruthanne Petters wasn't hard to find: Topanga, indeed, from where, her website explained, she did business as a 'Life Consultant' and 'Sacred Space Designer.' He paged through the site and read Ruthanne's 'poem prayer blog,' as well as details about the services she offered. There was 'intuitive counseling' (the intuition apparently a substitute for actual training), 'sacred space design for home and business' (which 'built on principles of hygge, lagom, and Feng Shui') and 'space cleansing and blessing' (which involved something called 'smudging' with something called 'palo santo'). Unable to resist, Waldo looked up 'palo santo.' One site said it was Spanish for 'holy wood.' Well, close.

Ruthanne's gifts – her clients all used her first name – were ballyhooed on a long page of testimonials, attributed only to one-letter initials and occupations, e.g. *T, studio executive*, or *W, financial consultant*, or *B, leading actor*. There was also a 'mart' with products for sale: crystals, candles and Himalayan salt lamps, plus, naturally, Ruthanne's videos.

Last, there was a contact page, with no phone number, only an online form to request a session. 'All pricing is project-based,' it noted, with 'corporate rates available.' Waldo filled it out and, in the comment box, said he'd like to come talk to her tomorrow, if she had time.

Dusk was falling by the time he reached Lorena's. He let himself in. Four candles on the living-room floor led the way to Lorena's bedroom. The lights in there were turned off, but a glow emanated from the bathroom.

Waldo pushed open the door and found Lorena in the tub, surrounded by candles and smoking a joint, something she almost never did. 'I know what you're going to say: candles, right? They're all terrible: paraffin, palm wax, beeswax. But these . . . are coconut. Look it up, you'll be proud of me. Actually, why don't you look it up later.'

'What's all this about?' Sex for them had always been bountiful and spontaneous, ceremony unnecessary.

'I wanted to celebrate. I thought today was kind of important.' She offered the joint. He passed, sat down and tipped his chin, asking her to say more. 'I took all that stuff to Goodwill. And you didn't go to Fontella. See? We can compromise. We can do this. So,' she said, extending a leg and draping it over the edge of the tub, 'you just going to sit on the toilet, or what?'

He felt guilty. And righteous. And trapped.

Also, aroused.

It would be easy to let not talking win, again, but he knew this time it would feel like cheating. He said, 'I did go see her.'

Lorena closed her eyes and slid down beneath the water. She came up, exhaled, and said, 'Jesus, Waldo.'

She killed the joint in the bathwater, flipped the drain with her big toe, stood up and reached for a towel. While she dressed, Waldo told her how Judge Ida lied about Ruth Petters, and also about Fontella's warnings.

Lorena didn't scold, didn't fire back. She silently pulled on a pair of gray sweats and went out to the skeletal dining area and did something on her laptop. Waldo assumed she was shopping. He sat across from her and read, or tried to.

In the quiet, it felt to him like they'd found their way onto the same page at last, albeit a blue one: neither of them angry, but both wounded and exhausted and out of words.

A bohemian enclave running from the west Valley to the ocean, Topanga was the closest thing L.A. had to a Seventies preservation society. Ruthanne Petters, with her poem prayers and space cleansing, could probably be elected mayor, if they had one. In some ways the town was a closer-by version of Idyllwild, which actually did have a mayor, a golden retriever named Max. Waldo wondered how the mayor made out in the fire.

He rode a bus for an hour out to Woodland Hills, and then his Brompton deep into Topanga Canyon. The shade and the nearby Pacific made it cooler than the other parts of town he'd been biking, but it was still a long way to go without certainty Ruthanne Petters would be there. She hadn't answered his contact. Right now, though, she was the best lead he had.

There was a car in her driveway, a small BMW convertible. What flavor of hippie was this? Waldo leaned his bike on an oversize flower pot and drank some water from his canteen, listening to a variety of chimes tinkling in the warm breeze. He found a doorbell, setting off more chimes inside.

Ruthanne opened the door, big blue eyes smiling from under flowing gray-blonde hair. She wore a peasant blouse with a Native American design and a huge necklace made from a shell. 'Welcome,' she said.

'My name's Charlie Waldo.'

'Oh: you're the one who sent me the session request. I saw that this morning.' She seemed neither to know who he was nor to recoil at his appearance. She pulled the front door shut behind her and led Waldo around to the back of her house. 'Did you travel far?'

'Hollywood.'

'You're in pain.'

'Why do you say that?'

'Not many people come all the way out here. Especially without an appointment.' There was a slow control to her movement, an airy equanimity to her voice.

Waldo said, 'How do you see your clients, then?'

'Most of them I FaceTime. Some I go to.'

Out back she had a round structure, like a huge tent made of bamboo walls and ribs, mostly covered with some kind of skins. Waldo was pretty sure you'd call it a yurt. If so, it was his first.

The interior was decorated like a living room, with furniture of carved branches and plush cushions. On a bookcase, an orange rock glowed, like something out of science fiction or maybe a superhero movie. 'What's this?' he said.

She found an electric cord and flipped it off and back on. 'This? This is a Himalayan salt lamp.'

'What's that supposed to do?'

'Not *supposed* to do; it's what it *does*. It releases negative ions. They increase the levels of serotonin in the body. Come, sit close to it. It's like a walk along the ocean – can you feel it? A slight euphoria?'

'Not yet.'

'You will.' She sat opposite him, inhaled, closed her eyes and let it out, then gazed at him with an unearthly serenity that began to disconcert him. She said, 'Your life is out of harmony.'

Well, shit, whose wasn't? It was the same crapola you'd get from any 'psychic' on Cahuenga Boulevard, only with a website and a BMW.

'Have you ever worked on your chakras?' she said.

'No.'

'Do you meditate?'

'Ms Petters—'

'I've been designing personal meditation studios for a number of my clients. If you have a space in your home, then with an aromatherapy diffuser, and the right oils—'

'Ms Petters, I'm a private detective.'

Her reaction to that was a little incongruous, a sympathetic lean in and widening of her already enormous eyes.

'What?' he said.

'Your work isn't going well, is it. It's not nourishing you.'

It was an odd way to put it, but it was also correct, even precise. 'No,' Waldo said, 'it's not.'

'It's not joyous.'

'I don't know that it's ever been "joyous."'

'Perhaps not, but in the past it's been more meaningful than you're finding it now.'

'Yes.'

'You're being compromised,' she said. 'Someone's clipping your wings.' Where was she getting this? Is this what intuitive counseling was? She leaned in a bit and squinted at him. 'Two people. One each wing, I think.' Waldo blinked, suddenly lightheaded. 'We have a spiritual anatomy, Mr Waldo, as well as a physical one. And if it's out of alignment, we're in pain. Your crown chakra, it's right here.' She ran her index finger back and forth a couple of times, high on the center of her forehead. 'It can be *too* powerful. Overactive. Our self-mastery can be too strong.'

He didn't understand it, quite, but he was reeling. He steadied himself, and said, 'I'm here to ask some questions. Not for counseling.'

'Don't worry,' she said, with that look of sympathy again, 'I'm not charging you.'

'You were married to Dave Petters.'

'You have questions about Dave?' It didn't seem to surprise her. But nothing did.

'More about your college years. Ida Tuttle was in your wedding?'

'Yes.'

'And Fontella Davis.'

'Fontella, yes.'

'You were close? With both of them?'

'In those days.'

'Your life took a very different direction.' He looked around the yurt.

'I've had some challenges, which I've processed into an awakened path.'

Waldo was sure he could get more by waiting her out. He was wrong. Instead she simply smiled gently until he was forced to say, 'What challenges?'

'We had a son, whom we lost as a baby. Then, Dave.'

'I'm sorry.'

'Even with all that, I have so much to be grateful for.' Without shifting or changing intonation, she said, 'What exactly are you investigating?'

Waldo told her he was doing background work on Judge Ida toward the harassment case, which she said she'd heard of but had chosen to avoid reading about. 'Why's that?' he said.

'I didn't see the value in it. Only bad energy.'

He circled around the subject awhile, asking what Ida was like in college, about their friendship, and how they fell away from each other. Ruthanne was nothing but positive. When they were in school, she said, she truly admired Ida's intellect and drive, and though she claimed not to have ever watched her television show, Ruthanne said she was 'deeply gratified' by Ida's success.

Waldo found his way to the subject of Anthony Branch's death. That made Ruthanne quiet. He brought up the slap incident and the rumors Anthony spread about Ida, and asked whether she remembered that. She nodded, but he could see her equanimity slipping. Bad energy.

He asked Ruthanne how angry Ida was at Anthony at the time he died. For the first time, she lost her composure. '*Ida?* Is that what this is about? You're not working for Ida on her lawsuit. You want to know whether Ida had something to do with Anthony dying. She didn't.'

The paroxysm made Waldo wonder whether Ruthanne might reach out to Judge Ida and tell her about this. She wasn't finished, either. 'Hell,' she said, '*I* had more reason to murder him.'

Before Waldo could even process that, Ruthanne gathered herself and brought the conversation back to her friend. 'Ida was the strongest woman I've ever known. She was always certain who she was. I'm sure that comes through on TV. I'm sure that's why she's so successful.'

He wanted to know what sort of reason Ruthanne would have had for killing Anthony, but knew not to come straight at it. So he said, 'Definitely.' And then: 'How did that manifest itself back then? Ida's strength.'

'She backed Anthony off.'

The penny dropped. Waldo said, 'Not everybody did.'

'No,' said Ruthanne, the equanimity entirely gone, not able, for the first time, to look him in the eye.

Anthony wasn't always what you'd call smooth with the ladies.

'I'm sorry,' said Waldo, 'but I *am* trying to figure out what happened to Anthony Branch, and I have to ask: did he assault—' He was about to say *you*, but swerved at the last moment. '—anyone?'

Ruthanne slowly inhaled and exhaled through slightly pursed lips, did that twice more, and still thought a while longer before answering, 'At the time, we didn't know to call it that.'

In an instant it seemed more likely Anthony Branch's death *wasn't* an accident, but that the suspect pool might have widened beyond imagining.

'Were there others? Look,' he said, trying to walk gingerly, 'I'm not asking for names. Well, yes, I guess I *would* like names. But only if you think they'd be willing to come forward.'

What was he asking for? Women to reach back decades to the most horrible moments of their lives? So they could turn themselves into murder suspects? Hell, if Anthony's killer had been his victim, Waldo wasn't even sure he wanted to solve the case. Especially looking at this poor woman in front of him, whom Waldo had managed to knock clean out of preternatural equilibrium and back into hell.

He said, 'I'm sorry. I want to walk all of that back. Forget I asked. And I want to apologize if I inadvertently opened old wounds. I definitely don't want to compromise anybody's pri—'

But she cut him off. 'There's one other I know: Fontella Davis.'

Waldo reeled again. 'Wait,' he said, 'why are you – I mean, I *really* don't want to compromise anyone's privacy. Maybe you shouldn't—'

'*Fuck* her privacy,' said Ruthanne Petters. 'It makes me sick, what she's done with her life. Criminal defense? After what happened to her? To me? To whoever else we don't know about? Every time I see Fontella on the news – *such* a betrayal. *Such* a sellout. Fuck her. Seriously.'

Ruthanne reached over, turned off the Himalayan salt lamp, and sat back into a deep shadow. Waldo sat there with her, neither speaking, for what felt like minutes.

Finally Ruthanne said, 'When you leave, I'm going to have to smudge the shit out of this room.' Waldo was tempted to laugh until he realized she was crying.

TWENTY

I n his woods, Waldo kept to a strict every-third-day shower
schedule. He tried to do the same in L.A., but soon moved it
up to every other day as a concession to socialization, and in
particular to cohabitation. He kept his water use to a minimum,
turning it off while he shampooed and again when he lathered.
He'd save his ablutions for the evening, after the worst of the day,
and luxuriate in a clean and comfortable night. With a second
straight day of triple-digit heat, though, and a meeting scheduled
for later that afternoon, he broke down and moved that night's
shower up by about six hours.

While he lathered his hair, he took stock. Whoever was behind
the Range Rover attack had something to do with Anthony Branch's
death. Could it have been Fontella? By Ruthanne's telling, she
had a stronger motive than Judge Ida. On the other hand, it would
have been tougher for her to get her hands on the map, assuming
it even existed; Fontella wasn't the one with the sort-of pledge-
captain boyfriend. More important, if someone other than Judge
Ida killed him, why was she the one getting blackmailed? Could
somebody, thirty-five years later, have conflated these two young
Black women?

That last gave him a Hoyt Lelong tingle. Did hand surgeons
blackmail, even racist ones? Lelong was clearly inflamed by
Judge Ida's coming payday; maybe the good doctor wanted to
score one of those one-day millions for himself, tax-free, and
thought he remembered something that could get it for him.
And now we were back to hippocampi and neocortices and
amygdalae, and maybe Ida was Fontella to him, and Fontella, Ida.

But then, it was definitely Ida, not Fontella, who lied to Waldo
about not knowing Ruthanne.

Could the women be in this together, somehow, one covering
for the other? No. Not the way they were whaling on each other
in the courts and in the press.

Waldo had gone to see Fontella Davis because she'd be happy

to hang the murder on Ida Mudge; maybe he needed to hear from Ida Mudge next, because she'd love to hang it on Fontella Davis.

But the outright lie about not knowing Ruthanne – that rankled him. In fact, since their last conversation, when Judge Ida soured on him and knocked him backwards, it felt like Waldo kept learning more ways in which his client was holding back important information. Why wouldn't she tell him that she'd slapped Anthony? Or about what happened between Anthony and Fontella, which she'd surely known, too?

If there *was* a map, and if Judge Ida knew about it, Waldo had no reason to believe she'd be straight with him about that, either.

He couldn't wait to brace her again. Fortunately, she was in town shooting episodes today and agreed to see him later on, when they wrapped. That's why he was taking a—

Suddenly he was cognizant of the water streaming down his back and realized that he'd forgotten to shut it off after rinsing his hair, and that he hadn't even started soaping. How many minutes had he stood there like this, letting gallons of California's precarious reserve flow down his drain?

This fucking case.

'What you got for me, Charlie Waldo? For all that money I'm payin' you.'

'I saw Hoyt Lelong and Matt Fishbein.'

'What *they* have to say?'

'That it was an accident.'

'Good. So we done?'

'Not quite yet. There's still a loose end or two.'

'I need to wrap this up.'

'Something change?'

'Rothbell got DigiTV to agree to a buyout.' In other words, the runway had been cleared for her syndication deal. 'Why ain't we done?'

He'd get to her lies in time. Now he just asked, 'Any more fan mail?' borrowing her flip locution, knowing it would provoke her. She scowled, then pointed to a corner of her desk, where another envelope sat. Waldo opened it.

Delivery in three days. Be ready.

He said, 'You getting money together?'

'Shit, I ain't givin' nothin' to no blackmailer when I ain't done nothin'. Anyway, I was countin' on you to get this shit fixed before that became an issue. 'Specially for what I'm payin'.' In less than a minute she'd complained twice about the fee she'd set herself.

It brought to mind what Fontella Davis had said about Judge Ida racking up debt, spending money before she had it. Waldo decided to poke a little harder: 'Paying? I haven't seen *my* money.' As opposed to the seventy-five grand for the plaintiff research. Those ten days were almost up, and Lorena and her ops had come up dry, except for the Man Nickerson stuff. Judge Ida was probably annoyed about that, too. Anyway, none of this was going to do much for Lorena's celebrity word of mouth.

'How many days you work?' said Judge Ida. '*This* case.'

'Six so far.'

'Thirty grand, and you ain't learned a damn thing. That it?'

'Not exactly,' he said, dropping onto her sofa. 'I heard you once slapped Anthony Branch at a party.'

'Who brought that up?'

'Why would you send me out to work this without telling me you'd assaulted the victim?'

Judge Ida burst out laughing. '*That* your loose end, Charlie Waldo? That maybe I *did* kill Anthony? That don't even make sense. If I killed him, why would I go payin' you thirty thousand dollars to figure that out?'

'I'll ask you again: why would you—'

'Because I forgot about it. Wasn't hardly a slap. Practically a love tap. I wasn't anywhere near them woods. Know what I'm gonna do? Get DeRaymond workin' that copy machine – print out a million pieces of paper that say, *Sit the fuck down and shut the fuck up*, and in three days I'll give *that* to this shitbird blackmailer instead.' She stood. 'We're finished now.'

But Waldo stayed seated. 'I went to see Ruthanne Petters, too.'

Judge Ida sighed. 'You went to see Ruthanne. After I told you not to.' She sat back down and eyed Waldo while she weighed that. 'Woo woo Ruthanne. She sell you any'a them five-thousand-dollar crystals? Man, I'd like a piece'a *that* business.'

All the rich people he was meeting on this case spent a lot of time counting each other's money. He said, 'You're doing all right.'

Judge Ida laughed. 'Yes, Charlie Waldo. Yes. I. Am.'

Waldo said, 'Ruthanne's an interesting woman.'

'She told you Fontella killed Anthony, right?'

Waldo wasn't sure what he was expecting, but it wasn't that.

She said, 'That's why I didn't send you over there. Ruthanne's been talkin' that crazy shit for years.'

'She didn't tell me that Fontella killed him. But she did tell me Anthony assaulted her. Assaulted both of them.'

Judge Ida gave that the back of her hand. 'I know the stories. There was a lot of drinkin' at those parties.'

'What are you saying?'

'You know what I'm sayin'. Lotta gray in tales people like to tell in black and white.'

'Maybe people just didn't give things the right names before.'

'You weren't there.'

'No,' he admitted, 'I wasn't.' But: 'Were you more sympathetic back then? When Fontella was your best friend?'

Judge Ida narrowed her eyes.

'The bigger question,' said Waldo, 'is why *you* didn't tell me any of this.'

'Their business. Not for me to go talking about. Not even when Fontella ain't my friend no more.'

'Did Ruthanne actually put it that way to you? That she thought Fontella was out there somehow, and pushed Anthony off the cliff?'

'She said that to me. Yeah. Exactly like that.'

'She said it at the time?'

She shook her head. 'Years after. There was tequila involved. And some other things. Ruthanne do enjoy her wacky tabacky. I don't know if she still believes it. Or believes it when she's sober.'

'Any chance she was right?'

Judge Ida laughed big. 'Man, I would love that. I would love *that*! Fontella Davis on trial for murder? Make a lot of shit in *my* life go away.' She sighed just as big. 'But, no. Ain't no way.'

'Say more.'

'Come on – how could she? She wasn't on that pledge hike. She didn't know where Anthony was gonna be, any more'n I did.'

'I heard there was a map.'

'A map? What kind of map?'

'A map of where each of the pledges was going to be placed.'

'I never heard'a no map. Where'd you get that one?'

'Matt Fishbein. He said he drew it up, and gave it to Morris and all the pledge captains.'

'*Matt Fishbein?* You're goin' on some shabalaba come outta *Matt Fishbein*? Matt Fishbein used to eat Dunkin' Donuts out a garbage can. Fontella didn't have no map! Fontella didn't have a way to *get* no map!'

'Was Fontella with you that night? While they were on the pledge hike?'

'No, but I know where she was, 'cause we talked about it the next day, when we were both all shook up.'

Waldo gestured for her to share it.

'She was with her study buddy from some science class she was tryin' not to flunk.'

'You remember her name?'

'*His* name. What, you gonna track him down, too? Ponciano Panerio. 'Ciano Pancrio. How's that for a handle? Study buddy, sniffed around her all year, wantin' to be her *booty* buddy. She let him *keep* sniffin', too – in exchange for doin' all her homework, is what *I* think.'

Judge Ida stood and went to her desk. 'Here's the thing,' she said, 'and yeah, I could've told you this up front: all you're gonna find out is there are boys who loved Anthony, and a couple girls who didn't. Thing is, there was only boys out there in the woods.

'I'm seein' how this is, Charlie Waldo. You walked in here thinkin' I was holdin' out on you all over the damn place – Ruthanne, Fontella, me introducin' Anthony to my talkin' hand. And maybe about some bullshit map only exists in Matt Fishbein's head, too. Go listenin' to *that* hot box'a cuckoo for cocoa puffs.' She unlocked a desk drawer and began taking out stacks of bills.

'Well, I hope I have disabused you of all your concerns. But whether I did or not, let me tell you how this goes from here.' She relocked the drawer. 'I'm gonna get my syndication deal closed, and announced, and then I'm gonna take my chances.' She pushed the cash in his direction. 'If you're as good as they say, and your best idea is, this was either me or Fontella findin' our

way out into the woods in the middle of the night and killin'
Anthony? Then for sure this is exactly what I always thought, and
what everybody's tellin' you: an accident, pure and simple. All
there is to it.'

Waldo started loading the money into his backpack, thinking,
tell that to the guy in the Range Rover.

TWENTY-ONE

Waldo knew he'd be giving Lorena something just by showing up at the office, and thought it would go over even bigger if he made a surprise of it. He was right. She actually hugged him in front of Reddix (whom she did have out front, doubling as receptionist).

The office smelled of paint, but the changes Lorena described when they visited had indeed transformed it. The space was bright and youthful and energetic. Or at least its doors and walls were; she still had Dumpster and Fat Dave in the staff room, giving the place a sour weight. Fat Dave barely glanced up at Waldo, but Dumpster grabbed another opportunity for fraternity and commiseration. 'Not like the old days, huh.'

In the corner office, Lorena took a seat behind a wooden partners desk; a swivel chair on the other side presumptuously awaited Waldo's arrival. He let that go without comment, but stayed on his feet. 'How'd you get all this done so quickly?'

'Preparation is half the battle. The other half is cash. Thank you, Judge Ida. Hey,' she said, 'did you notice the light bulbs? I replaced them all with fluorescents.' Waldo just nodded. 'What, should I have gotten the LEDs? They were more expensive.'

'Not over the long haul. The CFLs generate most of their energy in heat, like the old incandescents. And LEDs last longer, too.'

'OK, we'll switch.'

'No, no – you're better off sticking with these, now that you have them. You don't want to put extra mercury in a landfill.'

From the staff office, Fat Dave piped in: 'Hey, you two – get a room, huh?'

Waldo raised an eyebrow, and Lorena gave him an *I know* nod. He closed the door and dropped his voice. 'You're dumping them, right? Now that you can?'

'Oh, is this a personnel meeting? Is that your way of telling me you want to be a full partner?'

'Have these mooks found *anything* on those plaintiffs? What are they still doing, at this point?'

'What have *you* been doing?' she said. 'Do I want to know?'

Leavening the moment, Waldo skipped backwards and told her about the previous day's adventures in dog-catching. Still tickled by the fact of his visit, and given the context and contrast of their grim past with Don Q, everything about the story made her giggle, including the fact that this 'case' had drawn Waldo into the neighborhood where he used to live when they were first together.

Easing into a relaxed and companionable vibe, he told Lorena that he'd been to see Judge Ida. 'She wants me to shut it down. She says she'll take her chances with whatever the blackmailer thinks he's got.'

'You still think she might have done it?'

'I don't know. The motive is soft, right? That Anthony lied about having sex with her? She'd already slapped him; would she have to kill him over that, too?' Waldo rubbed his sore shoulder. 'Maybe she's playing some game on me that I can't figure out, but actually, she's got me back to thinking it was probably an accident after all.'

'Then what's the deal with the Range Rover?'

'Could be the blackmailer. Because of the timing, I automatically went to, someone's trying to get me because I'm looking into the death. But could just be whoever's trying to jack her.'

'And Ida lied about Ruthanne Petters because . . .?'

'Because Ruthanne's been pushing a different theory – for years, apparently. And Judge Ida didn't want me going down that rabbit hole.'

'What's the theory?'

'That Fontella Davis killed him.'

Lorena's eyes went big. 'Wait – why?'

'According to Ruthanne, Anthony had sex with each of them – Ruthanne and Fontella – which was, let's say, not consensual.'

'Date rape?'

'Nobody's using those words. But, yeah, acquaintance rape, sounds like.'

'Holy shit. That's awful.' She took a moment to work through all the implications. Waldo saw a sparkle behind her eyes. 'And it changes the whole picture.'

He said, 'Don't even.'

'Come on,' said Lorena. 'Nailing Fontella Davis for a thirty-five-year-old murder? What would *that* do for us? Any possibility Ruthanne's right?'

'Opportunity's even thinner than Judge Ida's. Fontella's access to the map – if there *is* a map – runs *through* Ida. Who's pushing back on the whole concept, like I said. And not just the murder; the sexual assault, too.'

'What do you mean? She's saying it *was* consensual?'

'Gray area.'

'Why would she doubt her friends?'

'Morris Thurmond said to me, "People remember what they want to remember." Judge Ida and Fontella hate each other now. For what it's worth, I believe Ruthanne on this one.' He sat in the chair across the desk from her – a pocket-size surrender, but he clocked Lorena clocking it. 'Thing is, even though she hates Fontella and is playing skeptical about the rapes, Ida totally rules out Ruthanne's take. She says Fontella was with a "study buddy" that night.'

'You check him out?'

Waldo said, 'Not yet. And what makes you sure it was a him?' Lorena gave Waldo a knowing tip of the head. As so often happened, a boy-girl thing he'd initially read wrong played obvious to her.

She said, 'You get his name, at least?'

Ponciano Panerio wasn't hard to find: a founding partner in a lower Manhattan law firm specializing in tax issues, he lived in Rumson, New Jersey and had a lot of Mathewson green on his Facebook page.

Lorena pitched the idea of making a trip east herself, making use of her powers of persuasion, especially with a male witness. Waldo said it couldn't possibly be worth a trip across country, financially or environmentally, just to confirm an alibi. She argued that confirming wasn't the point, that *puncturing* was the point, but backed down when Waldo reminded her that she wasn't even supposed to know about the case and that the blowback could be damaging if for some reason Panerio thought to reach out to Davis afterward.

Once they agreed to work the guy over the phone, the question was how to get him talking about such a specific and personal subject without raising his suspicions and giving him reason to flag her. Lorena said, 'We know he's still a rah-rah alum – what if you tell him you're from the school newspaper and you're doing a revisit piece about Anthony?'

'It's a good idea, but I'll sound too old for a college kid. You should call.'

Lorena thought a second, then opened the door. 'Hey, Reddix – come in here.'

Waldo started to protest but she jumped right into a briefing. She didn't tell Reddix about the blackmail, only what they were trying to confirm, in the narrowest terms. She practically wrote the kid a script, providing him with a fake name and telling him to try to befriend the guy to try to open him up but not to ask anything too directly.

Lorena jiggered her phone to hide behind an *Unknown* heading at the other end, then dialed with the speaker on. Reddix said the magic word 'Mathewson' to an assistant and they got through on the first try.

'Hey ho!' said Panerio. 'Is it fund-raising season already?' He had a shred of an accent Waldo couldn't place and an enthusiasm out of line with being asked for money.

'Actually,' said Reddix, 'I'm calling from the *Monitor.*'

'*The Mathewson Monitor!*' exclaimed Ponciano Panerio. The play was looking good. 'How can I be of service?'

Reddix worked Lorena's script. 'Well, as you may know, there have been several hazing-related deaths at fraternities around the country lately. So my editor asked me to do a look back at what happened to Anthony Branch at Chi Gamma Pi.'

'Oh.' The enthusiasm abated. 'I would always like to help *The Mathewson Monitor*, but I cannot say I knew Anthony Branch well.' Along with the accent, his speech had the formality of a man who'd learned his English elsewhere.

'No? Someone told us you guys were close friends. Maybe there was a picture of you two together in the yearbook, I think . . .?'

'I do not remember that. We were in the same freshman dorm, but not, I believe, on the same floor. We were familiar with each other, but to say we were friends would be an overstatement.'

'Oh,' said Reddix, 'I'm sorry to have bothered you.'

'Not a problem. Good luck with your—'

'Look, since I have you on the phone, though, could you just share any memories you have? If not of Anthony, of the whole event? The aftermath? What the campus was like?'

'Oh. Well. People became distressed. We were all at that age where you believe you are indestructible.'

'I can imagine. It must've felt like it could happen to anybody.'

'Yes. Very sobering.'

'I can't even. If that was us – man, I bet everyone would remember *everything*. Like, where we were when we heard, like, what we were doing ourselves the night it happened . . .'

'Exactly. Exactly. Like 9/11.'

'What were *you* doing?'

'Me, personally?'

'Yeah.'

'I was . . . well, I had this study date arranged, and . . .'

Reddix laughed.

'What?' said Panerio, suspicious. The kid was on the edge of blowing it.

'Just the way you said that. It was sounded like you were putting quotes around "study" date.' Reddix was off script now, winging it. Lorena leaned in her chair like she was trying to will a home run inside the foul pole.

'Funny you should put it that way!' Panerio's enthusiasm came roaring back.

'I feel you,' said Reddix, putting on a laugh.

'No, it wasn't like that.' Then, laughing himself: 'I mean, I *wanted* it to be like that!'

'Now I *really* feel you.' Reddix broadened his laugh, a brother in romantic failure.

'It sounds like you have been in this situation yourself!'

'For me,' Reddix said, 'it was Probability and Statistics. I mean, this girl – I *carried* her through that class . . .'

'You *do* feel me!' said Panerio, all in. Maybe the kid had some talent after all.

'So it didn't happen for you that night?'

'No!' said Panerio. 'The girl didn't even show!'

Waldo and Lorena froze. Reddix, picking up on their reactions, glanced from one of them to the other, though of course he didn't understand the implications.

Lorena rolled one forefinger over the other: *Keep it going.* They still needed confirmation that Fontella Davis was the girl he was talking about.

'Oh, *damn*!' said Reddix.

'Yeah!' Then Panerio sobered, realizing himself. 'I mean, this isn't funny. We're talking about a tragedy—'

Then Reddix blurted, interrupting, 'Was the girl Fontella Davis?'

Dead silence from the other end. The kid had snatched defeat from the jaws of victory.

Waldo scowled at him, then at Lorena. Three thousand miles away, Panerio stayed mute. He wasn't going to confirm now, and he well might be tempted to call her, too.

Reddix, though, was nothing but cool. 'The reason I ask is, I interviewed Ms Davis for this, and, as it happened, she told me a story about standing somebody up that night. But she didn't give me his name.'

After several more excruciating seconds, Panerio said, '. . . Really?'

'Really. She said she was kinda into the guy, too, but when the whole thing with Anthony Branch went down, she took it as, like, a sign never to get involved.'

'Huh,' said Panerio. 'That kind of makes sense. The way things all unfolded.'

They had their confirmation.

Reddix followed up with a couple of generic, open-ended questions, then asked Panerio if he'd be at the next Homecoming (a smooth touch) and wrapped up the call. Lorena excused Reddix with an approving wink. The kid, on a cloud, bopped out of the room, closing the door behind him without being asked.

Lorena said, 'She lied to her best friend!'

Waldo squirmed at her glee, particularly in light of what Fontella had gone through with Anthony Branch. 'Lot of reasons girls lie to each other.'

'On the night of a murder?'

'We don't know it was a murder.'

Lorena was too excited to stay in her chair. 'She's not right, and you know it. Here's my question, though: if it's Fontella who killed Anthony Branch, why is Ida Mudge the one getting blackmailed?'

Waldo told her about Lelong, and floated the possibility of his confusing the women. 'But we'd have long way to go to prove that's what's going on here. Long way until even *I'm* convinced.'

'Still.' Lorena sat back down with the satisfied look of a woman who, at last, had all she'd been striving for: a firm ready to rise, a career-maker on the blossom, even Waldo as a partner, more or less, and Waldo to take home.

Waldo had a lot more doubt about the case than she did, but the happiness she radiated was infectious. He said, 'Let's call it a night.'

Lorena told the guys to knock off and Reddix to lock up. Even with two retired LAPD on staff, it was the twenty-year-old she trusted with a key.

The office didn't come with parking and Lorena's Mercedes was on a side street a couple of blocks away. Waldo walked his Brompton alongside her. She said, 'Kid's good, right?'

'Might be, someday.'

'Listen to you.'

A minivan was parked flush behind Lorena, too tightly for Waldo to access the trunk. He folded his bike while Lorena maneuvered out of the space. She had to pull all the way to the far side of the street – the oncoming lane, had there been other cars around – because someone had left a rental scooter, L.A.'s new scourge, in what should have been her lane.

Waldo laid his bike in the trunk and slammed it closed. He took a moment to play the good citizen and pull the scooter to the sidewalk. Only as he opened the passenger door did he hear an engine crescendo and look up to see the red Range Rover in the vacated right lane, bearing down on him.

Waldo dove toward the curb and safety – barely – between parked cars.

He looked back just in time to see the Range Rover plow right through Lorena's open passenger door, shearing it clean off her beloved Mercedes.

She peeled out after it.

Waldo's bad shoulder took the worst of the impact again. Nursing it, he used one of the cars to haul himself to his feet. He watched Lorena tear down the street, her torrent of profanity ringing back at him in Doppler until she turned and disappeared onto Beverly Boulevard.

TWENTY-TWO

t was a more daring – one might say, stupider – attempt on his life than the one on Sepulveda: even if it worked, it'd leave Lorena an eyewitness who might be able to make the Range Rover. Of course, it could be stolen. But who'd use the same hot car for two attacks? Anyway, it was clear now that someone was following Waldo around, looking for another chance to run him down. He – she? – probably got frustrated waiting and took a wild swing.

Waldo didn't have a key to Lorena's office (he'd refused her offer of one, clinging to the symbolic distance), but he walked over in hope that someone would still be there and that he could get out of the heat while he waited. From the street, though, it looked like everyone was already gone. Waldo opened the door next to the Italian place anyhow, climbed the stairs and tried the doorknob. It turned in his hand.

Waldo cracked the door slowly, silently. The lights were off, the reception area empty.

He heard the floor creak.

He slipped off his backpack and took his Beretta from the inside pocket where it was secured. He eased the door open.

Another creak. It seemed to be coming from the staff room. That door was ajar. Pistol at the ready, Waldo crept toward it and gave it a sharp kick.

Reddix, sitting behind a laptop at Fat Dave's desk, threw up his hands. 'Don't shoot!'

Waldo lowered his gun. 'What are you doing?'

'I closed up to go home because Lorena said, but there was this thing I was working and I wanted to stick with it while it was fresh in my mind. So I came back and sat in here. Like, you know, the real detectives.' Reddix's brow furrowed. 'What happened?'

Waldo followed Reddix's eyes to the blood on his windbreaker sleeve. Reddix gestured at Waldo's forehead, too. Waldo touched it, then looked at his finger: red. 'Oh,' he said, and left the staff room without explaining.

They had access to a bathroom one floor down. The cut over his eye wasn't too bad; Waldo stopped the bleeding with cold water and a paper towel. His jeans were ripped at the knee, the skin underneath torn up more than he realized. His shoulder barked, too, but no worse than after the first wipeout on Sepulveda.

As he came out of the bathroom, Lorena was opening the door at the foot of the stairs. She said, 'Lost him right away. Fucking rush hour. You get my car door?'

'"You OK, Waldo?" "Yes, thank you for asking."'

'So you *didn't* get it.' She looked him over. 'You OK?' He nodded. She looked up at the open door to the office. 'Someone up there?'

'Reddix. Hung back to work late, trying to prove himself. I almost shot him.' They continued up the stairs.

'A for effort, right?'

'His or mine?'

They went into the corner office and sat opposite each other at the partners desk. Waldo said, 'It's not Fontella. That was the same Range Rover – she's too smart for that. And that scooter in the street was a setup. She's not going to walk around and expose herself, either.'

'You catch a plate?' Waldo shook his head. 'Me, neither.' Lorena took out her phone, searched out a number and dialed. '*Yeah*, it's me,' she said, in a come-hither voice Waldo wasn't expecting. 'Who do you *think* would be using my phone? . . . Yeah, but I'm not going to tell *you* about it . . .' She listened a moment and then let out a chuckle that belonged in the bedroom. It rattled Waldo's molars. She was giving him a little reminder of the promiscuity and jealousy of their bad old days and he had no idea why.

Still into the phone, she said, 'I need to find out what a guy named Immanuel Nickerson has registered. Immanuel, with an *I*. I'm looking for a Range Rover, red.' Lorena knew how to make even that sound filthy. She listened for a bit, then said, 'Good. I wouldn't want to think I was the only one. Bye, now.' She hung up, dropped the slinky voice and said, 'DMV.'

'Funny,' said Waldo, 'they usually make me come down and stand in line for two hours.'

'You dropped off the earth for three years, lover. I haven't seen him since you've been back. You want to know who's trying to kill you, or what?'

'You think it's Bailiff Man?'

'He's Fontella's client. Who knows what kind of installment plan she worked out for him.'

Reddix knocked at the closed door and said, 'Can I talk to you guys?'

Lorena stood and opened it but said, 'Can it wait until tomorrow—'

'I think I have something.'

She let him in. Reddix balanced his laptop on his forearm and referred to it for notes. 'OK, the two plaintiffs who were paralegals, Epstein and Vaught? They worked with Ida Mudge – back when she was Ida Tuttle – at different firms, so they didn't know each other then. But here's the thing: they *did* overlap a couple years later – we're talking nine years ago – for about three months, at an investment management company in D.C. called NorthStar.'

Lorena said, 'Coincidence.'

'That was my first thought. But then it turned out the *other* two, Markey and Rickenback? They played youth basketball together.'

Waldo said, 'How'd you get that?'

'They're Facebook friends, and it came up on Markey's feed. They've both become friends recently with this hot girl, Keesha Middleton.'

'Who's she?'

Reddix grinned. 'Me.' Waldo was starting to like him. 'There's also an overlap between the two pairs: Vaught used to be married to Markey's sister, like a starter marriage. So all the plaintiffs are connected: one knows the next knows the next knows the next.'

Lorena said, 'Did any of them know Fontella?'

'I haven't found anything yet.'

Waldo said, 'Three of them went to law school. Keep looking, you'll find a link to her.'

Reddix said, 'This is good, right?'

Waldo smiled and said, 'It's real good.' The kid practically levitated.

Lorena's phone rang. She winked at Waldo before steaming it

up again with her DMV guy. 'You don't waste any time jumping on it, do you . . . *Yeah* I remember . . .' She took notes on a pad. 'Thanks . . . You *know* I'll text you.' She hung up and, all business again, said to Waldo, 'I won't.'

Instead of rising to the flirtation bait again, he went for the scold. 'You could type that into your phone, you know, instead of wasting paper.'

She picked up the pad and jiggled it in front of him, playful provocation. 'These are Bailiff Man's plates. And it's not a Range Rover.'

Waldo nodded, started recalculating.

She smirked. 'It's a Ford Explorer. Red. Take a look.'

Waldo found pictures of both cars on his phone. Manufactured by related companies, the SUVs looked awfully similar, probably by design.

Lorena said, 'You still sure it was a Range Rover?'

He swiped from one to the other and back. 'No.'

'What's going on?' said Reddix.

Before they could decide whether to read Reddix all the way in, they heard feet clomping up the stairs.

Waldo and Lorena went on alert. Reddix looked from one to the other, confused. Waldo reached for his backpack. He put his hand on his Beretta again but kept it in the bag.

'Who's here?' bellowed Fat Dave. A moment later he was in Lorena's doorway.

'What's up?' she said.

'I left my rigatoni in the refrigerator.'

'OK,' said Lorena, 'both of you, go home.' Reddix looked crestfallen. 'Big day today,' she said to him, a consolation prize. 'You deserve a beer. Stand outside a package store and get somebody to buy you one.'

When the ops were gone, Waldo and Lorena recapped where they were and what they knew, or thought they knew.

Most of the signs now pointed to Fontella Davis. She had hired Bailiff Man Nickerson, her client, to kill Waldo to keep the truth interred – the truth presumably being that Davis, assaulted by Anthony Branch, found her way to him in the woods, probably with the help of Matt Fishbein's map, and killed him. Means, motive, opportunity.

That would make the blackmailing of Judge Ida a misfire: someone, perhaps Lelong, coming at the wrong target.

Also, thanks to Reddix, they now had dirt on Fontella's plaintiffs – and potentially on Fontella, as well – for suborning perjury. At the very least, that should speed Judge Ida's harassment case to a conclusion.

'Could this have gone better for us?' said Lorena.

Waldo wasn't ready to celebrate, and not just because of his multiple lacerations and throbbing shoulder. None of this was better than an educated guess. They had only the vaguest notion of whom the blackmailer might be, and no way to prove what they surmised Fontella Davis to have done.

Reading his doubt, Lorena said, 'That's the beauty of this case. It doesn't take hard solutions for us to win all around. Number one: Ida was willing to ignore the threat even without knowing why someone was blackmailing her, and now we can give her a decent theory.'

'And two, we've got the plaintiffs all connected, which'll be enough for Fontella to have to drop them, especially after the way she ripped Ida in that press conference. In fact, we get Fontella to make a statement, not only apologizing to Judge Ida, but thanking Nascimento-Waldo for their brilliant work uncovering the scam, of which she, after all, was an unwitting victim.'

'How do we get her to do that?'

'We tell her we're willing to back off the Anthony Branch investigation. Which also stops the attacks on you.' She leaned back and put her boots on the desk. 'You have Ida's direct line, right? Can we call her together? This is going to be great for us. People hate Fontella. We're going to make all sorts of new fans.'

'Whoa, what—? No.'

'This is way better than trying to crack a thirty-five-year-old crime.'

'You don't stop a murder investigation just as it's coming into focus.'

'It's not a "murder investigation." It's a blackmail case.'

'I'm investigating a murder.'

'Of a rapist.' She swung her feet to the floor.

'That didn't bother you an hour ago. Besides, you don't get to take the law into your own hands. Or avenge a rape with a murder.'

'OK, what client are you investigating for?' She leaned forward, intensity rising. 'Not Ida Mudge. She told you to shut it down.'

'For Anthony Branch.'

'Oh, please. You're not a cop catching a call. You're a PI. We're never going to be able to prove anything anyway, thirty-five years later. Come on, Waldo, this is a big win, which I need. Let's get Ida on the phone and start wrapping it up.'

'I'm going to Fontella.'

'To do what?'

'Ask questions,' said Waldo. 'Use what we have with the plaintiffs to shake her. Like you do with a suspect.'

'You can't.'

'What do you mean, I can't?'

'You wouldn't have the info, if it weren't for my guy.' She tipped her head toward Reddix's space in the outer room. 'You cannot go using it in a way that damages my agency.'

Suddenly she was casting it as a battle for control of the business, something Waldo truly didn't give a damn about.

But there was Anthony Branch, and his mother, and his father. And, in the shadows, Lydell Lipps.

So even though he didn't want to play his ace, Lorena had boxed him into it. He said, 'Judge Ida's my client.' She started to object. 'On the blackmail. You're still not even supposed to know about it.' He took out his phone and dialed Fontella Davis's office.

The receptionist placed him on hold. Lorena stared out at the Paramount lot. Waldo was sure she was thinking about ending it, all of it.

He knew he could lose here by winning. But if he didn't win this one, he'd be lost anyway.

TWENTY-THREE

Fontella Davis told him that she was on her way to an early dinner but that they could meet at her house in two hours. She gave him an address on Mulholland.

Waldo and Lorena didn't discuss it. They walked two blocks east to her car, then drove back in the other direction to find her severed door, which, it was quickly apparent, would fit neither in the trunk nor the passenger seat. Lorena called AAA, then told Waldo that he didn't have to hang around, and crossed her arms and cocked her hip like she was waiting for him to leave. He reminded her that he still needed his bike from her trunk. She looked daggers at him while she popped it with her remote.

Waldo chose to stick around anyway, not starting out himself until Lorena was safely in the tow truck and bumping down Melrose, with her baby, in pieces, strapped to its bed.

Even though he'd be relatively safe on his bike in the slow rush-hour traffic, he opted for the Metro up Laurel Canyon. The brazenness of the second attack had his nerves jangling, a condition that only worsened as he watched cars whiz past his bus like two-ton weapons. The city wasn't built for pedestrians, let alone cyclists, and if someone out there was hell-bent on taking him out, sooner or later Waldo was going to get walloped.

The sun was dropping behind the trees. Waldo's anxiety deepened with the shadows. At the top of the hill he got off the bus and stepped right off the road and into the brush, eyeing the traffic flow through two full stoplight cycles, watching for a red SUV or anything unusual. When he was confident that he hadn't been followed, he unfolded his bike and headed west on Mulholland.

Waldo didn't often ride at night and he was only moderately equipped for it. He did trick out his Brompton with the manufacturer's Cateye Volt 400 lighting system (which, though bought separately, he counted as part of the bike and not a separate Thing), but his windbreaker was not reflective, nor was his other clothing, and he didn't have a helmet light.

He stiffened with every approaching car and held his breath until it passed. He stayed on whichever side of the road ran along cliff rather than ravine, even when that meant crossing over and riding against traffic. Out past Coldwater a vehicle came up behind but didn't pass. Waldo cut his speed by half and pulled as far to the edge of the road as he could, but the driver followed suit and stayed on Waldo's tail, all the more menacing at lower speed.

After a quarter mile the driver suddenly accelerated. Waldo flinched and veered into a ditch, falling off his bike and landing in a patch of brambles. The car, a white Honda, zipped harmlessly past and disappeared into the night.

All was dark except the roadside flora over-illuminated by the lamp on his toppled Brompton. Waldo reminded himself to breathe, then stood and gathered himself – jumpy, vulnerable, and more alone than he ever felt during three years in the woods.

Fontella Davis's house didn't look like much from the street, a modest single-story Spanish on the canyon side. It did have privacy going for it; you couldn't see any other houses, even from the mouth of her driveway. Waldo rang the bell and started locking his bike to some decorative ironwork.

Fontella Davis opened the door in the designer suit she'd worn for work and her dinner, though her earrings had already been removed. 'You rode that up here, at night? I take back what I said about you being smart. And who do you think's going to steal it, the coyotes?'

He realized he'd been locking it out of habit and nerves. He needed to sharpen up.

She led him inside. Half the walls were glass, the other half dominated by large paintings, classical still-lifes and landscapes, each featured and flattered by carefully designed lighting. Davis led Waldo down a slate staircase, then down a second flight. The house was five times the size it appeared from the street, three sweeping stories built into the mountainside.

On the bottom floor she led him through sliding doors and out onto a fully furnished wooden deck which stretched out into the canyon, adding still more living space.

There was privacy out here, too, thanks to a geological jut which isolated Davis from anyone else on her side of the canyon. The city side twinkled off to the left, as did distant homes on the opposite ridge, but other than that and the light spill from inside the house, all was darkness.

'Something to drink?' said Fontella.

'I wouldn't say no to a glass of water.'

'I've got that. Enjoy the view – then you can tell me what couldn't wait.'

She went inside. Somewhere in the canyon, a coyote howled, drawing Waldo to the edge of the deck. He leaned over and peered into the darkness. The railing gave a little and he backed away.

He heard footsteps and the clinking of bottles and glassware. Too much noise for one person to be making? Who else might be in there? It might not be Davis coming back out with water, it could be Nickerson with a pistol. Or, if Bailiff Man was smart, a baseball bat. Clout Waldo on the head, then throw him through the creaky rail, or over it.

Not for the first time tonight, Waldo questioned his own judgment, coming up to Mulholland alone in the dark.

He sat on one of Fontella's plush outdoor chairs, set his backpack on his lap and slipped his right hand inside, checking his Beretta. He waited. He definitely heard more than one set of footsteps inside: the click of heels, plus squeaks from a pair of rubber soles.

But when the door opened, it was only Davis, in low pumps, carrying two glasses of wine. 'I decided you needed something a little stronger, Waldo, and that you should imbibe with me. You probably think I'm a lush – all I do around you is drink. Two glasses an evening is my limit. But the client I had dinner with tonight's a teetotaler. No fun.' She extended a glass. 'Pinot noir all right?'

Why the aggressive hospitality? Harder to taste, if she put something in it. 'No thanks,' said Waldo. 'I'm driving.'

'In that case,' said Davis, retreating to a chaise, 'these are my two.' She set one glass on a table and sipped from the other. 'So what's on your mind? You looking to re-open the JFK assassination?'

'Tonight I do want to talk about Judge Ida's case.'

'About time. All right, let's hear your opener.'

'My opener is, we don't go to the California Bar Association.'

'Say again?'

'Dewey Rickenback and Earnest Markey played youth basketball together. Earnest Markey's sister was briefly married to Austin Vaught. Austin Vaught worked as a paralegal at an investment firm with Martin Epstein. All your new plaintiffs knew each other beforehand. None of them worked with Ida Mudge *simultaneously*, so there was the illusion that these were four separate cases. But they were linked and communicating before they signed onto your suit. The connections were pretty well buried; I can see how everyone thought they'd get away with it.'

'It's the first I've heard of this. I'll look into it, and if what you say is true, I'll drop the case.'

'Three of them went to law school. We haven't found the place yet where you crossed paths with one of them. But we will.'

'I said I'd drop the case.'

'That's not enough.'

'I'll get all of *them* to drop it.'

He'd unnerved her. He pressed the advantage by rising, throwing his backpack on his shoulder, and crossing toward the house, setting himself in backlight so he could read Davis better than she could read him.

She said, 'What else do you want?'

'We'll let you make this go away quietly. If you'll help me on Anthony Branch.'

'I've got nothing to say about that.'

Waldo made the threat explicit. 'When we find that prior connection between you and one of the plaintiffs, everyone will assume you suborned perjury, even if no one can prove it. My partner would've taken this public yesterday.' Fontella Davis held very still. Waldo said, 'You know what happened.'

'Anthony fell.'

'Call me skeptical.'

More footsteps inside. The squeaky ones.

Davis said, 'Believe me: you want to leave this alone.'

'I don't.'

'Ida Tuttle did not kill that young man.'

'Who did?'

'Anthony fell.'

'Carter Gass was rich. Matt Fishbein was strange. Hoyt Lelong was white. Morris Thurmond was a hero.'

'You don't have to read me the transcript.'

'What about Anthony Branch? What was he?'

Davis held a neutral expression but shifted in her seat. She wasn't used to being pushed out of her comfort zone.

He let her dangle a moment longer, then said, 'It has made me curious. Of all the things you might have done with a law degree. After being the victim of an assault yourself.' She drew a sharp inhale. 'All that defense work. All those lawsuits against the police.'

'Police did nothing for me.' Metal in her voice now.

'Did you ask them to?' He knew the answer, of course.

'You come here and bring that up, and then ask me to explain myself? You do not lack for stones, that is for sure.' It *was* audacious, even indecent. But if she did kill Anthony, and if she was trying to kill Waldo, seemliness had to take a night off.

'Black girl,' said Davis, 'in those days, who'd been drinking at a fraternity party? Then goes to the police looking for justice? Goes to the college? How do you think that story ends?' He couldn't argue. 'Know what I learned at that school? Even if they let you in the room, doesn't mean they'll let you sit at the table. And the people who *have* seats aren't just standing up and offering you theirs.'

'You're telling me Anthony Branch had a seat at the table? I met his mom. She lives in a trailer park.'

'On his way to it. Not many born with Anthony Branch's gifts.'

'You managed to find a spot for yourself.'

'I fought for it. I got hard, when hard was called for.'

'Getting justice and getting yours.'

'Amen.'

'Justice being a flexible concept.'

'When it needs to be. You got questions,' she said, her voice almost a growl, 'ask them.'

'How long between the assault and Anthony's death?'

'A few months.'

'Did everyone know the pledge hike was going to be that night?'

'I didn't. I didn't know a thing about it until the next day, when all hell broke loose.'

'How many women had the same kind of experience with Anthony that you did?'

'Only one other I was aware of.'

'How well liked was Anthony by his fraternity brothers?'

'Extremely. That was the problem.'

'How well did you know each of them? No more word association. Carter Gass.'

'I knew all those guys a little, through Ida and Morris. Not very well. Anthony, I knew the best, actually. We had a late morning class together, and we used to get lunch afterward once or twice a week in the dining hall.' She added, '*Until.*'

'How well did you know Morris?'

'I knew him the way anyone knows their best friend's boyfriend. He'd try to fix me up sometimes, we'd double-date.'

'How often?'

'Five, six times.' Davis twisted in her seat as the realization dawned. '*This* is where we are.' A wicked grin crept across her face and she let out a low chuckle. 'You figured it out, didn't you. You took that famous detective brain of yours and put it together. *I* murdered Anthony. And all you still need is for me to tell you that I knew Morris well enough to get him to give me Matt Fishbein's map. Yeah, that's it. Right, Waldo?'

'The night Anthony died, where were you?'

'In the woods! There was this ravine, see, by a bridge?' She laughed. 'You tell *me* something: why are you working this so hard?'

'Because I don't believe it was an accident. The day after I asked all the pledge captains about the map, someone tried to run me down on Sepulveda.'

'Mm,' said Davis. 'Road rage. Terrible thing. What happened, you cut him off with that little scooter of yours?'

'We've ID'd the car, in case you're interested.'

'Why would I be interested?'

'Why did you lie about Ciano Panerio?'

'Ciano – what?'

'Ponciano Panerio. You said you were with him that night.'

'I did not. I haven't said the *name* "Ciano Panerio" since Ronald Reagan was president.'

'At the time. The day after Anthony. You told Ida, your best friend, that you were with Ciano Panerio. But you weren't.'

'Is that what happened.' She said it without the question mark. She was closing up shop on him.

'OK,' he said, 'we'll do it the other way,' renewing the Bar Association threat. He started for the house.

Her voice stopped him. 'I might have been with someone I shouldn't have.'

'Who?'

'Somebody's boyfriend.'

'I need a name.'

'I suppose it doesn't matter now. Dave Petters.'

Waldo couldn't suppress a sigh. More secrets. More twenty-year-olds' foolishness. *What were you thinking? I don't know.*

Davis said, 'He sneaked away from the frat after they came back from leaving the pledges in the woods. Nobody knew I was seeing him. Even Ida. *Especially* Ida. Who definitely would not approve.'

'Convenient that he isn't around to confirm this.'

'Not for him, it isn't,' she said, cold, and stood up from the chaise. She circled Waldo, moving closer to the house. 'I've gotten away with a murder all these years, *and* I'm going to let you nail me for it? Is that what you're thinking? You've got to know me better than that.'

Now Davis was backlit, so Waldo couldn't read her face. Was she being ironic? Literal? Threatening? And was there, buried in this confession – if it was one – a different explanation for her career as a defense attorney? Was it not about getting justice and getting hers, but, rather, about exculpating her fellow guilty, who too might have had their reasons?

There was a clattering from the house, behind Davis. It was louder than the noises before, probably closer to the sliding glass door.

Waldo backed further from the house, into the shadows near the edge.

Davis said, 'You're jumping into the private sector with both feet, did I hear that right? You're a full partner with your girlfriend now? *That* young lady wants a seat at the table, even if you don't. But for her to get it, *you're* going to have to get hard, too.'

'Hard how?'

'All these years, you've been tearing yourself up about that kid. You want to move forward? You want to *win*? There is no room for endless remorse. I learned it: no matter what you've done, what you're responsible for, you need to get – past – it.

'Take it from me, Waldo: let the dead bury the dead. We'll all be joining them soon enough.'

Again, he couldn't read her. Was this a philosophy lesson, or a shot she couldn't resist before having her hired killer attack?

Without thinking, Waldo leaned backward against the wood railing. When it gave again under his weight, he startled and instinctively raced for the open glass door, zipping past Davis, who was already cackling.

Inside, he looked around: no one visible on the lowest floor.

He made for the stairs. Halfway up the first flight he heard something and paused. Yes: again the squeaking of rubber-soled shoes.

Then it stopped.

Waldo reached into his backpack again. This time he took out the Beretta and readied it, safety off.

There were no sounds from downstairs or the deck beyond; Davis was staying clear.

Waldo took the steps one by one, silently as he could.

The first landing was the mouth of a hallway which looked like it led to bedrooms.

Waldo crept into that hallway, held still.

He heard the sneakers again, and waited.

A door on the left started to open, then stopped. Waldo cocked his pistol.

The sneakers again, then the door creaked open the rest of the way. A middle-aged Latina backed out of the room and turned to face Waldo, carrying a tall stack of towels which she steadied with her chin.

'Señor?' she said.

Waldo ran up the second flight and out into the night, chased by noises he no longer tried to distinguish, a coyote's howl or Fontella Davis's laughter or fresh pandemonium of his mind's own devising.

TWENTY-FOUR

After the tension of the night, even the short bike ride from the bus to Lorena's was unsteady, reaching her front door a major relief. He let himself in, instantly overcome by exhaustion and desperate for bed.

The bedroom was darkened, Lorena already asleep. Waldo moved quietly to the bathroom, where, struggling to keep his eyes open, he went about the nightly business of washing and hanging his clothing to dry.

When he opened the door, Lorena said, from the bed, 'How'd it go?'

He was quiet, not knowing how to begin describing the encounter.

She said, 'You tell her we know about the plaintiffs?'

'Mm-hmm.'

'What'd she say?'

'That she'll get them to drop out. So you can call Judge Ida tomorrow and let her know.'

His intention was to let Lorena take the victory lap with the client, but Lorena's mind was still on the opportunity Waldo was squandering. 'I don't suppose you talked to Fontella about making a statement,' she said. 'Mentioning us.' Waldo got into bed. Lorena sighed. 'Of course not.'

They lay there in the dark, not touching. He could feel her hostility build even before she said, 'And how'd the rest work out? She sign a confession?'

He knew falling asleep would only aggrieve her more, but there was nothing he could do about it.

And when he awoke, she was already gone for the day.

Waldo went to the kitchen, peeled an orange and thought about Davis's provocations. She hadn't exactly said that she'd killed Anthony Branch, but she came closer to saying that than that she hadn't. What she did make clear, what seemed her point, was that she *could* flirt with a confession because she knew Waldo would never be able to prove anything.

If Morris Thurmond were local, Waldo's next move would be to go see him again, to try to jog his memory about the map, or at least about Fontella. But was it worth going back to Oakland?

Arguing for the trip: pursuit of truth, pursuit of justice, the private vow to speak for Anthony, simple stubbornness.

Arguing against: the unlikelihood that it would yield anything, Lorena's wishes, carbon.

Without returning to Oakland, did he have any plays left? He could stay in L.A. and use himself as bait, hope that Nickerson came after him again in the SUV, and that this time Waldo could ID the plates. But that was kind of insane, and besides, now that he'd confronted Fontella about the attacks, they might well stop anyway.

His phone rang. He rinsed his hands in the sink and checked it: Freddie Dellamora. Waldo reminded himself to suggest they get a beer together.

'Freddie,' he said.

'Finally got the report on your John Doe.'

Ten days later. 'Put a rush on it, huh?'

'You want it or not? Diffuse axonal injury.'

'In English?'

'English? He bumped his head and he went to bed and he couldn't get up in the morning.'

'You saying he didn't drown?'

'No water in his lungs. Died and fell in, not fell in and died.'

'How do you hit a fountain so hard the impact kills you?'

'Not easy. Maybe if you're on ketamine or something. But this guy was clean. Not even alcohol.'

Which meant it wasn't an accident, either. 'What are they calling it?'

'What do you think? It's a John Doe.'

'His name's Dorian Strook. He was a professor at UC Riverside.'

'LAPD, his name's still John Doe.'

'It's Van Nuys, right? Who's on it?'

'What, I need to go find that, too?'

'It's a fucking *murder*, Freddie. You can't let them call it accidental.'

'Damn it, Waldo, it's not even mine—'

Waldo clicked off the call and steamed. If it weren't for Don Q's writer's block and this doppelgänger nonsense, nobody would even notice that a man was knocked dead and thrown into a fountain, nor that the MEs let him sit in a drawer for a week and a half. The cops who caught it didn't bother clocking it as an open homicide because they didn't need to. If nobody else gave a damn about this guy, why should they?

Unless there was something worse going on.

Because it was possible that Mikaela had it right, that the Professor *was* suing the city for seven million dollars, for mistreatment by the police. If so, his murder could have something to do with that.

What had Don Q led him into? Had he gone, in a single phone call, from chasing a dog to chasing a killer cop?

The Los Angeles Legal Aid Society wasn't even a storefront, it was a big one-room office *over* a storefront – a children's haircutter, to be specific – on Oxnard. There were two desks, one near the door, one near the back wall. Every inch of floor space had been given over to mismatched file cabinets, file cartons, loose files, and stacks of paper so loose you couldn't even call them files.

The young man at the front desk had a carefully manicured, half-inch-wide chinstrap of beard. He was on a phone, quickly fielding one incoming after another, taking information and promising almost everyone that Ms Carbonel would call as soon as she could. The woman at the far desk wasn't much older, probably in her late twenties. She wore a floral print blouse and had a pair of crutches next to her desk. She was on the phone, too, arguing with someone's employer about severance pay.

When the flood of calls hit a pause, the young man said to Waldo, 'Can we help you?'

Waldo nodded toward the woman and said, 'Is that Ms Carbonel?'

'Yes, but she's going to be tied up for a while. Is there an issue we might be able to help you with?'

'I'll wait. I'm an investigator.'

Ms Carbonel looked up from her call, then wound it down. She hung up and said to Waldo, 'Are you LAPD?'

'Private investigator.' It drew a blank, so he added, '*Former* LAPD.' *That* got a reaction, namely, disgust. Waldo said, 'Do you know a man named Dorian Strook?'

Ms Carbonel and the young man exchanged a look. 'Yes,' she said.

'He passed away – were you aware of that?'

'No. How did he die?'

'The police are calling it an accident. He may have fallen and hit his head.'

'"May have," huh.'

'What can you tell me about his lawsuit against the city?'

'Lawsuit? Dorian Strook? There was no lawsuit with Dorian Strook.'

'He told people you were helping him sue the city for seven million dollars.'

Ms Carbonel rolled her eyes. 'This office – the Valley office – it's a startup. We've got two part-time lawyers and three part-time assistants. We can't take every complaint into the courts, even if there is merit. Dorian Strook was not somebody you could put on a witness stand.'

'He was a university professor.'

'So he claims.'

'It's on their website. He told you that, and you didn't believe him?'

Ms Carbonel sighed irritation. 'He told people we filed a seven-million-dollar lawsuit for him. That's all you need to know about Dorian Strook.'

'*Did* his complaint have merit?'

'Uh, *yeah*, from the sound of it. You people took his shopping cart and claimed it was stolen property.'

'Wait, *I* didn't—'

'He said he found it in the wash. You put him in jail for half a day, then tossed him out into a forty-degree night, without his bedding, which you confiscated.'

'That's terrible. But I want to be clear, I was Robbery-Homicide—'

'This whole push to criminalize homelessness, confiscate citizens' property, or destroy it, until you harass them into going somewhere else – besides not being a solution, it's inhumane. And it doesn't absolve you, morally or legally, to say it was what your command instructed.'

'I'm not saying anything like that—'

'"I was only following orders" is not a defense.'

Waldo pushed past the Nazi allusion, and also resisted the temptation to justify himself with the story of his estrangement from the department. Instead, he said, 'Why not fight the policies with a lawsuit? Even if Strook wouldn't have been great on the stand?'

'I told you, we don't have the manpower. Here, this is what's on my desk today: I've got a ninety-year-old woman whose granddaughter cleaned out her life savings and she's about to get evicted; I've got a family in Pacoima, they *have* their money but the landlord won't *take* it because he wants to flip the apartment and raise the rent; I've got a woman whose ex-husband took her kids up to San Jose – she thinks – and hasn't let her see them in half a year; I've got a paraplegic veteran who's trying to figure out why they cut off his SSI; should I keep going?'

'No need.'

'Point is, I'm not going to get to all *them* today. Who else should I blow off so I can deal with your guy? Who's *gonzo*. Last time he was in here, he spent half an hour saying some crazy thing over and over, before Maximo could get the shopping cart story out of him.' She dipped her head in the younger guy's direction.

Maximo said, '"There's a hole under the fire! There's a hole under the fire!"'

'That's it,' said Ms Carbonel. 'Over and over. This was right when the first one of those fires started – the bad one up north, that killed people? I don't know what hole he thought was under it.'

Maximo said, 'That was the same day he kept taking the cardboard boxes he had on his feet and switching the left and right.'

Ms Carbonel said, 'Gonzo,' again.

Waldo said, 'Tell me this: how bad *were* his hassles with the police?'

'Obviously, pretty bad.'

'How physical?'

'He could get belligerent, I'm sure. And police *always* get belligerent.'

'I guess what I'm asking is: if it *wasn't* an accident, if Strook was killed, do you believe it could have been a cop?'

Ms Carbonel narrowed her eyes. 'Who's paying you? His family? What's he got, some sister someplace, wondering if she can go for wrongful death?'

Waldo said, 'Something like that.'

'Well. From what you're telling me, sounds like somebody killed him. Happens constantly. I doubt it was a cop. Dorian Strook was too far gone to be a danger to them in any way. But you want me to be honest?'

'Please.'

'I'm not surprised they're calling it an accident even if it's not. Give them half a chance not to give a damn, they won't. And that pisses me off, because it endangers the next homeless person, and the one after that.'

'It all depends what cop catches the call.'

'Easy to say now, when someone's paying you.'

'Mindy Steinman on one,' said Maximo.

Reaching for the phone, Ms Carbonel said to Waldo, 'You guys are all the same.'

TWENTY-FIVE

He could almost hear Pete Conady laughing at him. It was a taste of Waldo's own medicine, anyway, getting lumped in and derided with the whole department, how the rest of them must have felt when Waldo, after Lydell Lipps, torched the brass who deserved it and singed everyone else who didn't.

Waldo knew damn well, though, that if Dorian Strook were his, he wouldn't still be a John Doe, or an accidental. If he were Conady's, either.

But it was a relief, of sorts, that this was indifference to murder, rather than murderous corruption. And Waldo *wasn't* a cop, it *wasn't* his case, and his 'client,' Don Q, was already satisfied, or at least quieted. Waldo could just let it go.

Except he couldn't. Dorian Strook deserved somebody to speak for him, just like Anthony Branch did.

He waited until the sun set, then went back to the Professor's squat on Mary Ellen. Now that he was working a murder that the cops were ignoring, he wanted a fuller look at the main house. He'd break in, if need be.

The first time he'd been through the neighborhood, trying to identify the place Mikaela described, all the properties with activity – construction sites or *For Sale* signs – drew his closer scrutiny. In this still heated market, it was rare for a house to sit unoccupied for long before it was sold or torn down and replaced. Creeping around to the back this second time, the fact of the squat had Waldo wondering about how long it had been vacant, and why.

He leaned his Brompton against the converted guesthouse, which was still unlocked and still showed no signs of habitation. Waldo circled the main house again, testing all the windows and doors. One screen had a broken clasp. Waldo put his nose against it and shined the flashlight from his phone inside. Hookups on the wall suggested this would be the laundry room. Waldo studied the screen itself and saw that it was the kind with alarm wire threaded through the mesh. He wouldn't know whether the window was connected to an active system until he tried it. He decided to hold off that chance until he'd given the outdoor area a full study.

Squirrels scrabbled on the roof and rustled in the hedges which lined the perimeter, giving Waldo audio cover even though the lots in the neighborhood were small, the houses close together. The synthetic lawn in back was pool-table flat. Plastic yards were a recent trend; it had probably been installed in the last five years. The white vinyl picket fence in front was matched with a six-foot privacy fence of the same material on the other three sides. Between those and the hedges, none of the adjacent homes were even visible.

The jacuzzi, uncovered, had a thick layer of dead leaves on top, the most conspicuous sign of vacancy and disuse. The paint on the guesthouse was peeling even worse than the garage. Walking closer to the firepit, full of leaves too, Waldo felt his boot catch, then dragged a toe over what seemed a rise in the artificial grass. He knelt and ran his hand over the irregularity. It felt like there was an uneven seam, too, running perpendicular to the pit.

He shined his phone light at the turf to see more, but the rustling of some larger animal made him turn just in time to see the silhouette of a man approaching. Waldo stood, his light catching something cutting through the night. Waldo raised a defensive arm and caught a hard clout just below his good shoulder. It knocked him off balance and sent his phone tumbling away. The assailant, still just a shadow, drew back his weapon to strike again.

Waldo heard a shouted, 'Hey!' and then saw a light from across the yard.

He felt something hard graze the top of his head and the next thing he knew he was on the ground but couldn't remember going down. He heard the blows and grunts of a melee in the dark, and a clean thump and a voice crying out, then running footfalls.

Waldo crawled to the light of his own phone and, sitting beside the firepit, pointed the flashlight in the direction of the ruckus. Out on the street, a car started up and drove off.

Dumpster Williams was holding a hand against the brightness and limping in his direction. 'Sumbitch got me pretty good. Missed my knee, at least.'

'What are you doing here?'

'Been on you all day.'

'Why?'

'What the boss told me. Don't be looking pissed off, she's worried about you, man. You didn't spot me?' Waldo shook his head. 'I thought for sure you made me when you came out of that legal aid.'

'Nope.'

Dumpster beamed. 'Still got that, at least. I was a fuck-up in some ways, but I could always work a tail.'

'What was he swinging?'

'Tire iron, I think. You OK?'

Waldo nodded, but ran his fingers over the fresh bump on his skull.

Dumpster said, 'Sorry I wasn't here when he got you, but I was getting the plate on the car in front of the house.'

'Red SUV?'

'Yeah.'

'Ford Explorer?'

'Yeah, I'm pretty sure, yeah.'

'Good work. Guy's been trying to kill me. Been a lot worse if you hadn't been here. And you got the plate. We got him now. So, thank you.'

'Hey, the Over-the-Hill Gang got to stick together, right?'

Lorena's house wasn't exactly on Dumpster's way home, but it was close enough that Waldo let him drop him off, a minor bend of the rules out of deference to the mini-blackout he'd just suffered.

When Lorena saw Waldo's injuries, the tension of the previous night dissipated, or at least got put on hold. She cleaned the cut on his scalp, which had bled more than he realized, and held ice on it while Waldo, garrulous on the adrenaline, told her Freddie's surprising news about the Professor's clean tox report and about his frustrating meeting at legal aid, and then how stunned he was to see that sad sack Dumpster Williams play the hero.

Waldo asked Lorena if her DMV boyfriend had given her Man Nickerson's plate. She said yes, but that it was at the office. 'Why,' said Waldo, 'because you wrote it on a pad instead of your phone?' It meant they couldn't confirm a match to the plate Dumpster pulled off the Explorer until morning.

'Hey, if you need it now, I could ask him to go back to DMV after hours and run the plate again. He'd do it, too. But I'm sure he'd want me to meet him there in person.'

'We can wait till tomorrow,' said Waldo.

He started spinning out the ramifications of a match. Once they locked Nickerson as Waldo's assailant, they'd have Fontella Davis with something beyond a taunting flirtation with a confession; they'd now have a tangible connection to repeated attempted murder in order to impede his Anthony Branch investigation. 'You can see it,' he said, 'right? Now we *have* to go after her.'

Lorena checked to make sure the bleeding had fully stopped, and ran her fingers through his hair. 'I helped save your life.'

'You did. Thank you.'

'Don't make me sorry about that, OK?' She kissed his head, and with that they tabled the subject until morning.

They fell asleep curled against one another. Waldo slept uncharacteristically late and Lorena let him. Still at the house when he awoke, she said that she didn't want to go in to the office until she was sure he was OK. She made him an omelet, too, and then they drove in together.

Dumpster Williams was in the reception area, perched on the edge of Reddix's desk. '4645 Mary Ellen, and 9YDW298,' he said, proud and redeemed. 'That's the address, which you probably had already' (actually, Waldo didn't) 'and the license of that Explorer.'

'Nice work,' said Lorena, and she and Waldo continued into her office. Lorena sat behind the desk and looked at her notes. 'What's that plate again?' she called.

Dumpster repeated it.

She looked up at Waldo. 'Doesn't match.'

'It's a different red Explorer? He keeps coming after me, same car, but changing the plates?'

'Should I call my DMV guy?'

'Sure. You want me to leave the room?'

'Only if *you* need to.' She dialed her phone. Her guy picked up conspicuously quickly. Waldo raised an eyebrow. Lorena equaled it with one of her own, then spun her chair around for some artificial privacy. 'You're right, I guess I couldn't,' she breathed into the phone. 'Hey, I need you to run a plate for me

. . . What would I have to do to get you to run it while I hold . . .
Really? Mmm . . . I better close my office door first . . .'

Waldo made a guttural sound of mock revulsion. Lorena spun
back toward him and mouthed, *grow up*, then they held each
other's knowing grins while they waited out Lorena's hold. After
a minute she started writing on the same pad. 'I knew you'd be
good for a quickie. Thanks.' She hung up.

'Willie?' she called. Williams limped to the doorway. 'You
sure you saw an Explorer?'

'I . . . yeah.' Then, 'No.'

Lorena looked at Waldo. 'Range Rover.'

'Wait,' said Waldo. 'Man Nickerson has an Explorer.'

'This isn't Nickerson. You were right about the Range Rover
in the first place.'

'Two different cars?'

Lorena dismissed Dumpster with a, 'Thank you,' and he slumped
back to the staff room.

'You got the fucking *make* wrong?' they heard Fat Dave
Greenberg say, with a cruel chortle. 'You drinking again?' The
douchebaggery was enough to make Waldo feel sorry for
Dumpster, who after all, had saved his ass the night before.

Waldo said to Lorena, 'So who the hell's been trying to kill me?'

'The Range Rover is registered to a Leonard Culpepper.'

'Who's Leonard Culpepper?'

Another voice from outside: 'I know a *Florence* Culpepper.'
This time it was Reddix.

'Is that relevant?' said Lorena.

'Looks like it. I mean, I don't know her *personally*. When
you were calling DMV? I ran the address. You know, where you
guys were last night. It's owned by a Florence Culpepper. Has
been since 1956.'

The abandoned house where the Professor, Dorian Strook, was
squatting was owned by an old lady with the same name as the
man who'd attacked Waldo with a tire iron and who'd tried to kill
him on the road twice before that, following Waldo's first look at
the property.

The essential questions of connections and motives flitted across
Waldo's mind only briefly, displaced by a realization that sickened
and infuriated him, the realization that his relentlessness in trying

to figure out which of two brilliant and powerful women may have murdered a fraternity pledge thirty-five years ago, a relentlessness which was tearing apart his relationship with the love of his life, had, after all, no connection whatsoever to the series of attempts to murder him.

No.

Waldo had almost been killed – and not once, but three times – because he was trying to get Don Q's daughter a fucking dog.

TWENTY-SIX

Waldo, fixated now on the oddity of the Mary Ellen property sitting uninhabited without construction or a for sale sign, started researching on his phone through the real estate websites. From the other room he heard Lorena putting the ops to work filling in the gaps on Leonard Culpepper, whom they'd already ID'd as a developer living in Thousand Oaks. She sent Dumpster to the database sites and put Fat Dave on Culpepper's deeds and liens through the public records, telling him to split up what he found with Reddix for a deeper dive.

On Zillow, Waldo saw that the house had had almost no real estate activity for as long as the website kept track of these things: it had been listed on the market the previous March, then taken off again six weeks later, and that was it. Waldo could feel Lorena peering over his shoulder, only when he turned, it wasn't Lorena, it was Dumpster. Lorena came back into the room. 'Dumpster, I asked you to—'

'I know, I just wanted to see if Waldo needed any help. You know, because he and I are kind of partners now.'

Waldo said, 'That's OK, I got this.'

Waldo showed Lorena the funky real estate history. She said, 'Let me call this guy with Coldwell Banker.'

'Where do you know this one from?'

'The gym.'

'Good looking?'

'*So* hot.'

'Excellent.' He started to leave the room.

'And *so* gay.' She got the realtor on the phone right away. Waldo half-listened to Lorena asking questions while he browsed a couple other real estate sites, which repeated the same paltry history he'd found on Zillow.

She hung up and told Waldo, 'He remembered it from a realtor open house. An old couple lived there since the fifties or sixties, and after they died, their children put it on the market. But it was impossible to get a showing, and then they just took it off.'

Reddix knocked on the open door. Lorena said, 'Are you working with Dave on the public records?'

'He's doing something else.'

Lorena stood, exasperated, and started out. 'What are you—?'

Fat Dave, from the staff room, called back, 'I'm looking at the FBI criminal database. Nothing so far.'

'That's not what I told you to do.'

Reddix, in the doorway, said, 'Do you know about the brother?'

Lorena stopped. 'What about the brother?'

'While I was . . . *waiting* . . .' he tipped his head discreetly toward the staff room, 'I found Florence Culpepper's obituary, and there were two sons, Leonard and Shane. Shane lives down in Escondido.'

'And . . .?'

'And the *San Diego Union-Tribune* says he's been missing since April.'

Waldo looked at the dates on Zillow again. 'They took the house off the market in May.'

Lorena said, 'Even as a tear-down, that lot's seven figures. What they're giving up by holding onto it, plus taxes, insurance . . .'

'What if Culpepper had something to do with his brother disappearing, and it happened on the property? And Strook saw something that led to Culpepper killing Strook. Then I start investigating that, and he comes after me.'

'So what do you think? We go find this Culpepper?'

'Shit,' said Waldo, 'throw this one to LAPD. Let them do something.'

'Thank you,' said Lorena to Reddix, abruptly ushering him out the door and closing it. 'Don't even *think* about taking this to the cops.'

'Why not?'

'What are you going to tell them about how you got involved in the first place? That you were employed by Don Q? You *know* they'd find a way to get that into the press, just to fuck you.'

'*You* worked for him.'

'When I was young and new and had nothing to lose! Not when I was starting to build a business for real, with clients like Judge

Ida Mudge! It's hard enough to have the whole LAPD against you; we don't need this, too.'

'Now I'm a liability.'

'You know what I mean.'

'So what do you suggest we do? Wait for Culpepper to run me down again?'

'No, go right at him. Tell him we made the Range Rover and that you don't know what his problem is, but that multiple people here – five at this agency alone – know about it. If you ever see him again, you're taking it to the police; if anything happens to you, the rest of *us* do. But if he backs off, we'll let it be.'

'He might have killed somebody.'

'*Might* have.'

'We have an obligation to take it to the police.'

'Obligation? On a theory? The obligation you *have* is to your *client*. You think Don Q wants you bringing in LAPD?'

'I don't know what he wants.'

'Then ask him. Seriously: ask him.' She had a point: making that kind of move without Q's blessing had a lethal downside.

There was a knock at the door. Lorena opened it: Reddix again. 'Sorry to bother you, but I have my Google alerts set up for Judge Ida, and something just popped up. About Fontella Davis. You should check it out.'

Reddix went back to the staff room. Waldo found a report on CNN's website and Lorena one on the *L.A. Times*'. Both told the same story: one of the complainants, Austin Vaught, had dropped Davis and lawyered up with some downtowner neither Waldo nor Lorena had heard of. At a press conference in his office, the attorney claimed that Davis had approached his client and suborned his perjury in the Judge Ida Mudge harassment case.

'Shit,' muttered Lorena. 'No mention of us at all. We should have gotten Fontella in front of this, traded it off.'

Waldo wasn't going to revisit that spilled milk.

Lorena looked out the window, down Melrose. 'Is it bad that I'm disappointed it wasn't Fontella trying to kill you?'

Waldo laughed.

'So where are you on Anthony Branch,' she said, 'now that the Range Rover isn't part of it? Back to accident?'

'Fontella still feels wrong to me. That night at her house – it was like she was flirting with a confession. The woman has no problem proclaiming people innocent when she knows they're guilty; that's half her job. Instead, it was more like, "This is your last night on Earth, Mr Bond; I might as well tell you my whole evil plan." I think that's why I got so freaked out.'

'Maybe the idea *was* to freak you out. I mean, she can't stand you. *And* you're working for her rival, *and* you were threatening her with disbarment. Could just have been her idea of a good time.'

Waldo hiked a shoulder. It could be that simple; it just didn't feel like it. Of course, that would be exactly what Davis was going for.

Lorena said, 'How cool would that be, though? If we could actually nail Fontella for a thirty-five-year-old murder. Maybe after we make this Culpepper thing go away, it's worth another week, on spec. Just for giggles.'

'Two days ago, you couldn't run away from that fast enough.'

'Everything's changed. I was trying to nail down the win on the plaintiff, now we've already got that. I wanted to stop the attacks on you; we'll get that, too. And I wanted to jam Fontella to help us with publicity, but that ship's sailed.'

This time it was Fat Dave in the doorway. 'Feds have nothing on the guy.' He turned to Waldo. 'No puppies to chase today?' He burst out laughing. Reddix and Dumpster laughed from the other room. Lorena did, too.

'Sorry,' she said. 'I told them. The picture of you biking around your old neighborhood, looking for a Siberian Husky – I couldn't resist.' Even Waldo chuckled. With a little distance, the whole thing was kind of funny.

Then Fat Dave said, 'Shit, Waldo, you could've just asked LAPD for a transfer to K-9, instead of quitting after the Black kid and turning into a dick.' Waldo was the first to stop laughing.

Lorena said to Fat Dave, 'Get on the deeds and liens.' She stood, closed the door behind him and said to Waldo, 'Sorry.' She lowered her voice. 'When this is over,' she said, 'we'll do something about him. The other guys are useful, but I get it – douchebag isn't a skill.'

Waldo took the same bus he'd taken out to Topanga, got off near the Fallbrook shopping center and rode his Brompton to the Chuck E. Cheese. He'd long given up trying to figure out how Don Q picked his meets.

Waldo saw the Escalade about twenty yards from the entrance. He wheeled toward it, then heard a 'Yo!' and turned to see the dealer walking out the door. He tipped his head toward what looked like a random pair of minivans, and the two men stepped in between them to talk in relative privacy.

'You lookin' to create more drama with Nini, man, you're goin' 'bout it right.' He hiked a thumb toward the Chuck E. Cheese. 'Shit in there brings out the man's cantankerous side.'

'I didn't pick the spot. And why's he . . .?'

'Can't go leavin' Dulci unsupervised. I knew I was meetin' *you*, meant I needed Nini to come with. Tell you this, she make him go in that ball pit, that boy be lookin' to jack you *up*. What you want, anyway?'

Waldo got right to it. 'I've learned more about Dorian Strook, how he died.'

Don Q narrowed his eyes.

'For one thing, turns out he wasn't intoxicated, according to the medical examiner.'

'So it wasn't no accident.'

'Also, Strook had been squatting on an unused property, and the owner of that property has a brother who went missing. And that same owner has tried to kill me three times since I've been working this for you.'

'*Tried?* Boy must not've exerted hisself. You on that bike all the time – whenever I send Nini your way, I'm worried he gonna punch your ticket on happenstance.'

Waldo wondered if he was supposed to thank him for caring.

'So what you sayin', Waldo? This muthafucker with the real estate cancelled my boy Strook?'

Waldo nodded. 'And is trying to cancel me too because I'm investigating it. That's what I think. I want to bring in LAPD.'

'*LAPD?* Fuck, man? You burnt?'

'I can keep your name out of it.'

'No, man. *No.* LAPD? *Fuck.*'

'OK, then I'm going to come at the guy directly, back him off—'

'What's his name?'

It had occurred to Waldo, of course, that Don Q might want to take this into his own hands, but he'd thought it unlikely. Whatever happened between Culpepper and Strook wasn't the dealer's beef, after all, and wouldn't be worth the risk of a higher profile crime.

But now Q was asking. The last thing Waldo wanted was to be a conduit between Don Q and the general citizenry, so he hedged. 'Culpepper.'

'First name?'

'Not sure.'

Q tilted his head, disbelieving.

Waldo shaded again. 'One of Lorena's ops pulled the info. That's all he got me.'

Q shook his head slowly, then spit out the name. '*Culpepper.* You find out *what* Culpepper. And a domicile.'

'Why?'

'Bitch got to *pay.*'

'Wait a minute—'

'Get me that 411 and you're out. I'm gonna take care'a this myself.'

'You don't want to get near this. Guy's a taxpayer—'

'What are you now, Internal Revenue? Chancellor of the muthafuckin' Exchequer?'

'Chancellor of the what?'

'It's English, for, like, Secretary of the Treasury. But it sound better, don't it? More rhymes for it, too, if you're working, like, a terza rima or shit.'

Waldo stayed on subject. 'Culpepper's a real estate developer. Kind of guy makes political contributions.'

'He makes political contributions, all the more reason you can't go LAPD and expect nothin'. Muthafucker's the one gettin' cancelled. He disrespected my doppelgänger.' This again. 'I got to avenge that. Shit's gettin' literary.'

'Literary? What does—'

'Yes, literary, you *Judge Ida*-watchin' ignoramus. Disrespect a man's doppelgänger, shit is *on*. That's the rules, man. Literary obligation.'

The dealer's leg was twitching again. He looked distracted, a wreck. Was this really what writer's block looked like? Or was this part of the national meltdown Waldo kept dancing with himself, which he could feel himself being dragged toward again? 'You sure you're not making that up?'

'Not your problem, Waldo. Your problem is: first name, address, *tonight*.'

Waldo was jammed. Neither Don Q nor Lorena wanted him to go to the cops, but if he didn't, Q would kill Culpepper, and Waldo would be an accessory. His own leg started jumping. He said, 'I think he's abroad.'

Don Q scoffed. '"Abroad." Talk about makin' shit up.'

'What I heard. Europe.'

'*Where* in Europe?'

'Croatia. He has a return ticket, back a week from Wednesday. That's when I was going to come at him myself.'

Don Q leaned against one of the minivans and steamed. 'This is your fault, man. Flyin' 'round the country on somebody else's bullshit, all split focus and whatnot? You took too damn long. Let *my* muthafucker tip on out.'

He started toward the Chuck E. Cheese entrance, then turned back. 'I'm serious 'bout Nini, too. If Dulci got him eatin' that stank pizza? You best be gone by the time my boy come out.' He disappeared inside.

Even if Culpepper was a murderer, of his own brother, of hapless Professor Dorian Strook – hell, of Waldo, if things had broken differently – there was no way to square this with the catechism.

Don't affect. Don't hurt. So much for that.

And *don't want*. Well, Waldo *had* been wanting, hadn't he. That was the problem. He'd wanted some semblance of a normal life with Lorena. How was *that* working out?

Here's how: he was jammed. Culpepper wanted to kill him; Don Q wanted to kill Culpepper. Waldo felt that thing bubbling again, that thing he felt at the Apple Store, and in the cul-de-sac when the tears came.

Q's crazy was sucking Waldo back down, and this time there might be no coming back. This time somebody wasn't going to live through it.

Waldo's phone rang: Lorena.

Fucking Lorena, who should've just let him go to the cops in the first place.

Waldo let it ring, sat down on the asphalt with his head between his legs, and wondered if this would be the time the world never stopped tumbling.

TWENTY-SEVEN

The BevMo on Sepulveda carried Conady's blueberry-tasting stuff, Sea Dog, so that was something, at least, but as he approached the counter he couldn't bring himself to do it, couldn't consider the beer food (which didn't count as a Thing), since it wasn't for him to drink himself, and it wasn't even just 'beer,' but a *half-dozen* beers, and the cardboard holder. It was right there in the name – *six-pack* – six was six and the pack was a seventh, and if that meant shedding seven Things right now to keep it at an even Hundred, then that's what that meant. Not that he had much with him, but he could give the girl at the checkout Lena's pastel, which was still rolled up in his backpack, and he had his full change of clothes, which he'd taken to keeping in his pack, and his toothbrush was probably ready for replacing anyway, and that would get him down to ninety-three and he was good.

But he couldn't buy the beer and *then* get rid of his stuff, because who was kidding who, even without the pastel, he'd still be a hundred six for the interim. So he put the beer back in the cooler. Hopefully the Goodwill that used to be on Victory, the one he used like crazy when he divested four years ago, would still be there.

Then he could come back to BevMo for the Sea Dog.

Ridding seven articles of clothing just to buy beer that he wouldn't even let himself drink. He knew what Lorena would call it.

But he was past listening to any of that shit.

He'd do it, and then he could make his phone call.

With no electricity running outside the Mary Ellen house, the only light was what passed from the half moon through the trees. Waldo sat against the vinyl fence in full shadow, in a gap in the hedges near the firepit. The beers rested beside him, cool in a plastic bag of melting ice which Waldo had bought at Ralph's, after putting the beers in his backpack and the six-pack carrier into a recycling bin and thus dropping to ninety-nine. The ice was packaged, yes, but he wasn't eating it, so, fine.

He heard footsteps coming around from the other side of the house. 'Waldo?'

Waldo didn't answer, let him ask again.

'Waldo?'

'Over here,' he said, just loud enough to be heard.

Pete Conady turned on a flashlight and swung it in Waldo's direction. Waldo shielded his eyes. Conady pointed it on the ground and made his way to the firepit. 'Why'd you think I'd even answer?'

Waldo said, 'You gave me your card.' He hadn't kept it, of course, but there was no need; his old friend's cell number had been on his phone all these years anyway. Still on speed dial, in fact.

'Accident,' said Conady. 'Must've been stuck to one of the bills.' He snapped off his flashlight and sat down opposite Waldo and leaned against the firepit.

'Why'd you come, then?' said Waldo.

'Those texts you sent me. You sounded pretty fucked up.'

'Did I?'

'They barely made sense. All I really took out of them was that you might do yourself some harm.'

'I appreciate the concern.'

'Wasn't concern. Just wanted to make sure I'd be there to see it.'

'Still hate me. After all these years.'

'Like I hate the fucking Celtics.'

'Only the Celtics? Man, I thought I was down there with the Giants.'

'What can I say? Time, you know?'

'Heals all wounds?'

'And wounds all heels.' Conady said, 'You're not fucked up at all, are you. That was an act, those texts.'

'Have a beer.' Waldo handed him a Sea Dog.

Conady held it up to catch a slice of moonlight through the rustling leaves. 'My brand. You want something.'

'How about some manners, dude? I gave you a beer. Just drink with me.'

Conady twisted it open. 'You're not drinking.'

'Can't. It's bottled.'

'What, you're too good for a bottle now?'

Waldo walked his old friend through a summary of his lifestyle, starting with how he didn't eat or drink anything that had been packaged. He told him about the Hundred Things and the Brompton and the rest of it.

Conady said, 'I heard rumors about some of that. I figured it had to be bullshit.' They were quiet together a moment. It was surprisingly comfortable. After a while, Conady said, 'So what happened? What about that property you bought – in Idyllwild, right? Can't you sell it?'

'I don't want to sell it.'

'And Lorena? You two were doing stuff, right? PI work?'

'We tried. It's not happening.'

'Is it true Dumpster Williams's working for her?'

'And Fat Dave Greenberg.'

'No! She's got *both* of those jamokes? *Damn.*' Then, 'I'm still not getting this. Where do you sleep?'

'My cabin in Idyllwild. Or Lorena's, when I'm in town. We were talking about getting a place together, but I think we might bag that, too.'

Waldo could hear Conady shifting, as he recalculated his apprehension of Waldo's financial situation. 'So Panera,' he said. 'What the fuck was that? That dinner party.'

'I was working a case.'

'A *case*? What kind of case?'

'Transient they pulled out of a fountain on the Boulevard. Know it? Van Nuys Division.'

'No. And what are you saying? Someone's paying you to check the department's work? On *that*?'

Waldo wasn't going to answer that one directly. 'The department wasn't *doing* any work. That was the point. They treated it like an accident: passed out and banged his head.'

'So?'

'Tox was clean. No water in his lungs. Guy got bopped and dumped, and they took the easy way on the ticket.'

'Asking again: who's paying you?'

'Nobody.'

'So this is pro bono. Working outdoorsmen, for funsies.' He sounded kind of skeptical, but only kind of. Clearly he had no idea what to make of Waldo these days. He wasn't alone.

Waldo said, 'Fuck is the department doing with these people, anyway? Busting them for nothing, confiscating shopping carts—'

'What, you trying to make the homeless your new Lydell Lipps? If that's what this is, go fuck yourself. Seriously. But first give me another.' He pointed to the beers.

Waldo, knowing what he still needed, walked Conady through what he'd learned about the squatter Dorian Strook, about Culpepper and the Range Rover, and about the missing brother. He said that he didn't know if Culpepper had ever been a suspect in the disappearance, but he should've been.

Conady wasn't buying. 'So you've got a murder which isn't a murder—'

'It's a murder.'

'—and a second murder without a body.'

'Oh, we've got a body. That's the beautiful part.'

'Where.'

'Under your ass. Slide over.' Conady did. 'Feel that bump, where you were sitting?' Conady ran his hand over the artificial grass. 'Only one like it on this whole plastic lawn.'

'So?'

'There's a funky seam there, too, like somebody split it open to pull it back.'

'To bury a body.'

'Strook?' said Waldo. 'The guy in the fountain? Right before he got killed, he was in legal aid talking what sounded like gibberish. "There's a hole under the fire." That's what he kept saying. "There's a hole under the fire," over and over.' Waldo pointed to the pit.

'That's not under, that's next to.'

'Strook saw something that got him killed. Either on Ventura Boulevard in the middle of the night, or dumped there. Dude, you're sitting on a dead Culpepper, on property he probably co-owned with the killer. All you've got to do is dig him up.'

'"All I've got to do." With no probable cause, and not even on the right side of Coldwater.'

'Don't give me that division bullshit. You're Robbery-Homicide now.' Waldo had seen the step up on Conady's business card. 'I can hook you up with the legal aid lady.'

'You know that's not going to cut it. And when my captain asks how I knew, and your name comes up? Forget it.'

'Register me as a CI.'

Conady actually laughed. 'Yeah, I want *that* coming back on me. I don't even like taking a beer from you.'

'You can wipe down the empties for prints when we're done. I won't be offended.'

'Remind me.'

They fell quiet again. Lorena aside, this was the first moment that felt anything like reconnection with his previous life. One of these days he'd have to do this with Freddie Dellamora too. 'How's Gayle?' he said.

Conady said, 'Hates your guts.'

'And the twins?'

'Hate *my* guts.'

'What are they now, twelve?'

Conady took a beat before saying, 'Fifteen,' reminding them both of how much time had been lost, and why.

'Hey,' said Waldo. 'When I blew out? I could've done some things differently.'

'You think?' Even in the dark, Waldo could make out Conady shaking his head.

After another silence, Waldo said, 'We good?'

'"We good." Yeah, what the hell, Waldo. We're good.' Conady tipped back the rest of his beer. 'Long as you don't ask me to go digging up some homeless stiff.'

'This stiff isn't the homeless one. The homeless stiff was in the fountain.'

'Oh. In that case.'

'Fuck it,' said Waldo. 'Leave him. I'm not a cop anyway.'

'Good. I can still catch the end of the Dodgers.' Conady stood and picked up another beer.

But with Culpepper and Don Q looming, Waldo couldn't afford to let this go. 'Here's the deal,' he said. 'The guy who killed his brother' – he pointed to the bulge in the turf – 'he's been trying to kill me. And if I just back him down but don't take him off the street . . . well, my client is going to step in and take *him* out.'

'Fuck's sake, what am I supposed to do with *that*? You're either telling me too little, or too much.'

'You don't want to know more. Pete: pull up the body, do the right thing, everyone goes home a winner.'

Conady thought about it. 'Tell you what,' he said. 'We dig.

Tonight. Don't have to pull him out – just go deep enough that he's fragrant. Then you find a payphone somewhere and make an anonymous call, disturbance on the property. I'll swing back a few hours later, when FSD is on the scene, say I happened to be driving by. Whoever catches it, I'll keep half an eye.'

'Thanks.'

'But there's nothing under the carpet? This is done. *Done.*'

Waldo stood and reached out to shake his hand. Conady took it and pulled him into a hug.

Breaking, Waldo said, 'I saw a shovel behind the garage. Maybe there's a second one.'

'I don't think so,' said Conady, plucking the rest of the beers from their ice nest. 'I'm on lookout.' He headed for the front of the house. 'Charlie fucking Waldo.'

The body was right where Waldo thought it was. He stopped digging when he felt the torso, confirmed with Pete on the street, and talked him into getting rid of the shovel for them. They headed off in opposite directions.

On Ventura, Waldo spotted a crowd of millennials waiting for a car outside a gamer bar, and gave the drunkest-looking one a ten to call the police general line and complain about a loud fight happening at the address on Mary Ellen.

It was almost three by the time he made it to Lorena's house, filthy and spent. She was waiting up for him in the living room. 'I tried calling you.'

'Sorry.'

'Did you get my texts?'

'It's been a night. Can I wash these clothes while we talk? I had to give away my other ones.'

He could see her doing the math in her head – this was a Thing thing – and deciding it wasn't worth engaging with his shit anymore.

He left his work boots by the door and crossed through the bedroom into the bathroom. He stood in the tub and undressed there, trying to keep the dirt contained. Not bathing tonight wasn't an option.

Lorena said, 'Fontella called.'

'What does she want?'

'The complainant Vaught, the one who says Fontella put him up to the accusation?'

'Yeah?'

'She thinks *we* put *him* up to *that*.'

'That's ridiculous. Why?'

'Because of the enduring friendship between the two of you. And she says she's coming after *me* for it. Going after my license.'

'She's trying to scare you because you're the vulnerable one.'

'That's right, Waldo: I *am* the vulnerable one, and she *is* scaring me. We need to promise her we'll leave Anthony Branch alone. That *you'll* leave it alone. And you need to be the one to call her and say it. First thing in the morning.'

Waldo shook his head. 'This proves it, right? Fontella's scared. She's the one with something to hide.'

'On a non-case.'

'It's a case,' said Waldo.

'Not to the police.'

'To me. As a PI, it's my case.'

'A blackmail case.'

'In the beginning.'

'Your client's asked you to stop.'

'So I don't charge her.'

'Waldo: *this is my livelihood*.'

'This is a dead boy.'

'Dead rapist.'

'We're talking about a murderer,' said Waldo.

'A powerful one.'

'All the more reason.'

'How far,' she said, 'do you intend to take this?'

Waldo took off his underwear and started running hot water from the bathtub spigot. 'To the end.'

'Yeah?' she said, watching him shake off his jeans under the gush from the faucet. 'I think we're there.' She left the room.

Waldo flipped the flow to the top spigot and let the water run over him. A minute later, he thought he heard the front door slam.

TWENTY-EIGHT

S he left him alone all night in her house, a first. At a different
time in their relationship, he would have thought it meant
she was off distracting herself from him with her DMV friend
or the equivalent. But this wasn't about jealousy, or going each
other one better, or one worse. This was, she'd just had enough.
When she clocked the business about giving away his clothes, he
could see something snap behind her eyes. *Getting worse, getting
worse, getting worse.* And now he was going to take down everything she'd been working years to build.

Yeah, she'd had enough.

And she sure wouldn't want to hear that he was going back to
Oakland.

When the plane landed, Waldo already had a message waiting
from Pete Conady. They played phone tag while Waldo biked
across town (more easily, this time, with a working iPhone) and
connected when he was half a mile from Rev. Thurmond's church.

Body in hand, Conady told him, the Shane Culpepper case had
unfolded quickly. The brothers had been estranged for a decade
for reasons unknown. After Shane's disappearance was reported,
Escondido PD had talked to Leonard, but with no known recent
contact between them and with Leonard not a beneficiary of his
brother's estate, he'd been ruled out as a suspect in any possible
wrongdoing.

What Escondido hadn't thought to look at was the Mary Ellen
property, still part of the Florence Culpepper estate, of which,
Leonard, her elder son, was the executor. Even as a tear-down,
the property was now worth close to a million and a half, the
proceeds to be split between the two brothers – unless one of them
died before it was sold, in which case the survivor inherited it
solely. Of course, *missing* wasn't *dead*; not for five years, anyway,
in the State of California. So unless Shane was able to pull a
Lazarus from under the firepit in the next four, it would all be

Leonard's, and worth the wait. Besides, by then the land could be worth two mil.

Leonard was already downtown, lawyered up but not going anywhere. Waldo was sure Don Q would prefer to have taken Culpepper off the chessboard himself, but if this got the job done for him, he probably wouldn't kick too hard. And Waldo could finally get his MacBook back.

'I owe you a beer,' said Conady over the phone.

'You owe me six,' said Waldo. 'But drafts.'

The smile stayed on Waldo's face until he reached Wellspring AME and shifted gears to the business that had brought him there.

He walked his bike inside and followed the sound of female voices to the church office, where he found two older women and Brandi, the girl who'd been minding the Reverend the first time Waldo had come to see him. 'He's not here today,' she said right away, before Waldo had a chance at hello.

'When do you expect him?'

'It's hard to say. He's not well.'

'At home?'

'You can't go there,' said Brandi.

Waldo left the office.

'Sir—' said one of the other women, but Waldo was on his bike as soon as he hit the sidewalk and nobody would be able to stop him.

At the Reverend's apartment, Waldo folded his Brompton and carried it to the walk-up rectory. He knocked on the door and a young white man in hospital scrubs answered. 'Yes?'

'I'm here to see Rev. Thurmond.' The young man threw an uncertain glance back into the apartment. 'Who are you?' asked Waldo.

'I'm Bob.' Reading Waldo's questioning look, he added, 'From Mission Angels.' That still didn't mean anything. Bob lowered his voice and said, 'Hospice.'

'Who's that?' came the Reverend's voice from inside.

Waldo tried to look around Bob, and called, 'Charlie Waldo.'

'Let Mr Waldo in. And . . . give us . . . a minute, Bob.' His breathing sounded weaker than before.

Bob said, 'Where should I . . .?'

'You can . . . take a walk. Come . . . back . . . in ten minutes . . . and check on me. How's that?'

Bob stood aside to let Waldo in and left with a pleasant nod.

The minister was dressed in a sweat suit with food crumbs all over it, settled into an armchair next to the sofa. He said to Waldo, 'Hospice . . . makes it sound dire.'

'Doesn't make it sound good.'

'Well, I ain't . . . kicking . . . tonight. Put it that way.'

'Well, thank you for talking to me.'

'Come . . . a long way. Again. Can't believe . . . you're still . . . on this.'

'The more I look, Reverend, the less I think it was an accident.'

Rev. Thurmond deflated and gave Waldo a life-weary shake of the head, then blew out what little he had in his lungs.

Waldo said, 'Since I started, everybody keeps hiding cards. Everyone remembers what happened, or they *claim* to remember, but then they leave out pieces. And maybe that's just how memory works. I'm *sure* that's part of it, actually. But some of them, I think they're just shining me on, because they can – until somebody else fills in a gap, and then they go back and rearrange their stories to fit. After a while, I stopped trusting any of it.'

The Reverend, agitated, put his hands on the arms of his chair and tried to push himself up to stand. He wobbled and fell back. He said, 'You're still on that damn slap.'

'It's not so much that—'

'Ida . . . had reason . . . to slap Anthony. He was no . . . gentleman . . . believe me. But Ida Tuttle . . . had . . . no reason . . . to kill him.'

'How about Fontella?'

Rev. Thurmond gave Waldo a filthy look. 'Now you're flailing.'

'I've had two conversations with her—'

'You . . . have a problem . . . with . . . these strong . . . Black . . . women?'

Waldo felt blindsided. Sick. Flayed.

And he couldn't help but wonder: was there possibly something to the shot? Could there be something foul in his own heart? Something which he hadn't reckoned with, but had made him mistrustful?

No, he decided. It wasn't fair. These two women had taken turns lying to him, taunting him, giving him reason over and over to doubt their veracity. To ignore that *because* of race would be dishonest. Condescending, even.

And it occurred to him too that the Reverend knew exactly what he was doing. The man still knew more about Anthony's death than he was saying, and he was trying to knock Waldo backwards, using whatever he could.

Waldo said, 'You're going to make this that?'

'I don't know what . . . I'm making it . . . until I know . . . what *you're* . . . making it.'

Could be that Rev. Morris Thurmond knew that Fontella Davis had killed Anthony Branch, and why. And was fine with it.

'What do you think of Fontella? What she's done with her career.'

'Proud. Very. Like Ida.'

'How well did you two know each other? You and Fontella?'

The minister hiked a shoulder and shook his head, saving his breath.

Waldo tried to help him: 'Not very?'

'No.'

'She was your girlfriend's best friend.'

'That can . . . go . . . either way, right? Sometimes . . . girls love . . . their bestie's . . . boyfriend. Sometimes . . . they don't.'

'And Fontella didn't like you?'

'Fontella . . . always had a chip . . . on her shoulder. You may have noticed.'

'I guess I have.'

'I think . . . she might not . . . like men that much. Never . . . got married . . .'

Could also be that Morris Thurmond had no idea what Fontella Davis had been through. Waldo tested it. 'Maybe she had reason not to like men.'

'Liked . . . girls, maybe?'

It was true that Waldo had never seen Fontella Davis linked to anyone romantically, not that he necessarily would have. Anyway, he'd never given thought to her orientation. 'Was she gay? When you knew her?'

'Those days . . . even if she was . . .'

'She might not say,' Waldo finished the thought, again, to help. Rev. Thurmond pointed a shaky finger and nodded confirmation.

He was running out of breath and his hospice worker would be back soon. Waldo needed to swing this back to Anthony. 'You ever hear about her having a bad experience with a boy?'

'Never heard . . . her having . . . *any* experience . . . with a boy.' The minister's look was level, earnest. Did that mean he was speaking the truth as he knew it? Or a factual inaccuracy, honestly misremembered? Or was it a deliberate misremembrance, a dodge? Those questions had run underneath every exasperating interview Waldo had conducted for two weeks. And after all of it, he didn't know if he'd gotten anywhere near the truth. But he knew he was near the end.

Regardless, one more claim had opened one more discrepancy, and even as Rev. Thurmond's energy was running out, Waldo had to follow up. 'She said you used to double-date.'

'I don't . . . remember any . . . double-dates. Why,' he said with failing breath, 'do you . . . care . . . about this?' He started coughing, a long spell. Waldo didn't know if even the fit was legit, or one final stonewall.

Regardless, this was Waldo's last shot. He had means, he had motive, but Fontella's opportunity rested with her getting Matt Fishbein's map either from her secret boyfriend Dave Petters – if he *was* a secret boyfriend, if that wasn't just one more lie – or from her best friend's boyfriend Morris Thurmond.

Waldo waited for Morris's coughing to stop, then said, 'Tell me again about that night. About the pledge hike.'

That angered the minister. 'I . . . don't have . . . *wind* . . . to waste . . . on what—'

'OK, then,' said Waldo, 'answer me a new one. You told me it was somebody else that saw Anthony at the bottom of the gully. Not you.' The minister nodded. 'Who was it? Do you remember?'

'Dave. David Petters.'

'And you were with him all that night? Dave Petters?' The minister nodded. Dave Petters – the same Dave Petters Fontella was claiming *she* had been with.

The Reverend started coughing again. A key turned in the lock and Bob the hospice worker returned, now giving Waldo a less friendly look. 'He needs his rest.'

Waldo turned to Rev. Thurmond and asked another question before the coughing even stopped. 'Is there any way Fontella was out in the woods that night?'

'How . . .' the minister said, pulling himself together, 'would she . . . know where Anthony . . . was?'

'The map,' said Waldo.

'Back on that,' said Rev. Thurmond, scowling. 'I do not . . . know . . . anything about a map.'

'You never got one.'

'No.'

'Never saw one.'

'No.'

'Never gave one to Fontella.'

'No.'

'Was she close with any of the other pledge captains?'

'Not that I know of.'

'Not Dave Petters?'

'Mr Waldo—' said Bob.

'Why?' said Rev. Thurmond. 'Because . . . I just said . . . he found Anthony?'

'No,' said Waldo, 'something else. Something I heard. That she was close with Petters.'

Rev. Thurmond narrowed his eyes. 'Close, like . . .?' He tipped down his chin to finish the sentence without words.

Waldo nodded.

The minister waved it off. 'Who . . . told you . . . *that* bullshit?'

'*Mr Waldo*,' said Bob again.

The earth had taken thirty-five turns around the sun since Anthony Branch was killed, and now that sun was setting on his case for good. Morris Thurmond, in his final – what, weeks? days? – was the last witness who'd be able to hold Fontella Davis accountable. This dying legend. This dying saint.

Waldo made the last plea he could think of. 'Your whole life, sir, has been a fight for justice. Help me get justice for Anthony.'

The Reverend looked at Waldo for a long time, his chest shaking as his lungs strained for oxygen. 'Remember,' he finally said, 'what . . . we talked about? How . . . getting near the end . . . can . . . give you a . . . clarity?'

Waldo nodded. So did the Reverend. He *had* learned something.

Waldo leaned in; Anthony Branch and Fontella Davis and Judge Ida Mudge aside, he found himself hungry to hear what it was.

'Nothing . . . more important . . . than that fight . . . for justice. But sometimes . . . sometimes . . . you've got . . . to save . . . some of that . . . and fight . . . for mercy.'

With that, Rev. Thurmond signaled to the hospice worker. Whatever breath he had left, he wasn't spending on Charlie Waldo.

TWENTY-NINE

Two weeks of nothing but failure. Even on the Strook-Culpepper case, he'd needed help from Lorena's sorry band of ops, and had humiliated himself trying to wrest a dog from a little girl.

He'd failed Anthony Branch and had let Fontella Davis taunt and mock him in his defeat, getting in the digs she'd been wanting to since the Pinch case.

And along the way, he and Lorena had proven themselves so professionally incompatible that the personal was probably shot to hell now, too.

Plus these panic attacks, or whatever you'd call them.

It was time to start winding it down, and to tell Lorena. He hadn't heard from her since she'd walked out on him.

Going to Judge Ida's in Malibu, he texted her from the bus from LAX to Santa Monica. *Saying uncle.*

A few minutes later he texted her again. *Will catch bus home straight from Malibu after I wrap up.*

After he hit *send,* it occurred to him that it might not be clear that by 'home,' he'd meant his woods. But she'd get it at some point.

In Santa Monica he got off the 3 and walked the couple of blocks to the 534 stop. A ringing from his pocket: Don Q's burner.

'You lied to me, Waldo. Culpepper ain't in no Croatia. They got him in Men's Central.'

'That's a good thing, right?'

'Ain't how it *works.* Man of substance does not leave his doppelgänger to no *po*-lice.'

Waldo had a feeling he wasn't getting his laptop back today. 'You are definitely making this up as you go.'

'You gonna argue literary theory with *me,* muthafucker? *You,* who don't even *read?*'

'I read. Non-fiction,' said Waldo, getting cranky about the point. 'And I did you a favor. You mess with a connected citizen—'

'Not your call, Waldo. Know what else? I think you was bullshittin' me 'bout the blue cans.'

'What blue cans?'

'*Sancho*. My dog that you claim – unconvincingly – got run over by a recycling truck.'

'He's not your dog.'

'No. He ain't. Know why? Because you ain't got game enough to find him, for two G a day.' He could hear Don Q drawing long, slow breaths. 'I am fucked up behind this. I ain't been able to write a decent page since this whole thing started. Got me agitated like a tweaker with the IRS on his ass.'

The image befuddled Waldo. 'A tweaker with the IRS—'

'That's my fuckin' *point*: I can't even put together a what-do-you-call it. *I want Sancho*. Metaphor! – that's it. You're on notice, muthafucker: you are *bringin'* me that animal, or you're bringin' me proof of death.'

'What is "proof of death" for a homeless dog?'

'That's on you, Waldo. But I ain't playin', not when I'm blocked up like this. This shit began in a fountain, and you best know it can *end* in a fountain.'

He'd set the meeting with Judge Ida in Malibu by brief text. She stood in her doorway like she wasn't planning on letting him in. 'Unless I am misrememberin',' she said, 'you were dismissed.' She shifted her weight. 'Ain't givin' you no more money.'

He didn't want to talk on her porch. 'Glass of water? Could you spring for that?'

She snorted, turned and walked him inside. Waldo left his bike out front and closed the door behind himself. The place seemed especially still this time, with no agent, no Lorena. Waldo took the same spot on the sofa.

Judge Ida came back with his water. 'Why you still pesterin' me, Charlie Waldo?'

'I couldn't let this go. I kept talking to your old friends.'

Through her nose, Judge Ida drew a deep, displeased breath. 'Like I said, young man: you were dismissed.'

'Not by Anthony Branch.'

'Oh,' she said. 'You are one twisted mister, ain't you.'

'Fontella wasn't with Ciano Panerio that night.'

'How do you know? You talk to him, too?'

'I did. And even she admits it now.'

Judge Ida, pulling back to look at the larger story, said, 'How the fuck was Fontella Davis gonna find Anthony Branch out in the woods in the middle of the night?' She scoffed. 'Matt Fishbein's map? Anybody else tell you they seen that map?'

'Fontella, kind of.'

Judge Ida swatted away the notion with her hand. 'Fontella didn't tell you she had no map.'

'Not exactly. But she won't say she didn't.'

'Sounds like a Fontella Davis mind-fuck. Girl always got off on that kinda shit.'

'But if she wasn't with Ciano Panerio . . .'

'She say where she was?'

'With Dave Petters,' said Waldo.

'She was not.'

'She says it's why she told you Pancrio, to cover for that. You don't believe it?'

'Not for one hot second, the way Dave was all gooey on Ruthanne. Not that I'd put it past—' She stopped herself.

Waldo finished for her. '—Fontella?'

He watched Judge Ida shut down, fold into herself.

'Why would she say that?' said Waldo. 'Why lie at all?'

Judge Ida stared at a spot on her coffee table for a long time, wheels turning.

Waldo said, 'You never, ever thought Ruthanne might be onto something? Never had *any* reason?'

Her eyebrows knitted and she shifted in her seat, troubled. Then she said, 'Fontella did hate him.'

'Anthony?'

'That was her first time. She tell you that?'

Waldo shook his head. His stomach turned. With every revelation, every conversation, whether she was part of it or not, Fontella Davis kept getting more complicated, more maddening. Sadder, too.

'This one night, a while after it happened,' said Judge Ida, 'we got shitfaced on Kahlua and chocolate milk.' Anticipating his recoil, she said, 'Shit, we were eighteen. Anyway, she told me in great detail this fantasy she had 'bout bashin' Anthony's head in with a brick.' She leaned forward, coming around to it. 'And when we heard officially that it got ruled an accident? Fontella, she just kinda snorted. I remember that *real* good. I thought she just meant Anthony got what he deserved.'

'But maybe it was: she knew otherwise?'

Judge Ida drew up in her seat. 'What you plannin' on doin' with this, Charlie Waldo? Why you even botherin'? Got no evidence, got no witnesses, got no nothin'.'

'My partner keeps asking me the same question. I guess I've been thinking we live in a different world now. Buried stories come out, careers go down. You don't need a legal conviction to punish someone anymore. You don't need to get beyond reasonable doubt. Fame is fragile now. Status, too.'

'Who you tellin'? Why I hired you in the first place.' Judge Ida pondered it all a bit longer. 'Believe me, hearin' the *name* Fontella Davis makes me want to give back my lunch – but unlike Fontella, I won't get behind takin' down a lady's livelihood unless it's righteous. So my question is, Charlie Waldo: how damn certain *are* you?'

'I'm *not* certain. You need means, motive and opportunity. Means, we know. And you're telling me Fontella's motive was strong. But opportunity – that still hangs on the map. Which may not have even existed. And even if Matt Fishbein is honest and lucid and right . . . how would Fontella have gotten it? It would have to be Morris or Dave Petters, and you don't believe—'

'She got it from Morris.'

'Morris says they hardly knew each other. And even Fontella says she and Morris were just "casual friends," from when you guys would double-date.'

Somehow this, of all things, hit a nerve. Judge Ida's nostrils flared. 'Fontella Davis and Morris Thurmond weren't no casual friends,' she said. 'Fontella and Morris was *fuckin'*.'

'Fontella and Morris—'

'Fontella and Morris. *Yes*, sir. Morris and Fontella. Behind my back. And our good Reverend, he didn't have the stuffin' to man up and tell me straight.'

'When was that?'

'Started before Anthony died, and went on till I got wise right before Morris's graduation. Which was the end of Morris and me, *and* Morris and Fontella.'

'And *you* and Fontella.'

'You know it. Things got ugly after that. Both directions.' She looked out the window, stuck on some pointy detail of it. She blinked something back. It was as close to emotional as Waldo had seen Judge Ida get.

She pulled herself together and said, steel fully returned, 'Tell you this, though: if all you're worried 'bout is how Fontella Davis got her hands on a map, then it's on. Let's go. She had no right to kill that boy, no matter what he did to her. I mean it. Let's take that bitch down. Because gettin' her hands on that map ain't no mystery. Morris Thurmond gave it to her.'

Means, motive, opportunity.

Means, motive, opportunity.

Means, motive, opportunity.

And:

Ida Tuttle – she's smarter than damn near anybody.

Waldo said, 'Fontella didn't kill Anthony.'

'Say what, now?'

'I've spent two weeks trying to figure out how one of you two got to Anthony in the woods—'

'Whoa, whoa, whoa – you back on *me* now?'

'Not you. Morris. Morris killed Anthony.'

'*Fontella* killed Anthony. You just said—'

Waldo shook his head. 'She's been lying to cover for Morris.' Judge Ida screwed up her face. It didn't work for her. Waldo said, 'Why were you being blackmailed?'

'Somebody confused us. Two Black girls. I know that's how some'a them frat boys saw us. And one of them knew somethin' about Fontella—'

'There *was* no blackmailer.'

Judge Ida held out her hands, as if helpless in the face of his nonsense.

'You suspected Fontella killed Anthony, just like Ruthanne suspected her, but you kept quiet about it all these years. Until she came at you with the lawsuit, and then started ripping your show. In such a personal way – that stuff about "making Black people look like clowns" – that *had* to get under your skin. Especially with all that history.

'So you fake-blackmailed yourself and brought me in, expecting me to figure out what you believed to be true all along: that Fontella Davis had killed Anthony Branch and gotten away with it.

'You left out the slap because you knew I'd hear about it from one of those pledge captains, and you knew it would get me more intrigued, less likely to walk away when I hit a couple dead ends. And you left Dave Petters' name out on purpose, to make sure I'd get suspicious and go talk to Ruthanne, who you knew would put me onto Fontella. And then you sent me to Panerio to blow up her alibi.'

Judge Ida shrugged a confession to all that, but she wasn't buying Waldo's alternate solution. 'Morris Thurmond ain't no killer. If Fontella didn't do it, it *was* an accident.'

Waldo said, 'I never considered Morris because I couldn't see a motive. But he had one: rage, over what Anthony did to Fontella.'

'Just because he had motive don't mean it wasn't an accident.'

'No, but there are all of *his* lies. He lied to me about nobody on the hike having a beef with Anthony, *and* he left out your slap, *and* he lied about his relationship with Fontella. He was playing games with me, just like you and Fontella have been. Occam's Razor.'

'Whose razor?'

'It's from philosophy: the simplest answer is usually the right one. There wasn't any map – what'd you call Fishbein, a hot box of crazy? No map. Morris was right there; he pushed Anthony off that cliff.'

Waldo watched Judge Ida process it, rearranging certainties on which, for decades, she'd built her understanding of her own history.

But there was more. 'The thing is,' said Waldo, 'the phony blackmail is still a problem.'

'Why? I didn't commit no crime. I didn't lie to no authorities.'

'You jumped me through a lot of hoops.'

'So what?' she said. 'I paid you for your time. *Overpaid.*'

'Why? And why me?'

'*Because you're half out your fuckin' mind!* I read about you, and then I checked it out in person. Had to carry that money in a paper bag? Please. You were exactly who they said you were. Who *else* was gonna go all the way with a thirty-five-year-old case with no damn evidence? No police was gonna touch this. Your partner wouldn'ta done it – not ridin' it all the way, anyhow. But you – once I got you flyin' all over the country – *you, flyin'—*'

All that carbon waste hit him again like a ton of bricks.

'—I knew damn well that'd work like an investment for you, make it even more important that you rode it to the end. And I was right: you *did*. Just turned out to be a different end than I expected.'

What to him was living meritoriously, what to Lorena was Waldo 'getting worse,' was, to Judge Ida, simply a weakness, something to use as a lever. It was a perversion of his catechism, an insult to justice, an insult to everything, including the memory of Lydell Lipps.

Waldo closed his eyes and tried to push past that, to focus on whatever stray threads he still didn't understand.

'Go back,' he said. 'What did you think would happen if I *did* figure out it *was* Fontella? We'd have to tell the police about the blackmail, to know how I got involved.'

'Like I said: some racist dipshit from back in the day got us confused. Police spend a couple days dustin' for prints and come up empty, and that'd be it.'

'How will you explain it now?'

'What do you mean?'

'Can't say anybody mistook you for Morris.'

'Yeah, but you ain't goin' public with Morris.'

'I might. Then it turns into a story about you starting a phony blackmail to nail your celebrity frenemy, who didn't even do it. How's that going to play?'

'How's it gonna play with who?' There was ice in her voice, already knowing the answer.

'With the people who are thinking about paying you a million dollars a day. Like I said: fame is more fragile these days.'

Judge Ida said, 'What do you want?'

'To do the right thing.'

'What does that even mean?'

'You tell me. You're the judge.'

Waldo startled at the squeak of shoes down a marble hallway. The house had been so silent that he'd been sure they were alone.

He certainly didn't expect to see Davis's client, Judge Ida's estranged lover and co-star, Man Nickerson. Nor to see him holding a Glock 17.

'Go back in the bedroom,' said Judge Ida.

'Too much money,' said Bailiff Man. 'Can't risk it.'

'So this was all another act?' said Waldo. 'The break-up, the lawsuit? What was the point of that?'

'Oh, that was all real,' said Judge Ida. 'Lovers' quarrel. You know.'

Nickerson confirmed: 'How it be.'

Judge Ida said, 'We made up. Bailiff Man dropped the lawsuit, and he's comin' back, once we go syndicated. Show ain't been the same since he left.'

Waldo shrugged. 'I'm still in the middle of season one.'

Judge Ida said, 'You'll see.' She turned to Bailiff Man. 'You can put that away. Waldo's actin' all angry, but he ain't gonna do shit with this.'

Bailiff Man said, 'Why take the chance?'

Waldo said, 'She still paying you five percent?'

'Uh-huh,' said Bailiff Man.

Simultaneously, Judge Ida said, 'That's under negotiation.'

'Two-point-six mil a year, times five years?' Waldo chuckled. 'I *bet* that's under negotiation.' Bailiff Man scowled. Waldo said, 'I should probably remind you, Your Honor, that your deputy's smoked three people – I'm sure over way less money than that.'

'I should remind *you* to shut your *mouth*,' said Bailiff Man.

Judge Ida said to Waldo, 'You ain't makin' this situation better.'

Waldo said, 'No, but I'm making it more interesting.'

Then the doorbell rang.

'Put that away,' said Judge Ida, 'and see who it is.'

Bailiff Man stuffed the gun into the back of his pants and left the room. Waldo and Judge Ida eyed each other silently while they listened to the front door open and the shuffle of feet. They heard Bailiff Man say, 'In there.'

Waldo recognized the clack of stilettos. Lorena entered the room, Bailiff Man behind her, Glock again in hand.

Lorena looked from Judge Ida to Bailiff Man and then to Waldo, thoroughly baffled.

Waldo said, 'Feel like you missed some episodes?'

Lorena said, 'Maybe a whole season.'

Waldo explained that the blackmail was a fraud designed to get him to prove that Fontella Davis had pushed Anthony Branch off the cliff, only that he'd figured out it was actually Morris Thurmond. He explained also that there was still no evidence that would hold up in a court of law, but that there was probably enough to ruin both Rev. Thurmond and Judge Ida.

'That,' he concluded the recap, 'is what's currently under discussion. Hence the thug-turned-sidekick-turned-thug.'

Bailiff Man raised the Glock and looked down the sight at Waldo.

Waldo said, 'Settle down, killer. Your boss doesn't want my DNA all over her pretty rental.'

'No need for any of that,' Judge Ida confirmed to Bailiff Man, ''specially now this one showed up. She knows how to talk business.' To Lorena, she said, 'Million dollars to forget everything you've heard.'

'Hey,' said Waldo. 'I'm here.'

Judge Ida said to him, 'The million is for both of you.'

Waldo said, 'That's not my point.'

Judge Ida turned back to Lorena. 'How's that sound?'

Lorena said, 'You keep a million in cash in the house?'

'Two hundred today, the rest next week.'

Waldo said, 'We're not burying a murder and a fraud for a million dollars.'

Lorena said, 'No, we're not,' and Waldo breathed a quiet sigh of relief. For a moment he was worried she'd take the deal.

Lorena said, '*Two* million.'

Waldo looked at her, slack-jawed.

Judge Ida said, 'Fine. But I ain't doin' this 'less I know I got you both.'

Lorena said, 'I can bring him around.' She turned to Waldo. 'You said yourself, there's no evidence. All she's asking you to do is not go public with a theory you can't back up, about a dying man you don't really want to ruin. So why *not* take the money?'

Waldo said, 'What about the blackmail?'

Lorena said, 'What's the biggie? She paid you for your days.'

'*Overpaid*,' said Judge Ida for the second time. 'So what's the deal, Waldo? You in?'

Eyes steady on Lorena, Waldo shook his head *no*.

Lorena said, to no one in particular, 'What's the alternative here?'

Bailiff waved the gun a bit and said to Judge Ida, 'We could move them somewhere first.'

Waldo said, 'You could try.'

But Judge Ida was still presiding and everyone waited to see how she would rule.

When she hesitated, Lorena decided to speak. 'If I take the two hundred today to keep a murder quiet – technically, I'm in for conspiracy after the fact, right?'

'So?'

'So that'll keep Waldo from saying anything. However angry he is at me, he's not going to let me be jammed on a felony. Not over a case this thin.'

Judge Ida shook her head with a three-note hum of incredulity. 'Damn,' she said, cocking her head in Bailiff Man's direction. 'I thought me and *him* had some fucked-up shit.' Then she said, 'C'mon. Money's in the kitchen,' and started out of the room. The others followed.

Waldo exhaled, crushed. Lorena said, 'A million of it's yours. Plant a rainforest.'

In the kitchen, Judge Ida started removing a stack of bills from her freezer. 'Get me a bag,' she said to Bailiff Man. 'Paper.'

Bailiff Man did, and Lorena moved over to the counter next to him. The picture of the two of them working together, filling another Gelson's bag with cash, tweaked Waldo. He said to Judge Ida, 'You're taking this payoff out of his end, right? I mean, if this dumbshit hadn't let Lorena in the house in the first place—'

Bailiff Man slammed the Glock down on the kitchen counter with a rap that made the other three jump. 'Bitch,' he said to Waldo, 'I told you to shut your fuckin'—'

Lorena drove a stilettoed heel into the canvas top of Bailiff Man's sneaker. In the same move she grabbed his gun hand and sank her teeth into the fleshy part just below his thumb. The Glock dropped on the counter and went off, sending a 9mm round into the control panel of Judge Ida's microwave, right between the 4 and the 7, then bounced onto the floor near Judge Ida's feet.

The judge beat Waldo to the gun, then stepped back and held it on him.

Lorena released Bailiff Man's hand. He threatened her with a backhand fist, but didn't actually swing.

Then Judge Ida turned the Glock in Bailiff Man's direction, surprising everyone. Clearly she wasn't sure where she wanted this to go, either. Bailiff Man backed up.

Next she pointed it at Lorena, the only person she hadn't yet. 'This mean you ain't takin' the money?'

Lorena looked at Waldo with flat, tired eyes and said, 'Sadly, no.'

Waldo said to Judge Ida, 'Pick someone to shoot, huh? Or else make yourself useful and dial 911.'

Judge Ida turned the gun back on Waldo while she considered her options.

At length, she handed the pistol over to him, butt first.

Bailiff Man cursed under his breath. Waldo aimed the Glock at him and said, 'Face against the cabinet.'

The big man did as he was told. Lorena grabbed the hand she'd bitten, yanked it behind him and slapped on a handcuff. 'You'll notice I could fit these in my purse,' she said to Waldo, without warmth, cuffing Bailiff Man's other wrist. 'Know why? 'Cause they're the fucking disposables.'

THIRTY

I t was Lorena who actually called 911, but when the men from
the Sheriff's Department arrived, Judge Ida took over, to no
one's surprise. She told the officers that she kept a lot of cash
in the house and that her friend Man Nickerson (whom, she said,
slickly, they might recognize from her television show), overreacted
to unexpected visitors and drew a weapon to protect her. In the
resulting fracas, she told them, Ms Nascimento disarmed him and
the gun went off accidentally.

Bailiff Man wasn't going to contradict that, and Lorena decided
not to, either. Everybody waited on Waldo, who added only the
suggestion that they run a check on Nickerson to see if he had a
carry permit.

The officers detained him and let Waldo and Lorena leave.

They didn't talk about where they were going; Lorena just
turned her Mercedes onto Kanan Dume and headed toward the
ocean while Waldo stewed and hoped she'd explain herself.

She didn't.

He said, '*Please* tell me that was all an act to get Bailiff
Man's guard down. *Please* tell me you wouldn't have taken that
money.'

She hit the gas and shot down the hill, the first sign that she
too was furious. 'You mean, if it was actually an option? If I didn't
know you'd blow it for me somehow? Would I have taken two
million dollars, not to say anything when we had nothing to say
anyway? Yes, Waldo. Yes. I would have accepted two million
dollars for that.' She sped up to make a light which she didn't
really make, and took a wild, skidding left onto the Pacific Coast
Highway.

'And you're welcome,' she said, 'for saving your life.'

'I don't think he'd have shot me,' said Waldo.

Lorena slammed on the brake, just on general principles.

Waldo added, 'But thank you.'

They drove PCH for a while, Lorena slowing too fast at the lights and hitting the gas too hard in between.

'So, why were you there?' said Waldo. 'Besides the saving my life part.'

'You said on the message you were going there to wrap things up. I figured with Judge Ida, there was bound to be money involved, and I knew you'd leave too much on the table. I didn't think it'd be *two million*. But you know what?' she said. 'I don't want to talk about it.'

She did, though.

'This is what being a PI *is*, Waldo. People don't come to you because their life is the Disney Channel. They come to you because their life is messy and dirty and often as not they made it that way themselves. Sometimes you get stiffed, sometimes you get paid. And when you get paid, you take the money.

'And why *not* take money from Judge Ida Mudge? Even on my "peep shows," as you call them, I'm trying to help clients out of their pain by getting them the truth. Judge Ida? She finds people in pain and turns them into a carnival freak show. Only in this fucking sewer of a city would someone pay you a million dollars a day for *that*, and then brag about it in the trades. They'll probably give her awards, too, put her in a hall of fame someday as a pioneer of broadcasting.

'It's so much worse than what you bag on me for. So if *one time* some scuzzballs are throwing around stupid money and I get a chance to catch a little? And not hurt anybody? Damn it, Waldo, you've got to let me have that.'

Waldo didn't have an answer. It wasn't that she was wrong; it was just that he never wanted to be a private detective in the first place. He loved her, though, so he kept bending, into PI work and into the rest. But every bend came with a cost, and the costs had added up.

Lorena said, 'You know what really pisses me off? I had to walk away from two mil, and I know you're going to punish me for it anyway. You're going to use it as an excuse to bail.

'*I still want this*,' she said. 'I want to live with you. I want to work with you. I want that on the record. So that when we look back at this and say, *This is how it ended* – and you and I both know that's what this conversation is – I want there to be no doubt and no dispute that this was *your decision.*'

She wasn't finished. 'Even your rules – the Things, the cars, the food – you hang onto all that to help you keep a distance.

'You could change. You could raise the number of Things, or whatever. And when you don't – if you get *worse*, even – it's that much more of an excuse to put this on me. It's why you don't want to get any help. Not that I'm bothering to push that anymore. I know this is a lost cause.'

It was a fundamental misunderstanding of who he was, *why* he was, and he was tempted to correct it, for this 'record' – but to what purpose?

The idea that this was actually the end hadn't crystallized for Waldo until Lorena articulated it. But once she did, it sounded inevitable. Ahead of him again, like she always was.

Maybe this case, for all its blind alleys and disappointments, had finally answered the question the two of them had been scratching at together for a year, of whether their relationship and Waldo's redemption could, in the end, coexist.

He flashed on his cabin in Idyllwild, and the wildfire, which he'd heard that morning had at last been one hundred percent contained. A fitting bookend. A sign, if you were looking for one.

He said, 'There's a bus stop in Santa Monica. You can let me off there, if you want.'

That got her even madder. 'What, *that's* your idea of how we end this? You sit there and don't say anything, and then I drop you at a bus stop?'

'I don't want to fight.'

'I'm not talking about fighting. I'm talking about, I don't know, the *opposite* of that. Go for a walk on the beach or something. Make it sad instead of angry. Try and give it some kind of soft landing.'

She turned and looked at him for the first time since they got into the car. He hurt for her. He hurt for them. And he was grateful for what she was saying now. Maybe there was even a way for them to ring down the curtain with a little magic and grace.

There was one other thing, though.

'I've got to go see Fontella,' he said. 'Finish this off.'

She puffed out her cheeks and blew out the air slowly, bone weary. 'What's *left*?'

'A couple last things I need to say. Speaking for the victim.' As soon as it came out he knew he needed to stop talking like that, especially in a moment like this. He braced for another attack.

Instead, Lorena said, 'Want company?' To his surprise, she added, 'Think of it as our last date. Watching Fontella Davis squirm – beats dinner and a movie, right? Especially the shit you like to eat.'

He wasn't going to find another Lorena Nascimento.

She said, 'You're going to let the blackmail go, though. Judge Ida's fraud.'

'What makes you so sure?'

'I know you,' she said, squeezing her way into the left lane for the turn onto Santa Monica Boulevard. 'Yeah, you're pissed at her. But you want to her to keep making more episodes.'

'Anthony Branch,' said Waldo.

Fontella Davis rolled her eyes.

'Morris Thurmond,' he said, with enough certainty that she drew back deeper into her chair.

'What do you think you know?'

'I'm not telling *you* what I know. I'm telling the *San Francisco Chronicle*. Unless *you* tell *me* a good story, and I believe it.'

Davis stood. 'Put your phones on the table.' Waldo and Lorena did, and she checked both to see that they weren't recording. She crossed to her wine rack, took out a bottle and said, 'I'm not offering you any.' She took out her electric opener. 'First off, I want you to know I was scammed by those four phony plaintiffs and I'm as mad about it as anyone. I'm drawing up a suit against them myself.'

Waldo said, 'That's not what we care about.'

'No,' she said with a sigh. 'It's not.' She pulled the cork and set down the bottle.

'Freshman year,' she said. 'We both met Morris; Ida moved on him first. But Morris and I – it was going to happen; it was a matter of time. And after we started up, we didn't know how to tell Ida. Thing is, believe it or not, we both loved her.'

She poured a glass and came back over to her seat. 'After Morris and I got close, I told him about what had happened with Anthony, and he didn't know what to do with it. He took it on like poison, like, I don't know, maybe somehow his own rage could help me carry it. Which it couldn't. But that's how Morris is, always taking other people's pain on himself. I'm sure that's what all those people feel up in Oakland, why they love him.'

Waldo said, 'When you told him – how long was it before the pledge hike?'

'Two, three weeks. And that pledge hike – I didn't even know it was coming. That's the truth. Morris, I think him even deciding to go was a last-minute thing. Then he showed up at my room in the middle of the night and told me he had pushed him.'

'He said he was with Petters all night. You both told me you were with him.'

'The easiest alibi, right? Not around to contradict either of us.'

'What exactly did Morris tell you, in the middle of the night?'

'That they assigned him some pledges, and he dropped them off in the woods—'

'With a map?'

'No map, nothing about a map. He left them separated from each other, that's it. And he was walking back to where he was supposed to meet the other pledge captains, and he heard the pledges start calling out to each other in the dark to find each other, like they were supposed to. But one of the voices he heard was Anthony – drunk and laughing – and Morris's blood was still on the boil. And he followed Anthony's voice and found him stumbling around right near that gap by the bridge, and gave him a push. He wasn't trying to kill him, but he did want to hurt him. Anthony was blindfolded and Morris didn't speak, so Anthony would never be able to say who did it. Just impulse, he said.'

Waldo thought again about the adolescent brain. *What were you thinking? I don't know.*

'It was like he was half telling me he'd done it for me, and half feeling guilty about it. Then he left and went back to the frat house. He expected the pledges would find Anthony, at worst with a broken arm or something. Instead they never came back, and Morris and the older guys all went out, and he let someone else find Anthony.'

'And then he came back and told you he was dead.'

'He wanted to tell everyone else what he'd done. I worked on him for hours, not to. Him crying the whole time. And I was right. It would have ruined his life; I could see it. Let the dead bury the dead, I told him.

'He at least wanted to let Ida know what happened. I told him he couldn't even do that. What's that saying, Benjamin Franklin? Three can keep a secret, if two of them are dead?'

'Well, now there are a few more of us,' said Waldo. 'It shouldn't stop there, either.'

Davis took a deep breath. 'Morris doesn't have long. Do you know that? He has hospice there.'

So they *were* in touch. Another thing the minister had lied about. 'You still talk to him – all the time?'

'Regularly.' She blinked a few times. 'There's no need for you to do this to him.' When Waldo didn't soften, she sat up straighter and narrowed her eyes. 'I'll fight this *for* him.' Looking to Lorena, she said, 'File actions against whoever we need to.'

Whenever anyone got angry enough at Waldo, they started threatening Lorena; that hadn't been good for them, either. 'For God's sake,' he said to Davis, 'this all started with you representing fake accusers, and now you're blocking for a real killer. Are you *ever* on the right side?'

'I'm on the right side now. That man's suffered for this as much as he needs to. He spent his entire life punishing himself. Depriving himself. Did you see how he lives? A man with his intelligence and education? It's nothing but ashes. All he's done since that night is deny himself any bit of comfort or pleasure, trying to make it right with the world.'

Lorena turned his way, and the defeat in her eyes brought home the ring of familiarity in what they were hearing: Morris Thurmond, Waldo's own mortifying doppelgänger.

Fontella, for her part, was moving from stick to carrot. She said to Lorena, 'I'll put your firm on retainer.'

This, too, was familiar. 'What kind of retainer?' said Lorena.

Before Davis could answer, Waldo said, 'A thousand hours.'

Davis, taken aback by the number, said to Lorena, 'How much do you *charge* per hour?'

Waldo said, 'Not our hours. Not *her* hours. *Your* hours. Your firm. Can be associates, that's fine. Pro bono, for L.A. Legal Aid.'

Davis said, 'We already do well over a thousand hours' pro bono a year, for Innocence Matters, and California Lawyers for the Arts—'

'This needs to be on top of that. So I'm going to want to see an accounting – last year's hours, this year's, and next.'

Lorena glowered at him.

Davis protested. 'I've already lost the income from the harassment suit.'

'The fraudulent one?' said Waldo.

Fontella Davis's silence was her assent. She closed her eyes slowly, opened them more slowly, and turned her gaze to the distant island out her window. This had gotten to her, too. How could it not? The suffering on her face was uncomfortable to witness, but too powerful to turn away from. Was she lamenting her dying lover? Recalling the assault Waldo had dredged? Reflecting on the way the decades had twisted them all, or how dearly it had cost her to get that seat at the table?

When she finally spoke, she muttered so softly that Waldo almost couldn't hear it.

'That bitch,' she said, 'is going to make a million dollars a day.'

Though Waldo was breaking Lorena's heart and had again cost her a great deal of money, he noted her smiling to herself as they stepped into the elevator. She must have found the Fontella show splendid entertainment indeed.

Her phone rang. 'Greenberg,' she said to Waldo. 'FaceTime.' Waldo gave her a *why?* look and Lorena shrugged back, *No idea.*

She waited until they stepped off on the lobby floor to connect.

'Look what I've got!' shouted Fat Dave, over some barking.

Lorena showed Waldo the phone. The op had Sancho on a leash. 'What did you do?' said Waldo.

'I staked out your old neighborhood until I saw this mope walking your dog. I offered the guy two hundred bucks.'

'And he took it?'

'No, but he took *thirteen* hundred. If he didn't have his brat with him, I bet I could've gotten it for half that.'

Waldo said, 'Wait – you did that in front of his kid? Bid him up until he gave up her dog?'

'I had to follow them for like three blocks, but yeah. Balls, huh? Hey, Lorena!' he shouted.

Waldo handed her back the phone. 'What?' she said.

'You're going to reimburse me, right?'

She hung up on him.

Laughing, she said to Waldo, 'Well, now you can get Don Q off your ass.' With a nod toward the phone, she added, 'Turns out, douchebag *is* a skill.'

'He only did that so you can't fire him for a while.'

'Duh. But now you're going to have to keep working with him, too.'

'Me? Work with – wait, what do you think changed?'

'Waldo. Come on. Legal Aid? You wouldn't have screwed me over like that if you weren't staying.'

She stepped onto the escalator to ride down to the valet.

Waldo stopped short at the top. She was right, of course, though he'd had no idea in the moment, while he was doing it. He watched her ride down, feeling somehow bested once again, even though all the moves had been his own.

He got onto the escalator. She waited for him at the bottom. 'You can get that puss off your face,' she said. 'You're letting a good man die with his reputation intact, plus it bought you a thousand hours of top-flight legal work for the homeless. Do I have to spell out the moral for you?'

'Apparently,' said Waldo, at a total loss.

'Sometimes,' she said, 'the best way to speak for the victim is just to sit the fuck down and shut the fuck up.'

She slapped Waldo on the butt and handed her ticket to the valet.

GRATITUDE

Glenn Gers, Susan Dickes, Tony Quinn – sharp-eyed readers, irreplaceable friends.

Jay Mandel. Jared Levine, Aileen Gorospe, David McIlvain.

Charlie Hunnam and Tim Kirkby, who took Waldo into their enormous hearts and blessed him with their enormous talents. Christina Lurie, Brad Feinstein, and everyone else on the *Last Looks* movie. Mel Gibson.

Kate Lyall Grant, Rachel Slatter, and the rest of the Severn House team I've yet to meet.

Jess Renheim: *Jagska alltid vara tacksam.*

All the readers who've reached out with a note or shared on social media or showed up at an event. You have no idea how much it means.

The astonishing, welcoming community of crime authors. Especially William Kent Krueger and Lee Goldberg, whose generosity never ceases to amaze.

John Michael Higgins.

Laurie Gould.

Gary, Milo, Amanda. David, Rachel.

Terri Yenko Gould, my first and finest reader. Better, and amazingly, someone you can spend a year locked down in a house with, and never stop thinking how lucky you are.